Morning

A Novel by
Alan Parkinson

Preface

This book is a novel, in the genre of historical fiction, that traces the lives of three people—two Polish Jews, Rachel and Jacob, and a German soldier, Helmuth. The novel is set in Poland primarily from 1942 to 1943, a time when the Holocaust was ramping up to horrifying heights. Though each of the characters is on a unique journey, their journeys sometimes intersect.

While the main characters are fictional, many of the events of the narrative are taken from real accounts. I have done this for two reasons. First, I wanted to make these events better known, and in some cases, honor those involved. Second, I felt the novel would have much more credibility if based in fact. In some instances, I believe the reader will react by thinking, *that couldn't really happen*, but the reader will find in many cases *that really did happen*. I have acknowledged sources with notes at the end of the book. When I have based part of the narrative on a real account, I have always recast it in my own words and adapted it to fit the flow and characters of the story, often expanding a brief account significantly. I have also sometimes adjusted timelines. However, as I make clear in the notes, I have endeavored to remain true to the spirit and character of what actually happened.

I started this book some years ago. As a student of history, particularly World War II history, I was often struck by the brief mention of something—maybe just a few lines—in a memoir or history that caused me to think, *there is an amazing story there*. Once, while visiting Auschwitz, I resolved to try to write a book to bring some of these accounts together.

Any story grounded in the Holocaust is a story that includes violence. However, I did not want violence to be a main focus of the book. I have rather tried to focus on heroic events, virtues and dilemmas that resulted as people resisted this great evil. In doing so, I wished to give the utmost respect to the Jewish faith.

With the exception of a few cities, no Polish place names are given. This is because I would like the narrative to be representative of the hundreds of ghettos of Poland and not a particular ghetto (or two). I have also used the traditional English spellings for Jacob, Rachel, and Esther.

I close with this passage from a leaflet that especially impressed me. It was written while the Holocaust was happening:

> The world surveys this iniquity, more horrifying than anything in history, and is silent. The slaughter of millions of defenseless people is committed before a wall of universal, ominous silence. The henchmen, too, are silent; they do not vaunt their actions. Neither England nor America raises it voice; even influential international Jewry—in the past so sensitive to any harm done to one of their own—remains silent. The Poles too are silent. Polish political allies of the Jews confine themselves to journalism; Polish opponents of the Jews display a lack of interest in something alien to them. The dying Jews are surrounded by Pilates washing their hands. (From the leaflet *Protest* by Zofia Kossak-Szczucka, as given in Bartoszewski and Polonsky, 1991, p. 326)

Acknowledgments

I acknowledge the support of my wonderful wife, Christina. Kathryn Jenkins Oveson provided very helpful and encouraging mentoring and editing, and Sarah Ebel-Fraiman was gracious in giving valuable advice regarding Judaism and in proofing the text. Rabbi Sam Spector of Congregation Kol Ami in Utah, USA was kind enough to answer questions. Andrew Reed, Dean Hughes, David Shulz and Chris Crowe were generous in providing their time and suggestions. Bryan and Clay Dunford created the cover. I am also grateful for friends and family, including our long-time book group, who read the book and gave helpful feedback.

Chapter 1: The Loading
Rachel, Western Poland, Late Summer 1942

Twenty-year-old Rachel struggled to absorb the nightmarish scene around her. In front of her stood a row of battered railroad cars. The doors gaped open ominously, revealing nothing except a dark, forbidding interior. Before each car was a ramp and a straggling line of Jews—babies, children, adults, the elderly, most with their coats on, even though it was a warm day—three or four or five abreast. Everyone was holding something: the hands of children, suitcases, rolls of bedding tied with ropes, sacks large and small. Behind the lines, thousands of forlorn Jews sat on the dusty ground, waiting. There was no food or water or sanitation, and when the breeze changed direction, Rachel was assaulted by the smell. She couldn't help but think of a stockyard, though she had rarely seen one.

German soldiers with guns and dogs surrounded them. They were rough and impatient and yelled for the Jews to hurry. Rachel watched as anyone who didn't move fast enough was kicked or struck with the butt of a rifle. Babies were crying, but small children were silent, terrified by what was happening. Mothers held tightly onto their children. Fathers tried in vain to protect their wives and children from blows and indignities.

Rachel understood this was just one more step in the long process of imposed degradation. It had started with the loss of citizenship, prohibition from schools and professions, desecration of their synagogues, and, of course, the yellow star. Then it was forced relocation, work camps, and all the deprivations of the ghetto. Now they were treated as cattle—in fact, worse than cattle. The Germans at least cared whether cattle lived or died.

Waiting for her turn, Rachel saw those ahead of her scramble into the car with kicks and shouts. She noticed a little girl in a shabby dress, one hand in her mother's and one hand clutching a doll. This image seemed to symbolize the plight of her people—the march of innocence to hell.

Guards pushed Rachel into the car. The floor was covered with straw; in the middle sat an empty bucket and a bucket of water. The car was dark except for cracks in the sides where the boards had warped, allowing a little light to seep in, and a window of sorts at the top of one side, perhaps ten inches high and three feet wide. The window had bars over it and barbed wire strung along its width. The walls and floor exuded a stench that testified of previous trips.

Following instructions, people moved to the back. They expected to have enough space to sit down, but more people kept coming. They were pushed against each other tighter and tighter until everyone was packed up against his neighbor. Rachel overheard whispered apologies: "Excuse me," "Pardon me," "I'm sorry."

It seemed crazy. There was no room except to stand. *How can we travel like this, without even sitting down?* The guards counted off one hundred people and shoved the last of them into the car. With a metallic clank, the door was slammed and bolted shut. The bright shaft of light from the door was replaced by darkness that gradually gave way to shadows and haze.

They were locked in. The future loomed ahead of them. They would share this space and this journey together, and they knew that eventually the door would be opened, and they would share the destination. Inside, the car was filled with pleas to a merciful God; outside, Rachel could hear the shouts and curses of the guards and the cries of those yet to be loaded.

Rachel had been swept into a car with a crowd of people she did not know. Next to her stood a mother with an infant and a small child. The child clutched her mother's leg tenaciously and hid her face in her skirt. Rachel saw in the mother's eyes a look of anxiety and fear for her children.

"My name is Rachel," she whispered. "I will help you."

"Thank you," the mother replied. "I am Eva, and this is Esther." Upon hearing her name, the little girl raised her head. "And this," the mother continued, looking at the baby, "is Daniel."

Two hours passed before the train began moving. The car lurched forward, knocking some off their feet and causing others to cry out. Gradually the train gathered speed. Those near the walls peered through the cracks at the countryside, watching for any sign of where they were going. Some children sat on the shoulders of others so they could look out the small window at the top of one side.

Periods of slow, labored progress were punctuated with long waits on sidings. Rachel could hear the puffing of the engine and shouts of the guards stationed at the front and back of the train. With the door shut and the sun shining down, the car became warm and then hot and then stifling. Several older people fainted. They did not fall—there was no room. They slumped on neighbors who could not bear the weight and let them slide to the floor. People stood over them.

They became thirsty. Taking cups from their luggage, they dipped them into the bucket and passed them around. Most took only a gulp or two, to be fair. But those at the far end of the car didn't see a cup before it was empty. The other bucket was placed in a corner and became the toilet. Rachel saw that only with effort could a person squeeze past others to get there. Those nearby turned their backs so there was at least visual privacy.

It was a singular scene to witness. Rachel could make out the shapes of dim, yellow stars on armbands and coats. Faces were etched in fatigue and despair. People struggled to stand, leaning on each other, or sat jumbled together in awkward positions. They were unkempt and their clothes were dirty, but no one cared about appearances. The air was fetid with the smells of a cramped humanity.

As the hours crept by, people collapsed onto the floor in heaps, among them Rachel and Eva and the children. At least they were able to sit upright, even though knees and feet and elbows poked them. The baby became restless and needed to nurse. Rachel saw this and asked, "Can I hold your daughter while you nurse the baby?"

"That would be very kind."

Rachel held out her arms to Esther. "Would you let me hold you?" Esther hesitated and looked at her mother. When her mother whispered her approval, Esther squeezed herself into Rachel's lap. Esther had short, dark hair and an alert face sprinkled with freckles.

"How old are you, Esther?"

"Six."

"Six! You are getting to be a big girl! I'll bet you try to help your mother with Daniel."

Esther buried her face in Rachel's chest. "I am afraid," she whispered. "What is going to happen to us?"

"I am afraid too. Sometimes, if you have a friend, it helps you to be brave. Would you be my friend?"

"Yes," Esther whispered faintly.

"Why don't you try to sleep. Here, lean up against me."

Esther laid her head on Rachel's shoulder. Rachel could feel her breathing grow deeper and her arms go limp as she relaxed and fell asleep. It helped Rachel feel brave.

Rachel looked at Eva. The virtuous image of the mother nursing her child was in stark contrast to the stinking, cramped car and the persecuted Jews inside it. It reminded Rachel of the night before they had begun their march to the ghetto. More than six hundred Jews had been gathered into a field in anticipation of the morning's journey. The Germans had surrounded the field with barbed wire to make sure no one tried to escape during the night. Lacking other suitable places, mothers had hung out diapers and other clothes they had washed to dry on the barbed wire. There in the morning, fluttering in the breeze: diapers hanging on barbed wire.

While Esther slept and the baby nursed, Eva and Rachel talked. In their shared fate and misery, Eva and Rachel quickly formed a bond of friendship that made it seem natural to speak freely from their hearts.

"Tell me about your husband," Rachel said.

"Aaron was taken six months ago to work in a labor camp. He was given ten minutes to get ready and say goodbye. I haven't heard from him since."

"I'm so sorry. Still, there is hope."

"Yes," Eva said wistfully, "there is always hope. I think about Aaron a hundred times a day. I pray for him a hundred times a day. I wonder where he is and if he is well. Now I do not know who is in the greater danger—him or us. Until now, I thought we were safe."

"Did you have a good job?"

"I thought so. I was a seamstress. I took the furs collected from the Jews and made them into vests and coats for the soldiers fighting in Russia. The Germans assured me my job was essential. I guess they changed their minds, as all the mothers with children were selected this time. What about you, Rachel? Do you have a family? Are you alone?"

"I come from a small town south of Krakow. My father was a history teacher in the winter and a farmer in the summer. I was very close to him. My mother was a good Jewish mother, making sure we stayed kosher. I also had a little brother, four years younger than me.

They all died last winter of typhus during the epidemic that swept through the ghetto. I was also sick but recovered, so now I am alone."

"I am sad to hear about your family," Eva said.

"I suppose our stories are not that unusual anymore—you with your husband taken to a labor camp, me with my family taken by illness, and both of us now swept up in an *Aktion*[*]."

"Forgive me for being forward, but you seem like a nice girl. Are there any young men in the picture?" Eva asked.

Rachel blushed. "I suppose there is one. His name is Jacob."

"Tell me about him."

"Well, I haven't seen him since soon after the war started. His family left for eastern Poland, in the Russian-occupied zone, shortly after the Germans invaded. So I suppose I know a little of what it's like for you with Aaron, because I've not heard from Jacob either."

"Were the two of you serious?" Eva asked.

"We were becoming serious, I think. Or maybe I should say, I hope. I remember walking with him once along a river during the summer before the invasion. It was a beautiful day; I recall how the river sparkled with sun pennies of light. We were just walking and talking about the future—I mentioned I wanted to be an attorney, that I wanted to argue important cases. I was pleased he was supportive. He told me he wanted to be a teacher. He wants to help students have confidence in themselves, to dream. We didn't talk about being together; it was too early for that, but by not talking about it, the possibility seemed to be hovering around us, waiting. It seems unbelievable to me now..."

"What?"

"Well, at that point in my life my biggest concern was how I did on an exam or what I would wear to a party, not whether my family would be alive tomorrow."

"I know. I never could have imagined what has happened. How, for example, am I going to take care of these two little ones? They are so small, and I fear that I am not enough to protect them—not smart enough, not rich enough, not strong enough." Tears coursed down Eva's cheeks.

---

[*] *Aktion* was the term used by the Germans for a large-scale deportation.

11

Rachel teared up as well. "Sorry for being such dismal company," she said as she wiped away her tears. "I am not sure I am enough either, but I promise I will help you." Then trying to change the subject to something happier, Rachel asked, "What is one of your good memories?"

"When you mentioned walking with Jacob, it reminded me of a time when I was with Aaron before we were married. We went to a concert in a cathedral. It started with some Bach, played on a beautiful pipe organ. The music was perfect for that setting, soaring into the vaulted space above us. Then a small group of Polish music students played some Vivaldi. The music was bright and joyful and seemed to herald a bright future for us. When Aaron put his arm around me, I remember feeling everything was perfect."

Night fell, and with it, despair crowded in upon them. Exhausted from standing or sitting in awkward positions, the courtesy of the loading eroded into bickering and squabbles. As people nodded off, they sprawled over each other. There were kicks and yells as people became territorial and selfish. Periodically someone woke with a start and cried out, struggling to escape from under a pile of bodies. A young boy near Rachel, obviously still traumatized by the day's events, whimpered, "Don't shoot, don't shoot." Some, unable to sleep, prayed softly or sang. Occasionally someone lit a candle. In the eerie shadows, masses of bodies, slumped over, swayed with the rocking of the car. In the darkness Rachel felt even more that their journey had become a journey of terror, a journey into the abyss. Eva and Rachel huddled against each other for comfort and reassurance with the children in their laps.

Morning light filtered through cracks in the sides. The bucket of water had long since been emptied, and people were faint from thirst. Eva was drawn and gaunt, nursing having accelerated her dehydration. Her lips were parched and she had difficulty speaking. Someone nearby shared a small cup of wine, taken from a suitcase. Esther continued to sleep with her head nestled on Rachel's shoulder. Rachel began to softly sing Psalm 54:

> Save me, O God, by thy name, and judge me by thy strength.
> Hear my prayer, O God; give ear to the words of my mouth.

> For strangers are risen up against me, and oppressors seek after my soul: they have not set God before them. Selah.
> Behold God is mine helper: the Lord is with them that uphold my soul.
> He shall reward evil unto mine enemies: cut them off in thy truth.
> I will freely sacrifice unto thee: I will praise thy name, O Lord; for it is good.
> For he hath delivered me out of all trouble: and mine eye hath seen his desire upon mine enemies.

As she sang these words, a stillness and a resolve settled upon her. She spoke. "Eva, before I entered the train, I decided that I would not die passively, that I would fight." Eva nodded her understanding. "I had long thought that I should be prepared in case I was ever taken on the streets. And if I was forced into a transport, I would try to escape." Eva's expression changed to one of puzzlement. How did anyone escape from a transport? They were in a prison.

"Eva," Rachel repeated again, "we must try to escape."

Chapter 2: The Decision

Rachel, Western Poland, Late Summer 1942

Even to Rachel it sounded like she was talking nonsense. They were weak with fatigue and hunger; the door was locked; the window was barred by steel bars and barbed wire. Armed guards watched over the train. Having the war end tomorrow seemed more probable than escaping from the car.

Sensing Eva's incredulity, Rachel reached down inside her boot. For a few moments she struggled with some thread, pulling out stitches from a seam. Then she withdrew something silver and showed it to Eva. It was a piece of metal about twelve inches long, a half inch wide, about the thickness of a tin can, with little serrations running along one edge. What was it? Eva shook her head questioningly.

"Eva," Rachel said softly, "this is a hacksaw blade." Eva's questioning expression did not change. Rachel added, "This can cut through steel bars. We must try to escape. I will cut through the bars of the window and we will jump from the train."

Here Eva shook her head in disagreement. She spoke softly but firmly. "I cannot jump with Daniel. I will remain here. Our fates are sealed together. However, you must jump. You are a strong person, Rachel. I feel it. *You must yet live.*" Rachel felt it too.

After a pause, Eva continued. When Rachel reflected on this conversation later, it didn't seem real, but it was a time when the unreal was commonplace. "You must jump, but you must take my Esther with you. No matter what happens to me, Esther must live."

Rachel looked into Eva's eyes. In an instant a conviction welled up within her that she must do this. "All right," she said, "I will take Esther with me. We will face the hazards of the jump together. I will watch over her as my own daughter until we can find you once the war ends." Rachel took Eva's hands in hers and squeezed them to seal the promise. Both had tears in their eyes. A loving mother had entrusted her daughter into the safekeeping of another. It was a sacrifice Rachel could only imagine.

The morning had worn on mostly in silence. Their companions were too weary now to expend much energy speaking. A commotion started from the front of the car—an older man had died, the first casualty. His family wept, but there was nothing to be done.

Rachel made her way carefully to the space underneath the window. She approached some young men and asked for their help. "I am going to try to saw through these bars. Would you let me sit on your shoulders?" They stared at her wonderingly. This was an audacious and dangerous thing for anyone to suggest, much less for a woman to do. Rachel showed them her hacksaw blade. "I can do it. I used to practice in my father's shop. Just hoist me up on your shoulders."

Some nearby heard of Rachel's intent and began to object. What would the guards do if they found out? The Nazis were famous for punishing many indiscriminately when one person violated their rules. If one member of a family was guilty of some infraction, the whole family suffered. If one person tried to escape, they might shoot ten people at random. For what Rachel was proposing to do, they might shoot everyone in the whole car. And yet, many believed they were on their way to their deaths. If so, they had nothing to lose. A Hasid said, "If she escapes, she can become a witness. She can remain to tell the story of our people—let her try." This was persuasive.

"All right," a young man said, "Sit on my shoulders." He boosted her up, and she breathed deeply from the fresh air of the window. Rachel wrapped her fingers in her shawl, gripped the blade tightly, and began to stroke it against the bottom of the first bar. The blade made a shiny scratch on the dark metal. She made another stroke and then another until gradually a slot opened up. She worked with determination, being careful not to let the blade slip from her fingers. If it were dropped and somehow fell out of the window, all would be lost.

Her fingers became sore, but she was nearly finished with the first cut. Finally the blade slipped all the way through—the bar was severed. Two more to go. She slipped off the young man's shoulders a few minutes so they both could rest. He reached up, and with the bottom of the bar cut, he was able to bend it back until it was clear of the window. Others came forward to help. There was a sense of exhilaration in doing something to defy the Germans, even if it was just sawing through the bars of the window. After another bar, Rachel's fingers were raw and bleeding. One of her helpers offered to finish the job, promising he would be careful not to drop the blade. After the bars were bent back, they had to cut the barbed wire.

Although much thinner, it was not easy to cut, as it moved back and forth with the motion of the blade.

Everyone who was nearby followed her progress. When the last bar was cut and bent out of the way, a murmur of appreciation rippled through the crowd. "Look, look, she has done it! She has cut the bars." But some countered with, "We will all pay for this. The Germans will surely notice. She may get away, but we will not, and we will be the ones who pay." Rachel hoped this wasn't true, but she felt they had little to lose.

It was early afternoon when the last bar was cut. When should they try to escape? Immediately? Or should she try to time her leap when conditions were most favorable? It made sense that she should jump when the train was moving slowly, such as when it was going up a grade. It also made sense she should jump in the countryside, where she had the least chance of being observed and where the forest provided cover. But more important than timing the jump from the standpoint of the train's location and motion was timing the jump relative to when the guards were least likely to notice.

Here was a dilemma. Clearly the time to jump and not be noticed was at night. Could she afford to wait that long? No one knew their destination. As best observers could tell by peering through the cracks in the side, they had moved west—not east—toward Germany since they had left the day before. If she jumped during daylight and were noticed, the guards would surely fire at her. They might even halt the train and hunt her down. Yet if they reached their destination before nightfall, she would have no opportunity at all.

Rachel considered the situation. More than anything, she was a person of action. She would rather take a risk and act than be passive and wait. But it wasn't just her own life at stake anymore, it was Esther's life at stake as well. She needed Eva's advice.

***

When Rachel explained the situation, Eva did not immediately reply. She reflected on her decision to have Esther go with Rachel. *I have only known Rachel for twenty-four hours, yet I have asked for her to take Esther with her. Esther could be badly injured or even killed by the fall. How can I make such a choice?*

Eva looked up at Rachel, who was waiting for her reply. Rachel's manner inspired confidence. Already she had shown it was possible to find a way to escape. She not only believed it, she had done it—she had cut the bars of their prison. She seemed to be a person who made her own luck. *My intuition tells me this journey will not end well. By splitting up my family, it is more likely someone will survive. I feel I must do this. I must give Esther this chance.*

Yet she did not know how to advise Rachel.

One of the men who helped lift Rachel up to the window slowly made his way over to where Rachel and Eva were. "If you wait until the window of the car is on an outside curve, the guards will not be able to see you jump. They can see the side of the train on the inside of the curve, but not the outside. If you can roll into the bushes after making the jump, they will pass by and not see you."

That was all the persuasion Rachel needed, and after a moment Eva nodded her assent. Rachel and Esther would prepare to go now.

As yet, Esther did not know what was being planned. She had been asleep as Rachel and her mother talked. Now Eva spoke with her. She gathered Esther into her arms and clutched her tightly. "Esther, my daughter, I need to speak with you. You remember how I had to leave you with Aunt Sophia while I went to work." Esther nodded. "I left you there so you would be safe while I was gone."

Eva was referring to their last days in the ghetto. Of necessity, Eva had to keep Daniel with her while she worked. However, she left Esther with her friend Sophia who watched over her own child and Esther while hiding in an attic, in case the Germans came during the day. The attic was dark, with a few streaks of light, much like the car was now. During those days in the attic, Esther learned to be very quiet. Even though she was young, she somehow understood they were in danger.

"I need you to go with Rachel. Rachel is going to squeeze through the window and jump from this bad train. I want you to go with her. Mommy can't go; she needs to stay with baby Daniel. Whatever happens, I want you to know that Father and I love you. It is because we love you that I want you to go with Rachel. Do you understand?"

Esther nodded yes but held on to her mother all the more tightly.

"Now, my little one, you must be brave." Eva had hidden her wedding band in the lining of her coat. She retrieved it, slipped it onto a piece of twine, and tied it around Esther's neck. "This is the ring Daddy gave Mommy when we were married. Our names are inside. When you are afraid, hold it in your hand and know that we love you. You will feel us close by. Give me a kiss and a hug." As mother and daughter embraced, Rachel bowed her head. She felt she was witnessing a sacred moment.

***

They made their preparations. In reality, there was not much to do. Esther had a cloth sack she had carried onto the train—it was easier for her to carry than a suitcase. To the change of clothes already inside, Eva added an extra pair of shoes and a few remaining pieces of bread, wrapped in a cloth. Eva had Esther put on her coat and a hat to cushion her against the landing. Rachel put on her coat and filled her pockets with a few things. Having been pulled off the street, she didn't have much else.

Eva gave Rachel her last złoty. "I don't think I will need these," she said.

Rachel recognized the prudence of taking the money. "I will add this to what I already have," Rachel whispered, "hidden in my other boot."

Eva smiled. "For some reason, that doesn't surprise me." It was late afternoon.

Rachel understood she was approaching a defining moment in her life. She felt a strange mixture of foreboding and anticipation. She supposed her feelings were what an athlete feels as he approaches the starting line of a race for which he has trained all his life, or what a musician feels as she steps onto the stage for her debut. Her pulse quickened. Although she had moved toward this moment for some hours, now that it was here, she felt it rising up before her. Her life, and the life of another, would irrevocably be changed in the next few minutes.

She drew in a deep breath, took Esther by the hand, and moved toward the window.

Chapter 3: The Jump

Rachel, Western Poland, Late Summer 1942

Rachel asked the young men who had helped her cut the bars to stand next to her. She explained that she and the little girl were going to jump now. "I will go first," Rachel said, "so there is no chance Esther will be left outside alone. As soon as I jump, lower her from the window and throw her as gently as you can away from the train. Then throw out her sack of belongings."

"We understand," one of the young men answered.

Rachel continued, "I'll want you to lift me up on my back and slide my feet out the window a few inches and hold me there until I get in position. Don't do anything until I tell you."

Eva addressed them. "Esther is my daughter." Then to emphasize the point, she stated, "I am her mother. Her father is not here. As hard as it is for me to do this, it is my wish that she go with Rachel. I feel this will give her the best chance of surviving. As Jews in this car, I believe you understand. After Rachel jumps, no matter what Esther does or says, even if she screams, I want you to proceed. Is that understood?" The men nodded.

Eva looked at those around her. "I need two women to help me, one of them a mother." Two hands went up. "Yes, please," Eva said, "stand here next to me." One of them was a teenage girl, perhaps sixteen years old. The other appeared to be her mother. Both were dressed in dark, tattered skirts with long-sleeved blouses. "Here," Eva said to the teenager, "would you please hold my baby for me?" She handed over Daniel, who was content for now, having just nursed. Then she took the hands of the mother in her hands. "How many children do you have?" she asked.

"I have three still living."

"And this is one of them," she said, nodding towards the teenager.

"Yes."

"I'm sure you are proud of them."

"Yes, they are all good children."

"Here is what I need you to do. After I have said goodbye, and they are lifting Esther up to the window, I need you to hold me."

19

The mother instantly understood. She squeezed Eva's hands and said, "I will be here next to you, ready." To those around them, the sense of a mother's love was palpable.

They wanted to wait until the train was on an outside curve, preferably moving uphill. The minutes dragged by. Now that the decision was made, Rachel was impatient to act. When at last the train entered what appeared to be a long outside curve, grade or no grade, Rachel decided it was time. She was hoisted up to the opening. She slid her feet out the window, leaning back on the hands of her helpers, and then rotated onto her stomach. She had to wiggle to squeeze her body through the narrow opening. Strands of barbed wire scraped her back.

She was now outside, hanging on to the window ledge by her fingers, her body in a crouching position, her feet up against the side of the car. She was buffeted and chilled by the wind. After a day in the shadowy, confined space of the car, the expanse of the world—the blue sky open all around her—was almost overwhelming. She momentarily glanced down at the tracks. They were a blur of motion. The sense of speed was much greater than from inside the car. It didn't matter—she had set her course and she would follow it. She hoped she could spring out far enough to clear the tracks running alongside the train and land in the undergrowth next to the roadbed.

She steadied herself by repeating the first verse from Psalm 46: "God is my refuge and strength, a very present help in trouble," and closed her eyes. She became aware that her legs were trembling. *Am I trembling from excitement or fear? I guess it doesn't matter—I should not delay.* She leaned back and with all the strength she could summon, launched herself from the side of the train. There was a brief second where she was suspended in space, followed by a violent crash.

Then her world went black.

Chapter 4: Outside
Rachel, Western Poland, Late Summer 1942

When Rachel regained consciousness, it was dark. She was in a strange, twisted position, mostly on her back. One leg was bent up behind her, and her head throbbed terribly. She tried to assess her injuries. Her hair was matted, warm, and sticky. She probed a little with her fingers and could feel a long gash in her scalp. Her shoulder hurt. Both the knee and ankle of her right leg ached, and her whole body felt bruised. Yet, as she carefully checked, she was able to move all her limbs. As far as she could tell, she had not broken any bones. She struggled to sit up from underneath some bushes.

She could not understand what had happened. *Where am I? What am I doing here?* She crawled toward a space that looked somewhat clear in the moonlight. It was two sets of railroad tracks. *These somehow must be connected to me—they are so near—but I don't know how.* She seemed to be alone. As she struggled to her feet, she felt dizzy and nauseous. She dropped to her knees and vomited.

The night air was cold, and she pulled her coat tight around her. She would rest for a few minutes and then try to figure out what she should do. She knew that somehow the train tracks were important, but they were a puzzle to her. *How are they connected to me? Was I on a train? Was I pushed off? That's the only thing that seems to make sense.* One thing she was sure of—she was battered and hurt.

As her eyes adjusted to the moonlit scene, she could make out the profile of the forest nearby. Feeling exposed where she was, she gathered her strength and stumbled in that direction. She propped herself up against the trunk of a large tree and then slid to the ground, breathing heavily. The earth was soft and spongy. She became aware of an awful thirst. She could do no more for now. She slid down until her head was nestled in the cradle of some roots, closed her eyes, and slept.

When she awoke, dawn had come. She was stiff and sore, but the throbbing in her head had subsided some. She felt she could think more clearly now. She decided the tracks held the key to her being there. She rose slowly and made her way back to them. They stretched out before her, giving no hint as to their origin or destination. She arbitrarily turned in one direction and began to walk alongside the tracks.

As she walked, Rachel gradually became convinced that she had been on a train on these tracks. She had walked for about half an hour when she stumbled onto a little sack near the roadbed. *I know this sack. I'm sure of it!* She opened the sack and examined its contents. Children's clothing. She found a note. She opened it and read, *Esther, my darling, remember that Mother and Father love you. Be a good girl and do what Rachel says. May God keep you safe.*

A revelation washed over her. Rachel was so stunned she could not stand. "Oh, dear God!" she cried, "give me strength." There was a little girl attached to these clothes, a little girl named Esther. She and Rachel had jumped from the train. Wherever she was, she had been by herself now for many hours.

Rachel was frantic. Where was Esther? Since the bag had been thrown after the child, Esther must have landed somewhere between where Rachel had turned to walk down the tracks and where she was now. Rachel began to retrace her steps. Despite her injuries, she quickened her pace. She called out Esther's name. Was it possible she was injured and still lying by the tracks somewhere? Had she been killed by the fall? Rachel weaved in and out through the bushes near the tracks, checking under low branches, calling out Esther's name. Over and over she cried, "Please, God, help me find her!"

She reached her starting point without finding a trace of Esther. Rarely had Rachel felt such despair. Somewhere out there, a little six-year-old girl was alone and perhaps injured. Rachel would sacrifice anything to know where she was and reach her. "Dear God," she whispered, "watch over Esther. Guide me to her." Never had she prayed with such fervor.

Just then she heard a terrifying noise. In the distance she saw a train bearing down on her. Immediately she dropped to the ground and began to crawl to the cover of some bushes. It was, she saw, a train of cattle cars, the same kind of train of misery she had been on. Surely it was headed to the same destination. It did not slow as it passed.

Rachel rested for a few minutes and then drew herself up to try again. She would walk back to the place where she found the bag. She would zigzag back and forth between the forest and the tracks and carefully examine all the ground in between. Rachel was weak, but she drove herself on. Esther's coat was blue and should be easy to spot. It took almost an hour to reach the spot where she found the bag. There was no trace of Esther.

For the sake of thoroughness, she decided to return while searching the ground on the opposite side of the tracks. It seemed unlikely, but what if somehow Esther had crossed the tracks and collapsed on the other side? She began the walk back to her starting point, taking the little sack with her. With Esther's things in her hand, her search was even more agonizing. The sack was tangible evidence that Esther existed somewhere, but Rachel could not find her.

She had now walked several miles since morning. Rachel felt faint. She needed food and water, and she needed rest. She remembered the bread in Esther's sack and choked down a few bites, leaving the rest for when she found her.

Somewhere in the vast forest around her was Esther. Even if healthy, Rachel could search only the tiniest sliver of the immense woods. The odds of finding Esther now seemed impossibly small.

She made a small pile of rocks near the tracks in case she ever returned. She removed a sweater from the bag that had a pink ribbon at the neck. She drew out the ribbon and tied it to a tree branch opposite the rocks. You could not see it unless you were looking for it. She felt pathetic about these gestures, knowing that after she left this place, there was virtually no chance she would recognize it again. *Perhaps these will be the only markers of Esther's grave.*

Given her condition, she had done all she could. It was time to go. She had twice searched forward the distance to Esther's bag and back again. Not knowing what else to do, she began to walk in the backward direction, the direction the train had come from. *I'm leaving the only place I know for sure Esther has been. This is a goodbye.*

She held Esther's bag tightly in her hand as she walked. Tears rolled down her face and dripped onto her coat. She had spent the morning in her search to no avail, and she knew she had to move on. She likely had a long distance yet to walk, and she was desperate for water.

Rachel kept close to the forest's edge. It was harder to walk there, but she felt too exposed near the tracks. She didn't know how she could keep going, except that she had to. She repeatedly picked out a crooked tree or some feature of the forest in the distance and promised herself that she'd rest as soon as she reached it. She focused on putting one foot in front of the other and refused to let herself think too far ahead. Gradually each landmark came closer; after what seemed an interminable length of time and effort, she reached it. Then she rested and started the cycle over again.

In the early afternoon, she heard voices. She ducked into the forest and hid before she was noticed. It was a German patrol: four men walking along, talking with each other, smoking, guns slung over their shoulders. *They look bored; they've probably been this way many times before. How lucky they are not to be at the Russian front.* It was, she reflected, a stupid thought. Why should she care what happened to German soldiers? That thought was followed by a sober one: what if they found Esther? Earnestly she prayed this would not happen. Surely if they came upon her, it would not take long to deduce she was from a Jewish transport. They would probably execute her where they found her. No matter what Esther's situation was, Rachel prayed she would be able to retain her dearly purchased freedom.

Rachel walked within the obscurity of the forest until the patrol was no longer in sight. The sun was hanging low in the sky, and her body ached. She did not want to think about the possibility of another night in the forest. And then, so tired she felt she could not continue, she stumbled upon a road of sorts—two barely visible ruts in a wagon-sized swath cut through the trees, perpendicular to the tracks. Hope. Where there was a road, there were people. And no sooner had she followed the road for a short distance than, to her amazement, she came across a truck. It seemed quite out of place in the forest. She could see no one.

Of course. It was a German army truck, the truck of the patrol. She warily approached. As she cautiously looked the truck over, she saw a canteen on the front seat. Quickly she unscrewed the cap and brought the canteen to her lips. The cool water flowed into her like rain in the desert. She drank and drank, and then she drank some more. She luxuriated in the wetness and sweetness and refreshment of water. She felt its effects diffuse through her body. After a few minutes, she felt renewed enough to consider what to do next.

Rachel had a decision to make. Should she take the canteen, or leave it half empty on the seat? If she took it, she would have water for a while, and she could carry water with her when she found another source. But the Germans would miss it. If she put it back, they might wonder why it was half empty but not likely consider that a fugitive was on the loose. Suddenly the decision was made for her: she heard the sharp crack of a branch snapping behind her, and she bolted with the canteen into the woods. She half expected to hear a rifle shot and feel a bullet pierce her back. She did not turn around.

Rachel continued to follow the road from the edge of the forest. Gradually it became more substantial, turning from ruts overgrown with grass into three distinct tracks, two for wagon wheels and a third worn bare by horses' hooves. Although the water had given her a new surge of energy, this wore off quickly. She needed to find somewhere to stay for the night. After another hour of walking, she noticed a side trail connecting to the road, and she also thought she could smell smoke. She would follow this trail and hope for the best.

The trail wound through the trees for some distance and then opened into an expanse of fields. At the edge of the field stood a small cabin made of rough-sawn boards, interlocked at the corners, with smoke drifting up from the chimney. Across from it was a barn, big enough for a cow and a horse and some hay. Attached to the side of the barn was a lean-to, about four feet tall, which Rachel discerned from various screeches and clucks to be a chicken coop.

The house and barn formed two sides of a dirt courtyard. Stretching behind them was a large vegetable garden. It looked somewhat ragged; Rachel could tell the growing season for most of the garden was over, but she could see some pumpkin still on the vine. Behind the garden were some fruit trees. Although the tenants were obviously not wealthy, there was a tidiness about the place that encouraged her. *I like tidiness too. Perhaps I will find a friend here.*

Chapter 5: Marynka
Rachel, Western Poland, Late summer 1942

Rachel had no idea how she would be received. Her experience was that many Poles were glad to see the Jews deported, were willing to betray them, and were happy to "inherit" their possessions. Others were understandably afraid to put their own lives at risk to help them. The plight of the Jews was unfortunate, but what could they do? The Nazi war machine had crushed everything that stood in its path. To try to help was to stand as a blade of grass against a forest fire. She said a prayer and knocked.

The door opened a few inches. Standing before her was a peasant woman, sturdy-looking and shorter than Rachel, with a round face and ruddy complexion. Her hair was tied in a kerchief, and she wore an apron over her billowy blouse and skirt. In her hand was a rag. Her eyes showed apprehension.

In the strange way the mind takes in a scene, Rachel noticed the floor was wood, not dirt, and had been scrubbed till it was bleached almost white. Tentatively she said, "I was wondering if I might sleep in your barn."

The woman looked Rachel over. From her torn and tattered clothing, covered in dirt, to her ratty, tangled hair matted with blood, Rachel was a pitiful sight. The peasant woman seemed to be wrestling with what to do. At length her face softened. "Come in," she said, opening the door wider. "Come in and rest."

Rachel saw that the humble dwelling was just one room, with a bed on one side, covered with a quilt, and the kitchen with its cast-iron stove on the other. There was a table with some chairs, the seats and backs woven from hemp. All was neat and clean. Only with urging did Rachel sit down. In her condition, she felt better suited to being in the barn—she certainly looked and felt more like an animal than a person. "Thank you," she stammered. "My name is Rachel."

"And mine is Marynka. You are hungry. I have some soup I can heat up. It will only take a minute. First, though, I am sure you would like to wash. There is a basin over there." She motioned to a corner with a pitcher, a bowl, some soap, and a cloth. Rachel splashed the cold water on her face and used the gritty homemade soap to take off a layer of grime. She then washed her hands. It felt good to at least be this clean. What she would give for a bath and some clean clothes!

Rachel sat at the table, grateful to sit in a regular chair. "Here," Marynka offered, "let me get you something to drink." She took the kettle off the stove and poured some water into a mug, added a teaspoon of jam, and stirred. "I am sorry I don't have any real tea," she said as she handed the mug over.

Rachel gratefully accepted it with both hands and sipped slowly, appreciating its warmth. The soup was mostly beans and potatoes. She had a thick slice of bread with some butter, more jam, and a little milk. Her body had not had such abundance for a long time, and reason told her to eat slowly and sparingly.

It was understood in wartime that you didn't ask too many personal questions, and Rachel was relieved that Marynka didn't pry. Everyone was trying to survive, to get by, to hang on. Everyone had some sort of story that could get them in trouble—something bought or sold on the black market, a stolen ration book, a hidden radio, a relative in the resistance. Many families had been dislocated and displaced. Most had lost a brother or father or uncle. Rachel's appearance told much about her sad story, but it was not an uncommon story.

Marynka volunteered, "My husband went into town this morning to the market. He often spends the night at his brother's. I suspect I won't see him until tomorrow sometime."

"Children?" asked Rachel. Seeing Marynka wince, Rachel regretted the question as soon as she asked it.

"We've only been married two years—but no, no children yet."

"I am sure they will come in time," Rachel said, wanting to offer some encouragement. While trying to keep her expectations in check, Rachel asked, "I have been looking for a little girl. Six years old, short dark hair. Have you seen or heard of her?"

Marynka shook her head. "I'm sorry. But don't give up hope. I am quite isolated here, and I haven't been to town for several weeks."

Rachel asked about the direction and distance of the village, where nearby German outposts were, and other information about her location. She learned she was a little west of Krakow. From the information Marynka provided, Rachel concluded the train she had been on had probably been on its way to Oswiecim, a Polish town almost on the German border. Before the war, it was a medium-sized town, nondescript, a town of no significance. Now its new German name—Auschwitz—was spoken of only in hushed tones. The name summoned forth terrible rumors.

They sat silently for a few minutes, appreciating the warmth of the stove. Even without conversing, they enjoyed each other's company. Finally, Marynka said, "Normally I would be glad to have you sleep inside, where it is warm. But my husband would not like it. He gave me instructions not to let anyone in. If the Germans found out, there would be trouble."

"It is safer for me to sleep in the barn. I am sure I will be fine there. I will be gone by early morning. I am very grateful for your generosity."

"It has been nice for me to have a visitor. It gets lonely when my husband is away."

"Is there something I can do to help you?" Rachel asked.

"Well," Marynka paused, "I do have some chores to finish. I don't suppose—"

"Suppose what?" Rachel asked quickly. "What can I do?"

"Do you know how to milk a cow?"

Rachel smiled. Her father had been a gentleman farmer, and she knew how to milk a cow. "Yes," she said, "as a matter of fact, I do. I'd love to do that."

"While you're milking, I can scrub the kitchen floor," Marynka said with some enthusiasm. It was becoming clear to Rachel why the floor was so white.

Rachel washed up, grabbed the milk pail, and headed to the barn. Since she would be sleeping there, she thought it a fine idea to get acquainted with the cow.

Afterwards they sat until dusk became darkness. Marynka self-consciously mentioned that she could not read, and she asked if Rachel could read some from a Bible. Having become a little bit familiar with the Christian Bible from school, Rachel thought it would be safest if she picked something from the New Testament. As the evening wore on, Rachel excused herself and walked to the barn, taking a blanket from the house with her. A measure of her strength and spirits had been restored by good food and company and the recognition of her personhood by another human being.

***

Unnatural sounds. The whine of gears, the rumble of exhaust, the squeal of brakes. Doors slamming. Sharp voices. Through the fog of sleep, Rachel realized she was in danger. She jumped up from her bed of hay. She knew she had only seconds before she was discovered. There was no time to think. She had slept with her clothes and boots on. Noticing the blanket at her feet and realizing she must take it, quickly she scooped it up along with Esther's bag and slipped out the back of the barn into the night. She ran as fast as her sore and bruised legs could take her.

A German officer rapped at the door. Marynka answered. "Where is your husband?" he demanded in Polish.

"In town."

"We are looking for some Jews. Have you seen anyone you don't know milling around the farm?"

Marynka shook her head.

"Has anyone stopped to ask for help?"

"No."

"If you see anyone, you are to report it immediately."

"Yes, of course."

The officer ordered one of his soldiers to look around inside. Marynka stood aside as the soldier brushed past her.

"Sir," one of the German soldiers interrupted. He played his flashlight on something he had taken from the barn. It was the canteen Rachel had been carrying. The officer looked accusingly at Marynka. She said nothing, but her eyes confessed. The way she looked down at the ground, avoiding the officer's gaze, confirmed her guilt.

It was over in less than thirty seconds. The officer grabbed her roughly by her neck and twisted her arm behind her. He shoved her to the ground face down in the dirt and put his knee in the small of her back. He pulled out his pistol, placed it at the back of her head, and fired.

They left her in the courtyard for her husband to find.

Chapter 6: Morning
Rachel, Western Poland, Late Summer 1942

Rachel ran until she thought her heart would burst. Her side was aching, and her lungs burned from the cold night air. She would rest only for a minute or two and then push herself on. The night was clear and still, and she distinctly heard the report of the pistol. She continued for a few seconds more, and then, connecting the sound with Marynka, came to an abrupt halt. "Oh no, no, no!" she cried. The realization of what the sound meant struck her like a blow. As the certainty of what had happened sank in, she hugged her arms close about her and fell to her knees. She had largely repressed the emotions of the past two days. Now the floodgates opened, and she sobbed uncontrollably.

Rachel was used to taking risks, but always before the risks had been hers. She was not used to being responsible for others or for having others bear the consequences of her actions. In just two days, all that had changed. A six-year-old girl, whom she had promised to watch over as her own daughter, was gone—lost. A stranger, who had acted as a friend, was gone—murdered. Rachel felt the fault was hers. She reproached herself for her naiveté, for her audacity in thinking she could outwit the Nazi juggernaut of evil. She was a strong person, but she had been living by her wits for a long time, and her emotional reserves were exhausted.

The knowledge that her actions had cost Marynka her life drained her. Where was God? Why didn't He help her find Esther? How could He let Marynka die? She wanted to climb into her father's lap and feel his arms around her. She wondered if it would be better to die and leave this awful world than continue in the midst of this suffering.

She came up against a hedgerow separating two fields. Feeling she could go no further, she wrapped the blanket around her and collapsed at the foot of the hedge, curling up on the lumpy earth. She fell into a troubled sleep.

As she slept, she had a very vivid dream of something that had happened when she was a little girl. She had become very sick with influenza. Her mother was away tending the family of a relative who was also sick. Her father stayed at her bedside, wiping her forehead with a cool cloth. Besides a burning fever, she had sores in her mouth and throat that made it painful to swallow. The days wore on slowly, but nights were worse. The minutes dragged by. She would fall asleep for a few minutes and then wake with a start, gagging and crying from pain or fever. She would ask her father, "When will it be morning?" and he would have to tell her that it would not be morning for a long time, but that he would stay with her, and he loved her. Soothed by his presence, she would drop off for an hour before waking again and asking, "Father, is it morning yet?"

"No," he would reply, "Not yet. But I am here, and I love you."

This routine was repeated through the night until she finally drifted off for a few hours. The dream was so vivid it seemed like she was reliving the experience.

Rachel awoke. The sun was just coming up across the fields, bathing them in a soft radiance. A mist hung over the countryside. She shivered and drew the blanket more tightly around her. As she slowly got to her feet, she reflected that it might be safer for her to head back to the forest—she was clearly visible where she was. She angled back to the forest's edge. She would have to figure out a way to get to the village, but for now she would stay out of the fields. Her stomach growled. The food and hospitality of the previous evening seemed long ago.

As she wandered, she heard a gurgling sound. Following it, she came across a small stream. She washed her hands and face and drank water from her cupped hands. It was only then she remembered the canteen: she had left it in the barn. As it was, she felt very low in spirit. Now the realization that the canteen had probably given her away and been the cause of Marynka's death brought her even lower. *How ironic*, she thought, *that something could be a blessing one day and a curse the next. That it could restore life one day and take it the next.*

She looked across the fields, still and serene in the early morning light. They belied the struggle she faced. Another day stretched before her of foraging for food. Of throwing herself on the mercy of strangers, not knowing if they would respond with kindness or rejection. Of wondering, if she was fortunate enough to find a friend, whether she would endanger that person's life. The struggle of just staying alive one more day seemed monumental. Thinking of her dream, Rachel cried out, "Dear God, when will it be morning?"

Then something happened she had never before experienced. Gradually Rachel's whole body filled with a tangible warmth, with peace, with light. Her body was enveloped by some indescribable influence, not something that had come from within her, but something that had come over her from without. She felt loved and safe. And into her mind came the words of her dream, spoken in her father's voice, "It won't be morning for a while, but I am here, and I love you."

The experience lasted only a few minutes. Slowly the influence withdrew, leaving a lingering warmth. Rachel basked in the reflection of what had happened. She was still hungry, and she was still dirty, and she still faced a day of challenge. Those things hadn't changed. Nevertheless, a transformation had taken place, for Rachel knew that God was aware of her.

She struggled to her feet. Tears blurred her vision. Whereas before she was anxious and distressed, now, for the moment, she felt calm. She still didn't know what to do or what would happen or whether she would ever find Esther. Perhaps she would yet be caught and killed. But she would trust in God for whatever would come.

Rachel knew the general direction of the village. The village represented both danger and safety. If she fell into the wrong hands, she would be turned over to the Germans. If she happened upon the right ones, as she had with Marynka, she might find food and shelter. The fields, brown and uneven in a layer of stubble, were quiet. The harvest in these fields was over. She saw a footpath wandering in and out of view. It seemed foolhardy to leave the forest, but knowing that she could not stay where she was, she ventured out and followed the trail.

As Rachel thought about her night and morning, she felt she understood that God did not intervene often. God did not stop the train Eva was on. The train continued toward its destination, despite being filled with hundreds of innocent people. But she understood that God was there. Surely, if He knew Rachel, then He knew Eva and Esther and everyone else in the car.

God knew their suffering. That made a difference.

Chapter 7: Leaving

Jacob, Eastern Poland, Spring 1942

Jacob saw his father walk in the door, head bowed, his gray beard touching his chest, intently reading a paper he held in his hands. "What is it father?" he asked.

"It is what we feared might happen. We are to vacate our house in five days. We are to move to a ghetto ten miles away. We can take some belongings with us, but they all must fit in one wagon. We are to turn in our keys at the police station."

Jacob's sister, Mira, hearing the news, came into the room and leaned on Jacob's shoulder. Instinctively he put his arm around her—although still in their home, he sensed she felt like he did, like survivors on a raft surrounded by a hostile sea. They had lived in their home in eastern Poland for only two years. Initially the Germans had occupied the western half of Poland, and the Russians, through a secret pact made with Hitler before the war, had occupied the eastern half. Thinking that life under the Russians would be better than under the Germans, Jacob's family had left their comfortable home in the west and moved near Jacob's mother's family in the east, to the town where his mother, Sara, had grown up. After the Germans invaded Russia, they occupied all of Poland. Within a year, the Germans were concentrating Polish Jews in the east into ghettos just as they had in the west.

Upon hearing about their eviction notice, his mother, not really knowing what else to do, did what many good mothers would do: she cleaned. In a whirlwind of activity, she swept the floors, dusted the furniture, and wiped down the woodwork.

"Mama, what are you doing?" Jacob asked.

"I don't want whoever takes our home to think I was not a good housekeeper."

Given the circumstances, this struck Jacob as comical, and they all needed a laugh. "We are being forced out of our home, and you are worried about whether the people who move in will think our cupboards are dirty?"

"Now Jacob," said his father, "you know your mother prides herself on her housekeeping. Let's let her have her way. We will begin to pack tomorrow. Tonight, let us think of happier things. Tonight we still live in our house."

And so, with four nights left until they had to leave, they enjoyed the luxury of contrived normalcy, of doing mundane things as if life would go on the same as it always had. His mother cleaned. Mira wrote poetry. Jacob and his father studied the Talmud, as they did most nights. As he lay in bed that night, he wondered what the coming days would bring and where he would be sleeping in a few days. In the context of the war, there were many things worse than leaving one's home. At least, he thought, they were alive and together. But he feared this was the beginning of a long series of changes that had no foreseeable end.

He also thought of Rachel. He was the same age, twenty, and he had been in love with her since he was twelve or thirteen. Not only was she very pretty, but she was smart, and he liked that about her. He thought about the time when they were fifteen and they had both been in the annual math tournament. It was unusual for a girl to represent her class, so Jacob was impressed. But more than that, she seemed to bring out the best in him. The tournament had a format where each student in turn was asked a question by a teacher. When Jacob missed his first question because he was nervous, she passed him a note. "You can do this," it said. He saw the encouraging look in her face and took heart. He settled down and sailed through the rest of the questions.

After the math tournament, they became friends and often walked home from school together. Jacob found they shared a love of literature and music. He played chess with her father and taught her cousins how to build a toy helicopter. Rachel had ambitions to become a lawyer, and he thought that was laudable. With someone like Rachel beside him, he felt he could make something of his life. Now he wondered if he would ever see her again.

The next morning Jacob's father asked the family to gather in the front room. "You remember when we left our home in the west," he started. "We couldn't take much with us. We learned that we could get along without many things. Now, unfortunately, we must do this again."

"What will it be like where we are going?" asked Mira.

"I don't know for sure, but I have some idea from letters from relatives. It will be very crowded. We should bring as many warm clothes as we can. Each of you can take two suitcases. Bring only clothes that are practical. Bring warm underwear and socks and your best walking shoes and boots. We should also take as much food as we can."

"Can we bring any books?" asked Jacob. They would have some long days without anything to read.

"A few," his father replied. "We will still need to feed our minds as well as our bodies. Pick out several books that are favorites, and we'll put them all in a chest. You may also bring a photo album. We'll include the chess set, and you girls can bring your sewing—it doesn't take much room. Sara, you and Mira should pack up everything we will need from the kitchen. Bring only what we must have."

Josef continued, "Since we didn't bring much furniture when we moved here, we don't have much to leave, except Sara's parent's furniture, which we were given when we arrived. I hate to leave that behind, but we must. We'll take the mattresses and the kitchen table and chairs, if we can get them to fit. Everything else must stay." Sara didn't say anything, but her eyes were sad and a little teary. The furniture was about all she had left from her parents.

"Jacob, we will need a wagon to transport everything. How about you talk with Tomasz to see if we could hire him and his wagon for the day?"

"Sure, Papa." Tomasz, the milkman, had been a friend since they had moved there and would surely help if he could.

Later, when Jacob asked, Tomasz replied, "I am sorry you must ask me this. It is not right what the Germans are doing. I will be glad to help. We just need to start early enough so I can be back before curfew."

The night before they had to leave, Mira asked if they could have a "going away" party. Mama made a little cake to sweeten the bitterness of their leaving. They sang songs, and each recounted a favorite memory of the past, which brought a feeling of nostalgia to the family. Mira recounted learning to cook under her mother's direction. "I remember the first time I was allowed to braid the challah bread for Sabbath," she said. "I was very proud of myself."

"And you have done a wonderful job since," her mother added.

Jacob talked of nights studying at the kitchen table while the wind blew hard against the windows. "I loved the warmth of the stove on those nights."

Josef spoke of coming to town long ago to court their mother. He would stop before he arrived to gather some wildflowers. "At the time," he said, "that was all I could afford. But now, as you can see, I have given your mother everything she could want." He gestured at the meager belongings around them. They all laughed.

Sara told stories of growing up with lots of cousins. "After Sabbath a big group of relatives came to our house to talk and laugh and eat sugared shortbread or other desserts. My mother was very popular because of her good cooking."

Unexpectedly, there was a knock at the door. Mama looked up, and Jacob wondered who it could be. His mother, always concerned about appearances, began to tidy up the parlor, but Jacob said softly, "Here, Mama, let me do this. You go ahead and answer the door."

As she opened the door, Jacob could hear the surprise in his mother's voice as she greeted an acquaintance from Mira's school, Klara Czyzewska. Mira and Klara's daughter, Anna, were the same age, fourteen, and had been in several classes together. Jacob recalled seeing Anna at their home on several occasions. Yet Klara's visit was surprising, given the casual nature of their relationship, and the risk one took walking the streets of a Jewish neighborhood. German police had a habit of patrolling the Jewish part of town just so they could harass anyone who was out.

"Klara," Mama exclaimed, "come in. Is something wrong? Did something happen to Anna?"

"No, Sara," she replied, "everyone is fine, as least as fine as they can be under present circumstances. I heard you were leaving, and I just wanted to let you know how sorry we are."

Mama cast a quick glance at Father. They hadn't experienced much sympathy from their Gentile neighbors. Her visit seemed very nice, but something about her tone of voice seemed strange to Jacob. "Why thank you, Klara," Mama said, obviously touched by her concern. "Here, please sit down."

"Oh," replied Klara, "I won't stay long. I know you must be very busy. So, you are leaving in the morning?"

"Yes," replied Mama, "we start in the morning. We are to give our keys to the police before we go. It will be hard to leave. We will not be able to take much with us, just what we can fit in a wagon."

"Well," she said, "speaking of that . . ." and her voice trailed off. "I was hoping we might have something to remember you by, so we would not forget you."

"Ah," Jacob heard his father say quietly, "now the situation becomes clearer."

Mama, who never thought ill of anyone, didn't catch on. "Oh," Mama said, "it is good of you to want to remember us. I know just the thing. Wait just one moment." Mama disappeared into another room and shortly reappeared with a school photograph of Mira. It had been on a shelf in the kitchen and was in a nice frame. "I thought perhaps this would be something Anna might like."

*Pani** Czyzewska cleared her throat somewhat nervously. "Yes, we will treasure this. Thank you. However, I was thinking of something more along the lines of this sofa." As she spoke, she patted the rose-colored cushion gently.

"The sofa?" Mama questioned. "You want the sofa?" She turned to Father and said, "*Pani* Czyzewska would like our sofa, Josef." The tone of her voice betrayed her confusion.

Jacob's father helped her out. "Yes," he said, "it is thoughtful of *Pani* Czyzewska to relieve us of the worry of wondering who will take our possessions after we are forced from our home."

Pani Czyzewska blushed. "Well, *someone* will have them. I just thought you might like them to go to people you know."

Pani Czyzewska wasn't the only one now who was red in the face. Jacob had rarely seen his mother angry, but she was angry now. "How dare you!" she exclaimed. "How dare you come around like a vulture, not even waiting for us to leave!"

"Now, Sara," Jacob's father said gently, trying to keep her from getting too upset. After a moment Mama regained her composure and said sarcastically, "Thank you for your kind visit, which was clearly motivated by your concern for us. However, until tomorrow this is still our home, and I ask you to leave."

---

* *Pani* is Polish for "Mrs." and *Pan* for "Mr."

Pani Czyzewska rose to go. She was not ashamed, however. In a patronizing voice she replied, "Have it your way. We will be back tomorrow after you go. I won't be sorry to have our village *Judenrein**." With that she turned and walked out. Before she left, Sara grabbed the photograph away from her.

In the morning, having finished his milk deliveries, Tomasz came by with his horse and wagon. The horse, an old mare named Rosa, looked sturdy but a little tired. Her caramel-colored back bowed, but she had strong looking legs and large hooves covered in white hair. Jacob knew Tomasz and Rosa were old comrades. Rosa was used to many stops and starts during a day, and she would wait patiently for Jacob's family to load their belongings.

The police had told them to be out by noon, but they had to leave earlier than that so Tomasz could be back before curfew. First, Father, Jacob and Tomasz carried out the bigger things—the mattresses and table and chairs. There was one chest containing precious items: photographs, books, the Talmud, and two carefully wrapped vases that had been in Sara's family for many years. This was supplemented by two other chests full of bedding. Jacob carried out their suitcases. Packing their suitcases was different this time. There was no anticipation of the journey, no excitement of a trip to see relatives. Instead they felt the anxiety of the unknown and the solemnity of leaving home, not knowing what would happen to them. The food items were stowed away in the "in between" spaces. It occurred to Josef that firewood might come in handy—where they were going there would be lots of people in a small space. They didn't know what would be available, so he and Jacob piled firewood wherever it would fit. They were almost ready.

Mama made some sandwiches for lunch, and Mira filled a large thermos full of tea. As the wagon got fuller and the pile in the front room smaller, there was a feeling it was time to go. Their life was being transferred to the wagon. This was cemented by the arrival of the police, who wanted to collect the keys. Mama said they would have dropped them off and it was still early, but the police were in a hurry. They asked for the keys and Father turned them over. For Jacob, there was a great sense of finality in this act.

---

* Free of Jews.

Chapter 8: The Ghetto
Jacob, Eastern Poland, Spring 1942

Father sat up high in the seat with Tomasz; Mother and Mira made a place to sit in the wagon on top of suitcases. Jacob sat on the back edge with his legs dangling over. Then Tomasz gave a shake to the reins, and Rosa strained at the harness to start them on their journey. They were heading east, to join their Jewish brothers and sisters from several villages. Except for other wagons piled high like theirs, there was no one to be seen on the streets. The Jewish homes were all deserted, some with the front doors left open, displaying furniture left behind. It reminded Jacob of the Exodus when the Israelites left Egypt.

They stopped briefly at the cemetery so Mama could say farewell at the graves of her parents. Many of the headstones had been knocked over or broken in half since their last visit. Jacob had noticed many of the windows in the synagogue were also broken as they passed. He realized there were many Poles who wanted them and the other Jews gone. They were outcasts in their own country.

It was a slow journey. Rosa had one plodding pace, and Tomasz knew better than to try to hurry her up. She was slow but steady. Jacob noted their progress from the increased traffic on the road as they were joined by others traveling like them to their new home. They saw wagons and carts of all types, loaded even more heavily than their own. Some looked as if they had brought all their furniture, including sofas, chairs, tables, and beds. In one wagon Jacob spied a sideboard for china. There were people riding bicycles piled high with goods. They came upon a teenager laboriously pushing a baby carriage stuffed with clothes, its wheels squeaking loudly. Occasionally they passed groups of German soldiers standing with their guns slung over their shoulders. The soldiers yelled insults and told them they were going to have to work for a change.

By early afternoon, the dirt road widened into the main street of the town. Policemen shouted for them to continue to the synagogue and motioned in its direction. It was easy to find the way as they just had to follow the meandering line of wagons in front of them. As they got closer, Jacob could see the silhouette of the synagogue rise up on the left. It was finished in white stucco; towers on each side stood like sentinels watching over this strange pilgrimage. Policemen were at the corners to show them where to turn and to maintain some semblance of order. They yelled curtly for them to hurry, as if that were possible in a street clogged with wagons and masses of people.

Jacob's family approached the entrance of their new home. As soon as they turned off the main street, they passed through a gate in an eight-foot-high wooden fence. The makeshift fence, made from poles with the bark still on, was obviously hastily constructed. It was topped with barbed wire. They would be prisoners within the town. At least they would live among friends.

After turning into the ghetto, it was obvious they could ride no further. Thomaz got down from his seat and began to lead Rosa by her bridle. Jacob joined him. They snaked in and out of piles of goods and wagons and knots of people. As they got close to the synagogue, Jacob's father said, "Wait, let me go and find out what is going on. Everyone stay here. I hope to be back in a few minutes." With that he approached a long line of tables sitting outside the entrance. People were huddled around each one, asking questions, pointing at papers, emphatically gesturing and talking loudly, and just as emphatically being given answers they didn't seem to like.

After half an hour, Jacob's father, looking tired, rejoined them. "We will be spending the night in an old warehouse. It is not too far from here. Then we will move into a house shared with six other families."

"Six families?" they exclaimed in unison. "How will we fit?"

"We will figure out some way to make do," was all their father said.

As they made their way to the warehouse, Jacob surveyed the chaotic scene. The place was bedlam. Everywhere he looked, people were crowded into outbuildings, cellars, even the synagogue. To make more room, bathtubs, dressers, tables, and stoves were moved outside to add to the piles of belongings already left there. Not surprisingly, they saw people bathing, dressing, eating, and cooking outdoors. With so many people milling about and the jumble of colors and shapes of these incongruous objects, the atmosphere resembled one of a carnival. Children raced around exploring and playing games with newfound playmates. Some boys viewed the piles of furniture as challenging mountains to climb. Using dresser knobs or cupboard doors as handholds, they tried to reach the summit. Invariably a father yelled for the boy to get down, shouting "Don't you have any sense?" or "Do you want to break your neck?"

After leading Rosa for another block, they pulled up outside a concrete block warehouse. There were only a few windows in the two-story, front façade, and the interior was hazy with dust from the dirty cement floor. Dozens of families were inside trying to create some living space. Ropes had been stretched across the width of the building in a few places, allowing families to hang blankets to cordon off the large open area into smaller ones. Except for their suitcases and the mattresses, which they laid on some blankets spread out on the floor, Jacob's family piled everything against the back wall. They would move their things later when they knew where they would be living and how much space they would have.

The next day they made their way to the small house they had been assigned to live in. The clapboard siding had weathered to a blotchy brown, and a roof of tin, splashed with patches of green moss, tented the second story. Two wooden steps led to the front door, which was a faded pale green. Not surprisingly, there was a pile of furniture out front.

"Jacob, go upstairs and see what you find," his father said. Jacob entered the parlor where he could see several mattresses stacked up against a wall. Two teenage boys, sitting on the floor, reading, casually looked up at him as he crossed the room. Climbing the narrow staircase, he noticed the yellow railing had been worn down to bare wood in places. He thought of the many hands that had grasped it—hands of children and adults. There were three small rooms upstairs; the doors to them were all closed. As he knocked on the first door, a woman opened it. She was wearing a blue sweater over a nice floral print dress. She looked as if she might be going shopping, except, Jacob realized, there were no shops. Behind her, Jacob could see her entire family of five camped out in a space about eight by ten feet.

"Hello," he said. "I am Jacob Liebman. My family has been assigned to live here. Just wondering if there is any room upstairs for another family."

"We might have some room if we all remained standing," she replied with a smile. "If we are going to sleep laying down, you can see we are pretty crowded already."

Her husband interjected, "My name is David Walczak," and he extended his hand. "And this is Sara, my wife; my sons Abraham and Josef; and my daughter, Anna. I am thinking that we could put bunk beds up and get a little more room."

"My mother is also named Sara," Jacob replied, "and my father is Josef."

"Well," the man said, "it must be fate that we are put together."

"Do you know if there is any space in the other rooms?" Jacob asked.

"I am afraid they are like us—stepping on each other's toes. There are two families in the room next door, and another family of five in the third room. Let me come downstairs with you and see what we can find."

They met Jacob's father. "There is a family in the parlor and another family in the cellar," he reported.

"Here is my suggestion," *Pan* Walczak said. "Let's move the stove out of the kitchen for now and make it a bedroom. We can cook and eat outside while the weather is good. In the meantime, we can figure something out."

So that is what they did. *Pan* Walczak recruited his two sons, and together they moved the stove outside to a shady spot at the back of the house. Even then the kitchen was too small for Jacob's family. The family in the parlor offered to have Jacob sleep with them.

They lined up several tables outside so they could eat their meals together. It was a little like having a picnic. The food assignments were rotated—one day one family made soup, while another made bread and another provided dessert. It all became dinner for everyone. They soon got to know each other well.

Jacob liked *Pani* Moshkovski the best. She was short, about five feet tall, with an ample bosom and thick waist. She had a round face with a broad smile and eyes that crinkled when she laughed. Her hair was short and wavy. She reminded him of a favorite aunt. Hugging her was like hugging a marshmallow—she was soft and squishy and carried a faint aroma of fresh bread. She was cheerful in the morning, when Jacob was crabby, and always called him "my dear boy," which from anyone else would have been condescending, but from her it was fine and made Jacob laugh.

***

For a few days, things went along without any outside interference. Considering they had just been torn from their homes, Mira noticed that people were surprisingly cheerful. There was a sense of shared deprivation, and the persecution they faced acted as a strong unifying force. There was a long line for the public toilet (to Mira much nicer than the latrine), and a similar line for the public bath next to the synagogue. Mira met several girls her age, and they quickly became friends. The slow-moving line was a great place to catch up on the latest gossip.

"Did you sleep well last night?" Mira asked her friend Hanna.

"Well, I would have if *Pani* Solnicka had not snored so loudly," she replied.

"Oh, I know," Mira said sympathetically, "I thought my father snored loudly, but *Pan* Steinberg snores so loudly you can hear him downstairs with the door shut." They giggled.

"For me," Tatiana said, "it isn't just snoring. You should hear *Pani* Lanski yell out when her husband puts his cold feet on her." More giggling.

"Well, it's one thing to sleep in a room with your whole family, but another to sleep in a room with your family and two older boys you didn't know until a few days ago," Hanna observed. "I mean, I'm in my pajamas."

"So," Mira said, "are the boys cute?"

"After all, let's get to what is important," Tatiana added.

"I have picked one of them out for you," Hanna replied. "He's a little homely and doesn't talk much, but other than that I think he's a good catch." More giggling.

The girls arranged to rendezvous three times a day so they could share the latest news. It was understood if someone couldn't make it, but at least they tried to meet up.

There was much to do. Mira helped with the cooking and watched over the smaller children. The boys were busy organizing the living arrangements to make things easier and carrying water from the well. New latrines were constructed. Some of the furniture left in the yard was used to make bunks or other platforms for sleeping. The confusion of the first few days was gradually replaced with purposeful activity as they adapted to this new situation. Life was bearable and they were surviving.

But it was not to last for long. Mira felt as if she were in a zoo, for there were always guards outside looking in. Although she learned to ignore them, the fence served as a stark reminder of the limits of their new world. It was a small world, and it was not a world that would be practical when winter came. Also, it was not clear what was going to happen when the food ran out. So far, the guards had allowed only a limited amount of food to be brought in, and anyone who approached the gate was threatened and shooed away.

Chapter 9: Pails of Water
Jacob, Eastern Poland, Spring 1942

A week later, the hope that had gained slender purchase in the hearts of Jacob's family was shattered. Notices were posted that all Jews were to gather that evening in the courtyard next to the synagogue. The ostensible purpose was to elect a new governing body, the *Judenrat*. Each of the council of ten elders was to bring seven others. Jacob felt proud that one of the elders invited his father to come as one of his seven. Josef was already becoming known as a scholar and a man of sound judgment. For some unknown reason, each of these men was to bring along a pail for water.

While his father gathered with the other elders next to the synagogue, Jacob assumed responsibility to watch over his mother and sister. Normally, if they were out together, he wouldn't even think about this, but the atmosphere here made him protective of them. Things did not feel right. He positioned himself in the middle and put his arms around them.

The eighty men were ordered to line up in two rows. Soldiers of the SS, clad in gray field uniforms and wearing steel-toed boots, made a sort of corridor to the left tower of the synagogue by forming two lines stretching from the entrance to the well. Other soldiers climbed the steps. The soldiers were laughing and exchanging knowing glances with each other. They all held rifles, clubs, or metal bars. The Jews watched apprehensively as SS soldiers quietly ringed the crowd.

The SS commandant blew his whistle and silence fell over the square. "I thank you all for coming. The purpose of gathering here this evening is to select a new Jewish council, or what we refer to as the *Judenrat*. Its purpose is to keep order in the ghetto and follow orders with exactness."

An ominous feeling came over Jacob. *Why did they need to gather here like this? What were the Germans planning?*

"We will see tonight who can follow orders with exactness. I see the candidates have brought pails as instructed. That is good. Now here is what you are to do with them. You are to fill them up with water at the pump to within a half inch of the top." He gestured toward the pump. "Then you will carry the pails of water, on the double, from

45

the pump across the courtyard and up the stairs to the third floor of the synagogue without spilling a drop. Anyone who spills a drop will be punished for not following orders. Do you understand?"

Only a few responded. Those who didn't received a blow to the back. "Do you understand?" the commandant repeated. Now they all nodded. "Good. After reaching the third floor you will cross over to the other tower and descend the stairs. You will then enter the line to refill your buckets, if necessary. You will continue until I signal you may stop. Are there any questions?" He mocked them with his veneer of politeness. "When I blow my whistle, you will begin."

With a blast from his whistle, there commenced two hours of horror and outrage for the onlookers and two hours of humiliation and suffering for the participants. They started out slowly, trying to carry the water without spilling it. But this was not satisfactory. "I said on the double," yelled the commandant, "and I meant it," and the SS men on either side clubbed or pushed them to get them to move faster. Of course, this resulted in water sloshing out the sides of the pails. As soon as this happened, the SS beat them with a relish. They hit them on their backs and sides. They didn't want to disable them, at least not yet, so they avoided striking their heads or breaking their legs.

Jacob winced as he saw someone stumble, the pail crashing to the ground and the water spilling over the cobblestones. The unfortunate man was kicked savagely and told to get up. He gradually found the strength to pull himself to his feet, blows raining down on him while the guards told him to hurry up.

Jacob pulled his sister and mother tightly to him as they recoiled in shock and horror. They buried their faces into each other's coats, but they still heard the pails hit the ground and the thud of clubs and groans. His mother half shouted, half whispered, "Dear God, save Josef…save Josef!" The person next to him bent over and vomited.

After forty-five minutes, the men were exhausted and could only stumble along. One man fell, his strength sapped; after blows and kicks, he could not get up again. A nearby SS soldier pointed his rifle at his chest and fired. The body went limp. The soldier shoved the body out of the way. There were shrieks from the crowd, but the commandant yelled for silence. From this point on, a gunshot rang out every few minutes. With each gunshot his mother and Mira flinched as if they had been shot too. Bodies were thrown out the tower windows into the courtyard where they formed a bleeding, inert heap. Jacob could not bear to look for his father. It was too awful.

After two hours, the commandant called a halt. "I am glad a few of you are still standing. Otherwise, who would we select for the *Judenrat*? I hope, however, you will learn to obey orders better than you did tonight. If not, you see what will happen. Now everyone, go home. In the morning I expect a detail of twenty men to dispose of the bodies and twenty women to scrub the square clean. There is to be no sign of blood on the cobblestones. That is all." With that, he climbed into his black Mercedes and drove away. Those who lost loved ones stayed in the square, mourning their dead.

Twenty-eight men died that night; Josef survived. He came home with a face streaked with blood and dirt and missing a tooth—the result of falling on the stairs. Sara's first impulse was to embrace him, but he cried out in pain. Carefully they removed his ripped and blackened shirt. His back was a mass of bruises and swelling red lumps. His ribs ached, and it was hard for him to breathe. "Oh, Papa, I am so sorry," Mira sobbed as she knelt and hugged him around his knees.

Jacob felt an overpowering rage. "Someday," he promised himself, "they will pay for this." His father spent the night sitting up in a chair. The character of their German masters had been revealed. The Jews had not believed the stories they had heard. Now they had some first-hand experience.

The next morning at daybreak, there was a knock at the door. Twenty women were expected at the square in half an hour. Sara put on an old dress, added an apron, and tied a kerchief on her head. She took the same pail Josef had used and a brush and walked with others silently to the square. There they knelt and scrubbed the cobblestones and stairs clean from the night's horror while men loaded bodies on a cart to be buried outside the ghetto in a mass grave. In the days that followed, whenever Sara climbed the synagogue stairs to sit in the balcony, she was oppressed anew by the hatred and suffering that had taken place there. Her eyes caught several dull, rust-colored spots on the wall of the curving stairway—spots that had not been completely washed away and that stood as a testament to what had happened.

From that day on, Jacob and his family felt they were in an ever-tightening vise. The *Judenrat* became an instrument of German authority and oppression. It posted rules everyone was to follow—they were to wear the yellow star at all times, curfew was to be strictly obeyed, smuggling was forbidden, and everyone must carry an identity card. Disobedience was punishable by death. The circle of normal activity began to get smaller and smaller.

Chapter 10: Books and Scrolls
Jacob, Eastern Poland, Early Summer 1942

Several weeks after the selection of the *Judenrat*, Jacob noticed a group of Jews reading something that was posted on the synagogue wall. It was a decree instructing them to bring all written or printed materials to the square in two days. This was to include books, letters, photographs, documents, diaries—anything written or printed.

The decree said all written materials were to be "cataloged and approved." This sounded suspiciously euphemistic. Perhaps, some said optimistically, it will be alright—after all, the Germans were prodigious record keepers. But why did the Germans care? Did they believe the Talmud or a book of mathematics or Aunt Serena's picture was somehow going to lead to an uprising? The speculation, the fear, was that the books and records would be destroyed. Although any military justification for this action was ridiculous, no one doubted, after the *Judenrat* episode, that the Germans might do this.

When Josef came home that day from a *Judenrat* meeting, Mira immediately confronted him. "Is it true?" she asked. "Do we have to give up all of our photos and anything written?"

"Yes," her father said, "it is true."

Mira loved to write poetry, and she had painstakingly copied over her poems into one notebook she had brought with her. In the upheaval of their lives, it was a great solace for her to be able to write down her feelings and thoughts as poems. "My poems," she said, "are all I have. They are all I have left of my life! I will not give them up!" She was almost hysterical. Jacob, listening, understood this was about more than poems.

"Now, now, my darling," her father said tenderly. "Let me think. Let's not worry about this tonight. Let me see if I can think of something. Perhaps there is some way we can keep them."

The following morning, Mira brought her notebook to her father. "It is all right, Father. I am fine now. I will turn them in. I wouldn't want anything to happen to our family because of them. I will keep them inside of me." Her father bent down and kissed the top of her head.

The next day Jacob and Mira carried suitcases filled with books and papers to the square. They were joined by others as they walked, some of whom were pushing carts or wheelbarrows full of documents. In front of them stretched a line of tables where members of the *Judenrat*, forced into this detestable task by the SS, accepted the materials. Members of the SS stood nearby, making sure all was done according to orders. Periodically, one of them would yell out, "Form lines behind each station. Be ready to declare everything in your possession. You will have to leave everything here for approval and cataloging."

Jacob watched as Mira handed over her book of poems. She showed no emotion as she pushed the well-worn notebook towards *Pan* Birenbaum, a neighbor and a member of the *Judenrat*, who carefully placed it with the rest of their family's documents in a stack on his table. He was wearing gloves. Jacob guessed he didn't want to mar any photographs by leaving his fingerprints on them. If so, his care and concern were wasted, for as soon as a group of documents had been collected and a receipt given, German soldiers threw everything into a big pile, mixing everything up. They had no compunction about walking over everything in their boots, oblivious to the damage caused in the process. By afternoon, there was a small mountain of books and papers behind the tables.

A woman next to Jacob set a collection of things on the table, including, he could see, a photograph album. She pulled one photo from the pages. "I just," she said meekly, "want to keep this one." He could see it was a wedding picture. "I haven't seen my husband since he was taken to a labor camp. Please let me keep it."

The *Judenrat* official looked up into her eyes. How could he say no? But then a sharp voice intervened. "Leave it," it said. She put the photo down and turned quickly away. Jacob could see the anguish in her face.

Jacob's father didn't return until late afternoon. The family gathered around, as he was clearly downcast and troubled. "I felt I was erasing people's lives, destroying the evidence of their existence," he said. "We are to come back at five p.m. tomorrow. It doesn't matter that it is the Sabbath." They shared glances with each other. They all knew what would happen to their books and heirlooms. They understood they would never see them again.

But they did not know what else the Germans had in store. When the appointed hour came, Jacob was surprised to see Rabbi

Goldstein standing in front of the mountain of documents. The Rabbi was a short man, with a balding head partially covered with a skullcap and full white beard. He was holding the Torah scrolls from the synagogue. People bowed their heads. They sensed the scrolls were about to be desecrated.

"Now," said the commandant, "let me have your attention. If any of you have things you have held back, you may bring them here tomorrow after the Sabbath is over—I wouldn't want to upset your religious observances." Soldiers snickered. "After that, anyone found in possession of anything written, or any photo, except your registration papers, will be shot. Do I make myself clear?" Knowing he expected a response, people nodded their understanding.

"The good rabbi here holds something written, and like everything else, it must go. It will be placed on the top of the pile, and then it all will be set on fire." People absorbed this news with little overt reaction, but it struck an inward blow. "But I will try to protect these sacred writings. We will use water to save them from the fire." The crowd wondered what he could mean. And then, with a gleam in his eye, he said, "Rabbi, spit on them," and pointed at the scrolls.

Rabbi Goldstein looked at the commandant and looked at his people. These scrolls represented what he had dedicated his life to. There are some things a person cannot do, even though it may cost him his life. The rabbi turned to the commandant and said simply, "I cannot do this."

"Do you dare to disobey me? I order you to spit on these rolls of trash." And with that, the commandant motioned to a soldier standing near him, who took the butt of his rifle and struck the rabbi in the back so hard he fell to his knees. He then kicked him so hard that the rabbi moaned and fell face down on the ground. "Now," said the commandant, "get up."

The rabbi, dazed and in pain, could not rise. The soldier pulled him roughly to his feet and held him there. The commandant decided to provide some persuasion. He grabbed a young girl, perhaps ten years of age, from the crowd. She began to cry as he held her tightly by the arm. He put his pistol to her head and said again, "Spit on them, or I will shoot everyone here until you do, starting with her." No one doubted he would keep his word.

The rabbi had no choice. "God forgive me," he said, and then he spit on the sacred scrolls.

"Keep going," growled the commandant, "until I say you can stop." After five minutes the rabbi could no longer spit. His mouth was dry. Perceiving the problem, the commandant ordered several SS men to stand in front of the rabbi. "We need to save these scrolls," he said sarcastically. "If they aren't wet, they will burn. The honorable rabbi is doing a poor job." He then told the rabbi to open his mouth. Now, he told his men, "help him out." It didn't take long for the SS to comprehend this order. They spit all over the rabbi's face and into his mouth. The commandant invited others to join in. A line formed. Soon a dozen men took turns spitting on the rabbi. The spittle ran down his face and dribbled onto his beard. After enjoying this spectacle for a few minutes, the commandant told the rabbi to resume spitting.

When he had had his fun, the commandant released the terrified girl. "Douse this pile of rubbish with gasoline," he ordered his men. They emptied several cans of fuel on the books and papers at the base of the pile. Of course, not much would be needed, since the small mountain was primarily made of paper. He then ordered the Torah scrolls to be put on top. "Let us see," he said, "if your God will save your scrolls. I have done my part to help."

A match was struck, and the pile burst into flames. Jacob and his family watched as their precious documents—their scrolls and sacred texts, histories, prayer books, school texts, photograph albums, family records, the accumulated knowledge and evidence of their religion and their lives—were turned to ashes before their eyes. Their bodies were gradually being worn down physically. But this was an assault on their spirits. This destroyed the fabric of who they were. Burning the scrolls was like severing the link between themselves and their God. Burning their keepsakes was like severing their link with their past. They were castaways.

Jacob thought of Rachel. She came from a family that revered books. Books contained the word of God. Books explained the words of the great rabbis. In Rachel's family, books were handled carefully. Your hands were to be clean, and when you were finished, the book was to be put away. Every year she made covers for her schoolbooks. When a boy took one of her books to tease her and threw it on the ground, she gave him a bloody nose. To see books trampled underfoot, to have the Torah scrolls spit on and burned, would have wrenched her heart.

The fire cast an eerie glow around it. "It is all right," said the commandant, in a pretend caring tone, "you can leave now. I realize evening has come. Please enjoy your Sabbath." A few people, including Josef, came forward to help the rabbi, who was still sitting on the ground with his face in his hands. Attention had been drawn elsewhere. Spittle hung down in threads from his beard. In a quiet voice, he was asking God for forgiveness. Although few noticed, he had rent his coat.

For hours afterwards, black snow fell across the ghetto—snow made from the ashes of the fire. The symbolism was not lost on Jacob. The black snow settled on their hearts like it did on the streets and roofs.

Chapter 11: Samuel
Jacob, Eastern Poland, Early Summer 1942

Their lives began to fall into a routine. Each day the *Judenrat* organized the men of the ghetto into work details, according to assignments given by the Germans. At first there was a big demand for crews to clean streets and clear rubble. Another group, including Jacob, was taken under guard to the forest to cut down trees. Those with certain useful skills were marched out of the ghetto to some former government offices, now deserted, where they were organized into a collection of small "shops." They would make or repair shoes, clothes, furniture, clocks, and tack for horses. There was a carpentry shop, an electrical shop, and even a mechanical shop to repair vehicles. Jacob's father, who was a watchmaker and jeweler, was lucky enough to be assigned to these shops. Since Jacob had worked with his father at times, Josef was determined to get him transferred to the shops as his apprentice.

One evening Jacob's family heard a knock at the door. It was a member of the Jewish police force. The Germans wanted a gang of men to work that evening and Jacob was requested to be part of it. Although exhausted from the day's labors, he nevertheless felt he must go. He grabbed his coat and some gloves and kissed his mother goodbye. His father wasn't home. He could see concern in Mira's eyes, and he wondered if it was justified. About the only certainty in their lives these days was uncertainty. The policeman could only tell him that the Germans had decided to enclose the shops where his father worked with a fence. For some reason they wanted this done tonight.

With a group of about fifty men, Jacob was marched outside the ghetto to the town market square. They were watched over by mounted SS and Lithuanian guards, who were in a perverse mood and who whipped or beat them with little provocation. Apparently the guards weren't happy either about working this night shift. At the square, they were to disassemble and then transport an already built fence to the shops. First, they had to break the existing fence into sections.

With picks, sledges, crowbars and shovels they dug up the posts and then separated the sections between posts. The fence was made of poles that over the years had absorbed a lot of moisture and were very heavy. They were to carry the sections, which were roughly eight feet long and six feet tall and weighed several hundred pounds, a mile to the shops. Eight men hoisted each section horizontally onto their shoulders. Jacob groaned as his slight frame absorbed the weight. He felt as if his legs would buckle. *How would he manage to last the night? In fact, how would he manage to last one trip?*

They only had moonlight to light the way. As they struggled down a dirt path to the shops, it was not unusual for someone to trip or collapse under the weight of their load. Sometimes that meant the whole section would tumble down, in which case they were beaten by the guards. Anyone who could not get back up again was shot; the body was thrown on the fence section, increasing the load for everyone else, to be buried in a mass grave. Jacob struggled along. With each step he felt his strength ebbing away, till he could barely put one foot in front of the other.

In Jacob's group was a young man named Samuel. Midway through the dark night, Jacob began to stumble as if he were drunk. Samuel could see Jacob would soon go down.

"Hang on," Samuel encouraged, and then, more insistently, "Listen to me. You have to keep going. Don't give up. You *must* go on." Jacob wanted to listen, but the words seemed far away and disconnected to him. "Keep going. You *cannot* let yourself stop. I'll help you." Samuel's voice willed determination into Jacob's body.

"I can't go much further," Jacob replied, slurring his words.

Seeing Jacob needed immediate help, Samuel told him, "Come closer to me. Move to the inside." Jacob moved closer to Samuel. He could feel Samuel lift the fence up enough so Jacob's load was reduced. Somehow he made it until morning. There was no doubt Samuel saved his life.

***

Thus began the friendship between Jacob and Samuel. They were in some respects very different, but the shared experiences of the ghetto drew people together. While Jacob was quite introspective and self-critical, Samuel was open and friendly, a person without guile. Physically they were also different—Jacob was lean and wiry while

Samuel was solid and sturdy. His broad shoulders and thick neck contrasted with Jacob's slender build. Samuel's warm smile reflected a general attitude of goodwill towards others, and his positive outlook was a tonic for Jacob's more serious nature.

At the end of each day, if they had any energy left, they talked. Samuel could sense in Jacob a fine intellect. Samuel had grown up on a farm and had not had a lot of schooling. He partially made up for that now as he asked Jacob a lot of questions, especially about books Jacob had read. Somewhat surprisingly to Jacob, Samuel was interested in literature. He had Jacob recount all he could remember from Shakespeare's plays. They went through the novels of Henryk Sienkiewicz, a famous Polish author. They both enjoyed these discussions, which made them feel human again.

In time, Josef was able to get Jacob a job in the shops as his apprentice. Jacob began a campaign to also get Samuel a job in the shops as well—Samuel had done a little bit of everything on the farm—and eventually Jacob was able to get Samuel brought inside as a carpenter. The work in the shops was sheltered from the weather and not as physically demanding as the outside work. They received better food rations. But more importantly, they created things the Germans wanted, which made them feel more secure.

Chapter 12: The *Aktions*
Jacob, Eastern Poland, Summer 1942

It was clear to Jacob that something would have to change. There were now more than three thousand people in the ghetto, with more arriving every day, and that was too many. There was not enough space for that many people to live in the ghetto during the winter.

Jacob wasn't surprised, therefore, when he saw notices go up one morning indicating that twelve hundred people were needed for work camps in the east. The notices stated they would be expected to work hard but they would have adequate housing and enough to eat. For those who volunteered, there would be two loaves of bread and a jar of marmalade given as they started their journey. They were to report to the square in two days at eight a.m. with a maximum of thirty pounds of luggage per person. From there they would be taken to the train station.

The *Judenrat* was given the assignment to make sure twelve hundred showed up. The ghetto had a Jewish police force that operated under the direction of the *Judenrat*. If not enough came, they would be responsible to round up families and force them into the square and onto the trucks. This created the sort of spectacle the Germans enjoyed: Jews oppressing Jews.

Jacob's family gathered in their small room, now shared with another family. Should they volunteer? They were always hungry. The backdrop of any day was a craving for food. It would be wonderful to have enough—that was the promise of the eastern work camps. "What do you think we should do, Father?" asked Jacob.

"I frankly do not know. We are gradually starving here. Mira looks like a skeleton already."

Mira was very thin, despite receiving some of her parent's rations. She must have taken this comment as a reprimand because she said dejectedly, "I can't help it."

"I'm sorry," Josef said. "I didn't mean to sound like I was blaming you." He reached over and squeezed her hand. Then he continued, "Do we take a chance on the transports, which lead to an end we do not know, or stay here, in the desolation we do know? It is a devil's choice."

57

Sara spoke up. "There are rumors there are no eastern work camps. That the Germans are lying."

"That is my problem as well," said Josef. "Can we believe anything the Nazis tell us? I can believe they want to destroy us—that I can believe, but anything else, anything supposedly better, I do not trust. I think for now we should stay. Perhaps things will get clearer soon, and we will know better what to do. What do you think?" Their father was a good and wise man, and they had faith in him. They agreed, though they knew it meant more hunger.

But many, out of desperation, did go. When the morning came, hundreds filed past their door on the way to the square. There they formed into lines while their names were taken. To their satisfaction and delight, the Germans provided them with loaves of bread and jars of marmalade. "You see," they said, "it will be alright. We will be fine. The Germans are keeping their word. They need us to work."

Jacob could hear quarreling among some of those who remained behind. "We should have gone," they said. But enough had come. Those left behind watched the loaves of bread and marmalade with keen disappointment and hunger pains. The volunteers were loaded into trucks to be driven to the station.

***

Several days later, a few of the volunteers made it back to the ghetto to tell what had happened. The trucks drove several miles outside of town, where large pits had been dug. People were ordered out of the trucks. They were told to leave their luggage. SS soldiers with clubs and dogs were waiting for them.

"Everyone line up," they shouted, "four abreast." The line stretched for two hundred yards. "Be ready to hand over your jewelry and your valuables. Anyone caught holding anything back will be shot. Move!" The guards collected their watches and rings and demanded their money and gold. If a person wasn't fast enough, the guards yanked off the rings, leaving bloody fingers. It was quickly becoming apparent they weren't going to the east to labor camps.

The next command further deepened their shock. "Take off your clothes. Everything. Then lie on the ground." People looked around at each other in confusion. Was this command real? Modesty was an important principle for a Jew. Did they really expect men, women, and children to disrobe out in the countryside in front of each other?

The answer was *yes*. The guards repeated their order: "Take off all your clothes. Everyone. Put them into piles." The soldiers struck anyone who was reluctant. They grabbed shirts and ripped them open. They yanked off coats. A few Jews instinctively resisted; they were beaten or shot. Dogs lunged at them. Occasionally a soldier gave his dog enough leash to savagely attack their pale, bare bodies.

Naked, humiliated, and cowering from blows and bites, the men, women, and children were ordered to the brink of the pits eight at a time, where they were shot. Babies were thrown into the pits alive. As they stood waiting to be executed, they saw before them the naked layers of their friends and neighbors covered in blood. There were no words to describe the horror of this scene, except to say, *this is Gehenna. This is hell on earth.*

Occasionally some movement in the pits was spotted and the wounded person was dispatched by an additional bullet. Amazingly, a few survived. Hidden by the bodies on top of them, they crawled out of the pits at night covered in blood; a few made it back to the ghetto. As their stories circulated through the ghetto, some felt they must be wildly exaggerated. How could such things be? In a quiet moment, Jacob asked his father if he thought the rumors were true. His father put his arms on Jacob's shoulders, looked him in the eyes, and nodded.

***

It was from this time forward that the decimation of the ghetto began. Three weeks after the first deportation, the ghetto was hit with a surprise *Aktion* where police, including Jewish police, cordoned off sections of the ghetto so no one could escape, and went house by house forcing people into the streets and onto trucks. On "Black Monday" as it was later called, another thousand Jews were "resettled" in the east.

Sometime afterwards, new identity cards were issued. A few, including members of the police force and the *Judenrat*, received a special stamp indicating their occupations were protected. Jacob felt fortunate that the tradesmen who worked in the shops also received the stamp. With the stamp, your immediate family was declared as having a protected status as well. Everyone understood what this meant: those without the special stamp would be selected next. They were only half right.

Two weeks later, on Thursday evening, Jacob and everyone else in the shops were not allowed to go home. "You will spend the night here," they were told.

"What about our families?" they asked the guards.

"Your families will be fine. You will see them tomorrow."

Jacob was usually with his father, but not this day. For some reason, his father had declined that morning to come to the shops. "You go, but I need to stay with your mother," he said. Now, as evening came on without his family, he felt alone and worried.

Jacob knew anything out of the ordinary usually did not bode well for the Jews. That night he lay on the floor, with a thin blanket over him, wide awake. Sometime after midnight, far away, he could hear trucks, whistles, and dogs barking.

He knew what these sounds meant. Jacob felt sick as he imagined families and neighbors, his people, being roused from their beds and forced into trucks. Yet he wanted to hope—to hope that this time things were different, to hope his family was spared, because of the special stamp. After all, his father was not only a member of *Judenrat*, but he and his father worked in the shops.

Unfortunately, his hope was in vain.

Chapter 13: Outcast
Rachel, Western Poland, Fall 1942

    Rachel followed the trail through a mix of undulating fields intermixed with pockets of forest. As she crossed over a shallow rise, the village came into view. She could see twenty-five or thirty houses scattered along the main road and several cross streets. The houses were separated from each other by gardens, outbuildings, and small pastures. The steeple of a church rose beyond the trees and the tin roofs. It was too dangerous for Rachel to approach in the daytime—she would have to wait until dark. The Nazis would have imposed a curfew, so she had to get to the village before that. She walked back over the crest of the hill and continued until she could sit secluded within a grove of trees. There she found a few berries to eat.

    She started toward the village late in the afternoon. At the top of the hill, she studied the layout of the village. She had no idea where to start, so she picked out the cluster of homes closest to her. She memorized where they were relative to her path and the main road. She would try to approach them from the fields behind. She picked her way carefully along the path and through some trees until she was close to a group of three or four houses. As she considered which to approach, one especially appealed to her. From the rear she could see it had a stable and some other small buildings. A horse was picketed in a grassy area. Next to it, she noticed some junk—wagon parts, farm implements, a rusty tractor. What was it about this odd collection of stuff that she liked? She sifted these images for a moment until she realized they reminded her of home—they were the sorts of things her father had worked on. There was a friendliness in their familiarity. Perhaps someone like her father lived here.

    Rachel knew that her life could very well depend on selecting the right house. She decided to wait a while and just observe and settle her nerves. Perhaps she could get a look at someone who was inside. At length, the back door opened, and she heard the master call for the dog. A black-and-white, flop-eared collie mix came running. Rachel hadn't seen the dog. If she had walked much further, the dog would have certainly barked. With two good omens—familiar junk and a dog now confined indoors—she thought she shouldn't wait any longer. She screwed up her courage, walked across the backyard, and climbed a couple of steps to the back door. She knocked and stepped back.

Immediately the dog barked. Then there was silence for a few seconds and a shuffling noise. A man with a weathered face and deeply tanned skin opened the door, holding out a lamp so he could see.

"I wondered if I might sleep in your stable."

Half of the man's face was cast in shadows by the lamp, but she could still see his expression. At first, he appeared confused, and he held the lamp out further so he could get a good look at Rachel. He looked her over as Marynka had, examining her from head to toe. His brow furrowed. "Are you a Jew?"

"Yes."

A look of utter repugnance came over him. "Leave," he said harshly. "Leave, and don't come back. I thought we were rid of the damn Jews."

Rachel backed up, tears of hot anger coming to her eyes as surely as if she'd been slapped. She backed up a few more steps and then she turned and ran.

It was a clear night, and stars filled the sky. Rachel only knew that she was hungry and cold and demoralized. She walked until she entered a small grove of trees. She would be warmer on a clear night under a tree than in the open fields. She made a bed of some boughs and curled up in her coat and blanket and tried to sleep. Although hunger pains gnawed at her, it was the sting of being hated by a person she had never met before that kept her awake.

She arose with the dawn, cold and stiff. She had passed a small lake the day before. Now she returned to wash the sleep out of her eyes and to drink. She followed the perimeter until she found a stream running into the lake. This would be better water, less prone to contamination. She washed and then drank some of the bracingly cold water as her breakfast.

She did not want to go back into the village. Yet she needed the help of other people if she was to get any food.

It was the middle of September. The wheat harvest was over, but the potato harvest was still underway. Since the farmers would have fields scattered outside the village, she decided to observe the comings and goings during the early morning to see if they might present an opportunity for her. As she reached a point where she could watch the village from adjacent hills, she noticed several wagons with a few peasants riding along leaving for the countryside.

Labor was scarce during the harvest, especially now, with many of the men having been taken to labor camps in Germany. It was a race against winter to get the crop in, so another field hand was usually welcome. Rachel watched as one of the wagons turned into the fields in her direction. The horse pulling the wagon was plodding along at a slow pace, and she thought she could keep up walking a little distance behind. After an hour, the field came into view, green with the tops of potatoes. Workers collected a shovel or pitchfork from a pile in the wagon and began to disperse in groups to rows that had not yet been harvested.

Feeling exposed but driven by hunger, she approached a group of five or six women working together. "Can I work with you?" she asked. They looked up briefly and nodded. Rachel realized they probably guessed her story, but they did not question her. One gave her a shovel. Then they continued their work, digging up the mounded plants with a shovel or lifting them with the tines of the pitchfork, shaking them to get rid of the dirt and exposing the potatoes. The potatoes were left in rows to be piled on the wagon later.

After several hours of steady work, they stopped to have lunch, brought by the farmer's wife. Having worked hard all morning and with little to eat for two days, Rachel was faint with hunger, so the slices of bread and sour milk were welcome. With lunch provided and a field of potatoes at her feet, Rachel knew at least she wouldn't starve. Toward the end of the day, she put a few small potatoes in Esther's bag. A woman who had been friendly to her approached her with an extra slice of bread, saying quietly, "In case you get hungry later." Rachel knew this woman would not ask, nor would she tell.

While the others walked or rode the wagon, now piled high with the day's harvest, Rachel hurried off to where she could not be observed. The farmer had agreed she could come back the next day, and that was enough for now. She surveyed the area. She noticed a small shed about a half mile away standing next to a hedgerow; she knew it would be the storage shed of a farmer who lived in town and would be a place he kept tools or hay for when he was out in his fields. It would be undisturbed in the evenings. As dusk fell, she made her way to it and pushed the door open. Straw was scattered on the floor, and a couple of bales of hay were stacked on one side. There was enough room to make a small bed on the floor. She would feel more secure here. She left the door open a little for some light and had a dinner of raw potatoes and the slice of bread.

Rachel worked for the farmer for ten more days, each day receiving lunch and something extra from her friend, Krystyna, for dinner. On the third day Krystyna gave her a cloth bundle. It was a peasant's blouse and skirt in a soft gray and blue.

Rachel was deeply touched. "Thank you," she said. After the experiences of the past week, she needed some new clothes.

"I hope they fit," replied Krystyna, somewhat bashfully. "I had to guess at some of the alterations. Fortunately, you are smaller than I am."

"I am very grateful," replied Rachel. She took Krystyna's hands and kissed her cheek, reflecting on how goodness seemed to exist in great measure among the poor and common people of the earth. With a clean, mended blouse and skirt, she would not stand out as much.

The next day, as they worked side by side digging up potatoes, Rachel said, "Krystyna, I want to ask you a question."

"All right; I hope it is something I can answer."

"I am looking for a little girl, six years old, with short, dark hair. We became separated a few days ago, a few miles from here. Have you heard of anything?"

"I am sorry, I haven't. Would you like me to ask around?"

Rachel had to think about this. "No, I don't think that is a good idea. But if you hear something, please let me know."

"Certainly."

At the end of the tenth day, the farmer told her he was sorry he had no more work for her. Assuming from her circumstances that she was Jewish, he told her to be careful, as some in the town would gladly turn her in, if not for spite, then for the reward the Germans were offering for Jews: a new pair of boots. Rachel nodded. She was thinking of her first encounter in the village. As a parting gift, the farmer gave her a sack containing a few potatoes and turnips.

For almost two weeks, she had lived close to the land. She slept on the earth, dropping off to sleep to a chorus of crickets and night birds and the wind blowing through the fields and trees. She rose with the sun, worked until it was low on the horizon, and retired when it was dark. She ate simple meals and she washed in a stream. Her cheeks were sunburned, and she was developing calluses on her hands and feet. At the end of the day, her arms and back were sore and tired, but it was a good fatigue born of exertion rather than the fatigue of emotional stress or physical terror. She slept relatively well, but the slightest unusual sound woke her in alarm. She never felt safe.

She felt the keenness of separation every evening as her co-workers left for their homes and she left for her hovel in the fields. She was a hunted creature, someone others thought did not deserve to live. She missed her family and her people. She thought about Jacob. Would she see him again? She wondered about Esther—was she alive? She thought of Eva and her courage in giving Esther a chance to live. Rachel's inner voice told her Eva was now gone. Would Rachel ever be able to keep her promise? She prayed for Esther's safety every night. Her loneliness was deepest just before she fell asleep in the darkness. At those times, she tried to remember hearing her father's voice and the security and comfort she felt then.

Now that the potato harvest was over, she needed to find someplace else to stay. It was just as well—enough people knew about her presence in the fields that sooner or later someone would turn her in. Winter was coming on, and she had to find someplace where she could be inside. She wondered how this could happen.

She decided to travel parallel to the main road in an easterly direction, away from Germany. She knew the next town was some ten miles away and was quite a bit bigger in size. Although she was somewhat more accustomed to seeing people in the fields, she was still very cautious. Germans weren't the only threat; bandits roamed the countryside, plundering as a means of survival. Many would not hesitate to rape or kill. And of course, even ordinary people might give her away. It was with some consternation, then, that she crossed paths with a trio, two men and a woman, traveling in her same direction. They saw her before she had a chance to flee.

"Hello," the woman greeted her. "Are you traveling to town?"

"Yes," Rachel responded. And then as an afterthought she added rather too honestly, "I suppose."

All three smiled. "Would you like to travel with us?" the woman offered.

Rachel weighed this offer. The woman seemed genuine. These men did not look like bandits. Their clothes were a cut above normal peasant fare, more fashionable—she could see that the woman's blouse, visible under her open coat, was tailored.

One of the men, sensing Rachel's discomfort, tried to make her feel more at ease. "My name is Alan," he said. "And this is Marek and Laura. We liberate vegetables in the countryside and sell them in the city."

At this the woman laughed. "You make it sound like we take them at gunpoint. We *buy* vegetables in the countryside and sell them in Krakow. It is a way to help out our families and make ends meet."

Rachel understood. They sold food on the black market. Their openness encouraged her. "Thank you for your offer," she said, "I would like to travel with you."

Each of the three shouldered a large knapsack. "Have you had anything to eat?" asked Laura.

"A little."

"Here," Laura said as she handed Rachel an apple, something she had not had for more than a year. Rachel introduced herself as Helena, a good non-Jewish name, and offered that she was a survivor of a village that had been burned down by the Germans. Her companions accepted her story at face value.

She enjoyed being part of the little group. There was an easy banter between the three, and it became clear they were good friends. From some of their comments, Rachel surmised they had been at university together. She reflected on her own hopes to attend university someday. At one point they discussed the novels of Joseph Conrad (a.k.a Józef Teodor Konrad Korzeniowski), particularly *Heart of Darkness*. After some back-and-forth exchanges, one of the young men posed the question, "Would Conrad have been as great a writer if he had stayed in Poland and not gone to England in his twenties?"

Laura, wanting to pull Rachel into the conversation, asked, "And what do you think, Helena?"

"If he was a great novelist in England, he would have been even greater in Poland, because the Poles have had to suffer. And suffering makes a great novelist." Rachel was pleased her comment was deemed worthy of smiles and further discussion.

They made their way down to the main road and into town. The town was much larger than the village, with many shops along the cobblestone streets. In the center of town, buildings adjoined each other, shutting in either side of the street with walls of brick and windows. The streets were crowded with people who paid little attention to each other. It would be easy to be anonymous here.

Before they reached the train station, they ducked into an alleyway and from there entered the first floor of a drab apartment. The tenants greeted them and were cordial to Rachel, but no one offered a name. Her companions had stored some suitcases here, and they transferred their goods so they would be less conspicuous. After making the transfer and having a cup of tea with their hosts, they headed out again.

The train station was not a desirable destination for Rachel, for she had no papers. The Germans often conducted random searches at critical points, such as transportation centers, and anyone without papers would be immediately arrested and interrogated. This would be fatal for her. Not wanting to part with her newfound acquaintances and resume her lonely existence, she walked with them until just before they reached the entrance to the station.

The station was a large, gray, hulking building just off the town square. It was three stories high, with a foundation of rough stones topped with gray walls and an overhanging gabled roof of black tiles that blended in with the overcast sky. The only real color was the deep crimson of several Nazi flags hanging vertically down the sides. The building was surrounded by steps leading up a half story to the train platforms. As expected, it was a busy place, with people coming and going and vendors selling an assortment of goods from small carts. At the foot of the stairs, Rachel stopped. "I need to say goodbye," she said. "I cannot travel with you."

"Do you need money?" Laura asked.

"No," Rachel shook her head, "but I need to stay here." They did not press. Laura gave her a hug, and the men said goodbye and wished her luck. Then the three were off. Rachel turned around to walk away.

She had taken only a few steps when she was frozen by the shrill sound of a whistle and a voice yelling, "Halt!"

Chapter 14: The Young Man
Rachel, Western Poland, Fall 1942

A cold chill raced up Rachel's spine. Every element of her being cried out for her to run, to drop her belongings and try to escape. Perhaps she could get enough of a head start that she could disappear into a shop or alleyway before they could catch her. If caught, her lack of papers would be her doom. She must get away.

But, as had happened a number of times before, an inner voice counseled a different course of action—to go on the offensive. Resisting mightily the urge to run, she whirled around, defiant, ready to give a tongue lashing to anyone who accosted her. What she saw was not what she expected: a tall young man in a brown suit and brown coat was leaping down the stairs and heading straight at her. Behind him about twenty yards were uniformed Polish and German police. Their guns were drawn, and they again shouted, "Halt!"

He did not halt. Instinctively Rachel pulled back as the young man passed her. Shots rang out. Everyone scattered or fell to the steps. She could see the impact of the bullets push the young man forward and make ragged holes in the back of his coat. His stride broke; he stumbled for a few more feet and then fell hard to the pavement, his suitcase skidding down the street. A pool of red began to spread on the cobblestones. Rachel could see his face clearly. He was Jewish.

Rachel heard him take his last breath. Police gathered round and prodded him with their boots until they were convinced he was dead. They commandeered a wagon and loaded the body in the back. One of the officers noticed Rachel staring blankly at the blood-stained stones. "Are you all right, Miss?" he asked.

"Yes—yes, I think so," she slowly said. "Just a little shaken up."

"I am sorry this had to happen right in front of you. Fortunately, you weren't hurt. Would you like to sit down?"

Rachel nodded. Touching her elbow, the officer gently led her to a bench. She sat for a few minutes trying to regain her composure.

In a strange sort of way, Rachel felt a connection to the young man, as if he had acted on her behalf. He had died, but she was safe, at least for now. They had been within a few feet of each other. Her perceived danger had been his real danger. How was it she was spared and he was not?

Rachel wandered the streets for the next hour. Although she had felt brave during the shooting, now she shook and trembled all over. She wanted to be somewhere warm where she could close her eyes and make the world go away. She used a little of her money to buy some food. Gradually she came to grips with the fact she still had to find a place to sleep that night.

The first place that came to mind was the apartment where her "black market companions" had stored their suitcases. She was not at all sure she would be welcome, but it did not matter. The trauma of the afternoon had left her unable to remember exactly where they lived. She tried to retrace her steps back to the alleyway, but every time she turned off the main street, thinking she was on the right path, nothing seemed familiar. After an hour she gave up and headed back toward the main part of town, avoiding the train station.

Although she had money, she could not consider a hotel—papers were required to get a room. Evening was coming on, and the temperature was dropping. At some point—she wasn't even quite sure where she was—she passed a church. In churches, at least, you didn't need papers.

She went inside.

Chapter 15: Father Sobieski
Rachel, Western Poland, Fall 1942

The church was cold, both physically and emotionally. The floor and walls were stone; the dark wooden pews showed many years of wear. Behind the altar Rachel recognized a figure of Jesus hanging on the cross. A few worshippers were sprinkled about, praying softly, heads bowed, fingering their rosaries. She couldn't see a priest. She kept to the back and decided to stay until she could formulate some sort of plan.

As night fell, the sanctuary became a place of shadows, lit by a few candles. Rachel scooted to the far side of the chapel and slumped down in the pew. Then, without a better idea, she crawled down under the bench in the near darkness and lay on the floor to spend the night.

It was not a comfortable bed. The floor was hard and cold, but it wasn't the floor that most affected Rachel—it was how hard and cold life had become. Though she was in the middle of a large town, she had never felt more alone, even when she slept in the countryside. At least nature did not despise her. She understood how it was that some people escaped the ghetto only to come back because they could not cope with being on the outside. Her emptiness was compounded by the loss of Esther. How would she ever find her, even if she was still alive? She held Esther's bag tightly; it gave her some comfort—it was something she could touch.

As the stained-glass windows began to glow with early morning light, she stood to get the blood circulating in her hands and feet. Assuming she was alone, she sat down on the bench and wept quietly but earnestly. The tears were a release, and with them poured out her loneliness and the ache in her heart.

Suddenly she felt the presence of someone nearby. She looked up and saw she was being watched. In the middle of the chapel stood a priest, clothed in a dark suit and white collar, looking at her. She searched his face for a clue of his reaction at finding a woman weeping in the chapel in early morning.

"Hello," he said softly.

"Hello," she answered weakly.

"Can I help you?" he asked.

"No, I don't think so," she replied. "No one can help me." Bitterly she blurted out, "It is illegal to help me."

"Perhaps on earth," he said, "but not in heaven. And it is heaven we worry about here."

Rachel wasn't sure what to make of this remark. She had heard of priests sanctioning the persecution of the Jews. After all, they said, the Jews had murdered Jesus. And if a priest said anything even remotely against the Nazis or their methods, he disappeared. Those who were left were often sympathetic to their occupiers.

He walked slowly down the pew in front of her, and she saw the lined face of an older man. His thinning hair was streaked with gray. He was slight of frame and of medium height. But while his physical features were unimpressive, the light from his eyes and the countenance of his face said to her, *this is a good man*. He addressed her with kindness, as he would a daughter. "Come," he said. "Let me show you where you can wash." He took her to the front of the chapel where there were some rooms. "When you are done," he said, "come to the kitchen and share some bread."

Rachel was grateful for the chance to wash her face and hands. As she did so, she thought of the priest. Was her first impression correct? Or was he trying to gain her trust just so he could betray her? She determined to stay on her guard.

She joined the priest in a small kitchen with a table and a few chairs. Bread and jam were on a cutting board; the kettle sang softly on the stove. A woman busied herself with some preparations. He introduced himself as Father Sobieski and the woman as Maria. "Maria is my housekeeper. She works in the chapel and prepares my meals. But more than that, she is the one who keeps me on the straight and narrow path."

The woman gave him an affectionate look and laughed. "Oh, yes," she joked, "that's what I do all right—keep the Father from sin. He's very inclined that way, you know."

Despite her previous admission, Rachel decided to be cautious. "My name is Helena," she stated.

"Please," said Father Sobieski, "sit down and have some breakfast with us."

What the Father did next left Rachel slightly stunned. "God," he said to Maria, "has brought an important person to us. We should thank God for this blessing." Then he bowed his head and said a simple prayer from his heart. After thanking God for their daily bread, he thanked God that a daughter of Israel had found her way to their church. He asked for a blessing upon her and upon all other Jews who were in hiding. "Help them," he implored, "to escape the evil which has come upon them."

Was it true that someone could feel this way? Tears filled Rachel's eyes and her chest burned within her. Yes, she felt, it was true. Rachel looked at the priest and whispered, "Thank you. My name is Rachel."

"Now Rachel," Father Sobieski said while spreading some jam on his bread, "God has brought you here. How can we help you?"

Rachel recounted her story—of sawing through the bars, of jumping from the train. About Eva and Esther. About Marynka and the young man who was shot at the train station. Father Sobieski listened attentively.

"Well," he said after she finished, "I believe there is a reason you have survived. God has a purpose for your life. You are, as you have said, a witness. But perhaps there is something more. I may know a place where you can stay over the winter. Would you like me to see if I can make the arrangements?"

She nodded. Although she had known him for only an hour, she trusted him implicitly.

"Let me ask you a few questions first. Tell me about your schooling."

Rachel recounted some about her school days. He seemed especially pleased when she told him she had won a medal in math and of her love of science.

"Any university study?" he asked.

"I was admitted but the war intervened."

"What languages do you speak?"

"Polish and German" (she figured Yiddish wouldn't really help here).

"Any French?"

"No, I am sorry, I didn't learn French."

His smile was now replaced by a frown. "Music?"

"I can play the piano reasonably well."

"Ah, well, that is something." She felt a rush of gratitude to her mother for her extravagance at having a piano in the house.

"Now, if you will excuse me, I have some business I must attend to. Maria will take care of you. It will be safer today for you to stay in the chapel as a worshipper in case we are searched. You can stay here a night or two, but then we must find another place. I am being watched, and it is not safe for you here."

Rachel helped Maria clean up. She was still grappling with what had happened during breakfast. "Tell me more about the Father."

"What would you like to know?"

"Have you known him a long time? Is he really the way he seems?"

"He has been the priest in the parish for more than twenty years. I have known him since I was a girl of nine or ten. And yes, he is really the way he seems. He is the foundation stone of the neighborhood.

"The people love him. He is always in demand for advice, always called for at times of sorrow or rejoicing. He is the one trusted to perform their baptisms and marriages and burials. People consider him a member of their families."

Maria continued in a somewhat more philosophical, deeper vein. "Father Sobieski's only concern," she told Rachel, "is to serve God. Wherever God calls him to be, that's where he is content to be. He has served here, in an obscure parish, for many years without concern for recognition." Then Maria paid him the ultimate compliment. "I know God better because I know Father Sobieski."

Rachel struggled to phrase her next question. "Does he, um, help a lot of people like me?"

Maria was careful in her reply. "Let me just say you are in good hands. If someone is in trouble, he will try to help. Especially if that person is a child." At hearing this, a longing filled Rachel's heart as she thought of Esther.

"Here," Maria said, as she sawed off a slab of bread. "Take this for your lunch today. We will see you again this evening when the Father has returned."

Rachel felt it would be best if she did not spend too much time at the church, for everyone's sake. She made sure she knew where it was by memorizing its relationship to several landmarks. A river was just three blocks to the north, and down the road east a half mile was the train station. She wandered the town feeling quite safe. She looked the part of a peasant, along with many others. It was a nice morning for late September with a pale-blue sky and crisp autumn air. Many people were out.

She did not have any ration books, so she could not legally purchase food. There was always the black market, but Rachel did not want to tempt fate today by doing anything risky. By late morning, she wandered down by the river where she sat on a patch of grass and basked in the warm sunshine. She retrieved the slice of bread from a pocket and had a few mouthfuls. She had not felt this safe, this human, in a long time.

In late afternoon she returned to the church. Maria was in the chapel cleaning. She had her hair tied up but was wearing the same apron as at breakfast, and she was mopping the floor. When she saw Rachel enter, she gave a brief smile of recognition.

That smile meant a lot to Rachel.

Chapter 16: A New Life
Rachel, Western Poland, Fall 1942

After spending the day alone, Rachel was glad she could share dinner with Maria and Father Sobieski. Although the meal was simple—potato-and-cabbage soup with bread—it tasted delicious to her. While the food fed her body, their conversation and friendliness fed her spirit.

During dinner, Father Sobieski told her, "I have suggested that you be a governess for a family who lives on the outskirts of town. Sometimes," he said, "I think the best strategy is to hide in plain sight. You are fortunate you have Polish looks. And you are doubly fortunate," he said somewhat grimly, "you are not male." Rachel blushed. She knew what he meant. Circumcision had been the downfall of many Jewish men in hiding.

The Kohler family was a prominent family in town. Father Sobieski explained that *Herr* Kohler ran a factory in the timely business of making ammunition for small-caliber weapons such as pistols and rifles. *Herr* Kohler was *Volksdeutsche*, an ethnic German with Polish citizenship. His family had been among the Germans who had been made part of Poland at the end of World War I, when Germany lost territory and Poland was reborn as an independent country. He had met *Frau* Kohler at university. She was native Polish, originally from Katowice.

"He has two sons, ages twelve and ten, and a six-year-old daughter." At mention of the six-year-old, the same age as Esther, Rachel again felt a pang in her heart. "He wants them to have an excellent education, better than the public schools can provide, especially during times such as these. Although they want to meet you before deciding, I have spoken to them about you, and I am relatively confident you will be offered the position. At any rate, we will have you meet them in a few days. Before that we need to make an honest woman out of you.

"We need to provide you with a backstory and Aryan papers," Father Sobieski continued. "First, I want you to study this." He handed Rachel *The Catechism for Adolescents*. "You need to become a reasonably good Catholic, at least good enough you can speak their language. You will also need to attend mass and take communion.

Before you leave, we can practice. But please don't misunderstand—in God's eyes, and in mine, you will always be Jewish. This is an expediency we must adopt to save your life.

"Tomorrow we will start the process of getting you some papers. This means we will give you a new name and birthdate. We'll use a name from a list of people who have died whose deaths were not recorded in the parish records. We will assign such a name to you, and if anyone decides to check, you will have a birth and baptism that can be confirmed. You will also need to create a simple background—where you grew up, your family, and so on. People don't expect a lot of details, and they understand that many people would prefer not to talk about what has happened to them. If you work hard and take good care of the children, that should be sufficient to keep you out of danger.

"After tonight, Maria has suggested you stay at her apartment for a week until we can get everything in order." He paused to give an appreciative look to Maria. "She is not only a great help to me, but a brave and courageous woman."

"Thank you, Maria, I am very grateful," Rachel said with deep feeling.

"Tonight," he said with a twinkle in his eye, "you have the privilege of sleeping in the birdhouse." When Rachel gave him a questioning look, he said, "Don't worry—birds won't share your bed. But you will see what I mean. Please, follow me."

Carrying a lighted candle, Father Sobieski opened a narrow door at the front of the chapel. Inside was a circular staircase with steps about two feet wide. They made a steep, winding ascent two stories to a narrow hall. "This direction," he said with a nod, "leads to the belfry. Over here," he motioned in the opposite direction, "is the birdhouse."

Rachel could see a door made of wooden planks, about six feet high, with an old-fashioned wooden latch. Behind the door was a small closet about two feet deep. The candle cast a shadowy light on some nails, hand tools, and a few wooden shingles. Father Sobieski knelt and confidently placed his fingertips on a plank in the back wall and squeezed. The plank yielded, and the wall swung away to reveal a small room beyond. On one side lay a cot and a pillow. In one corner was a basin with some water and a chamber pot. A small table completed the furnishings. "I am sorry the accommodations are rather spare. But I do think it will be more comfortable than sleeping under a pew."

Rachel laughed. "I'm sure it will be fine."

"It will get cold up here tonight. Maria has left some blankets," he said, pointing to a bundle on the cot. "I will leave the candle—and, oh, before I forget"—he pulled a piece of bread from a pocket— "in case you get hungry. After I leave, lock the door behind me. Please come down in the morning when you hear we are up and about, and if," he paused for emphasis, "it sounds like all is well. Happy reading and sweet dreams."

Rachel surveyed her little nest. The room was cleverly devised and prepared. She wasn't the first person to spend the night here. How was it that she had stumbled upon such a place and such a person as Father Sobieski? She was filled with wonder. "Dear God," she said softly, "thank you." Rachel sat on the cot with her back to the wall. She held the book for a moment, enjoying the feel of it in her hands and letting the pages flip through her fingers. Then she opened it and began to read the first chapter, "The Nature of God."

***

Rachel awoke early and lay in bed watching the dawn come as pinpoints of light crept through cracks in the attic. Presently she heard talking downstairs, though she couldn't make out the words. She crept silently down the stairs until she could hear Maria and the Father conversing normally. She knocked softly on the door to the kitchen and opened it slowly.

"Ah, there you are," said the Father. "I trust you slept well? Please come join us after you have had a chance to wash up."

They had an enjoyable breakfast, though the fare was plain. Father Sobieski liked to tease Maria, and he was naturally outgoing and cheerful. As they finished breakfast, he said to Rachel, "To begin the process of creating your new identity, you will need to visit the druggist on Smolensk Street today. Ask for Karl, and tell him your mother has the rheumatism. Ask if he has the treatment mentioned in this note." As he said this, Father Sobieski handed Rachel a thick envelope. "Then do as he says. It will be best if we don't see you again before nightfall. Maria will fix you a lunch."

Rachel made the trip to Smolensk Street, where she met with Karl the druggist. He invited her into a back room, where he opened the envelope from Father Sobieski. Rachel saw that it contained at least 2,000 złoty[*]. "I know it seems like a lot of money," he said, when he noticed Rachel's look of surprise, "but everyone involved will take their cut. It is a dangerous business and people need to live." He then took her photograph. "What is your age?" he asked.

"Twenty."

"Well, I would suggest you take the identity of Julia Niemczyk. She was a year older than you, which is close enough, and was killed at the beginning of the war when the Germans bombed Warsaw. Her death was never recorded. What do you think?"

"I think that is fine."

"Do you like the name Julia?"

"Yes, I like it fine."

"It is a pretty name, I think. She was born in Konin. Are you familiar with it?"

"I've only heard of it. I've not been there."

"A nice little town in the country. A good place to be from. Big enough that not everyone knows everyone else, and small enough that few people would know you anyway. When you come back, I'll have a birth certificate and your identification document—your *Kennkarte*—for you. It will take me seven days."

While she was out, Rachel used some of her remaining money to buy a second-hand suitcase, some personal items, and some second-hand clothes. She couldn't show up as a governess with no luggage. Through all of this, she carefully protected Esther's little bag of belongings.

When Rachel returned seven days later, she didn't really know what to expect. She was amazed to receive a *Kennkarte* that looked exactly like ones she was familiar with. It bore her photo along with numerous signatures and official stamps. It lacked only her fingerprints, which were taken on the spot.

---

[*]In 1939, one złoty was approximately $0.20.

Like all Polish citizens older than fifteen, Rachel had been required to have a *Kennkarte* since shortly after the war started. There was, however, one important difference between this card and her previous one: this card was gray, indicating she was of Polish ethnicity; her previous card had been yellow, indicating she was Jewish. She was now officially a Gentile.

Rachel held this card in her hand and considered its significance. *The color of a card determines whether I should live or die,* she thought. *I will be a Gentile to live, but I will always have a Jewish heart.*

Chapter 17: Governess
Rachel, Western Poland, Fall 1942

Rachel had butterflies in her stomach as she rode in a wagon to her new home. After they had traveled for twenty minutes, the busy streets gave way to fashionable residences and then to country estates surrounded by high walls. Rachel could only catch a glimpse of the grandeur behind the walls when they went past an entrance. At length, the driver turned into one of the driveways and proceeded along a gravel drive past an expanse of lawn with a pond off to one side. There were many large trees around the perimeter of the grounds. The home was two stories high with pale-yellow walls, large latticed windows, and dormers jutting out from the steeply pitched, gray tile roof.

Rachel met her charges, Ralph, Christof, and Joanna. Ralph and Christof bowed, and Joanna gave a somewhat unsteady curtsy. The overall effect was quite pleasing. "Hello," Rachel said, "I am glad to meet you. My name is Julia."

"Nikola," *Frau* Kohler spoke to the maid, "please show Julia to her room and help her with her things." Speaking to Rachel, she said, "dinner will be in an hour. I'm sure you'll want to get settled until then."

The children looked her over carefully. Ralph and Christof had sandy hair and fair skin; Joanna was a little more olive in complexion and had thick, dark hair that fell to her shoulders. They were well dressed, the boys in nice pants and Joanna in a crisp yellow smock. As Rachel glanced about, she noticed curtains of rich fabrics and dark floors covered by plush rugs. She couldn't help but think of the contrast between these surroundings and the living conditions of the Jews under German occupation—or, for that matter, the living conditions of most Poles.

Her room was in the attic, with a dormer window that looked over the back of the estate. She was pleased she could see out over the countryside, even though today the trees were shrouded in a mist after a few hundred yards.

Her room had a real bed, with a real mattress, tucked into an alcove in the wall. She sat on it slowly and felt it sink under her weight. Could she still sleep on such a bed? It might be too soft for her now. She reflected that just two weeks ago she was living in a hut in the countryside and sleeping on the ground. *How strange my life is*, she thought. Believing it wouldn't last, she resolved not to let herself become accustomed to such luxury.

Along one side of the room was an old wardrobe with paneled doors that sagged in the middle. She opened it to discover a few serviceable and attractive dresses and a coat, worn but in good condition. Her old one showed the wear of the past few months and wouldn't last another winter. A note pinned to one of the dresses indicated she was welcome to wear anything that fit. Obviously, the mistress of the house understood she would not be coming with much. She would take good advantage of these clothes in the days ahead. As she put away her few belongings, she heard a bell announce supper. She hoped she could remember her manners, or even how to eat with silverware. "I've become a regular savage," she said to herself in a mocking voice.

Herr Kohler often worked late, so the family had supper without him most evenings. Occasionally *Frau* Kohler was gone as well, entertaining with her husband. Attending or hosting lavish dinners for their German clientele was considered the oil that lubricated the wheels of business. Rachel bowed her head as they said grace and remembered to put her napkin in her lap. She had wondered what dinner here would be like. She was pleased to discover it was not a dinner of potatoes and bread. No, this was a pre-war-like meal that included meat.

At first, she didn't recognize the meat until she realized it was pork, something she had never eaten, since it was forbidden in Judaism, except in circumstances where it would save a life. Now that she was ostensibly a Catholic rather than a Jew, she would have to get used to it. She also thought of what Father Sobieski had said—that God would always know she was Jewish. Surely, He would understand. Dessert was a favorite—*Jabłecznik*—apple cake.

Thus began some halcyon days for Rachel. She arose early while most of the family was still asleep and walked the grounds. The grounds behind the house were quite extensive, with a garden and some woods. There were several paths and a few benches located in shady spots. She felt renewed each day as she wandered and sat and listened. She then made her way back to the house where she had a simple breakfast, usually with the maid and cook. She was able to take time to say her morning prayers.

Around nine she started her day with the children. They met in the sunroom, where each of the children had a desk and where there was a slate chalkboard on which she could write. She usually began with mathematics because they were all fresh, and the children liked to get that subject out of the way. This was followed by grammar and writing, and then some study time before lunch. After lunch they had science and history, and then an activity period where they played outside if the weather was good or improvised something inside if it was bad. This was followed by literature and some time for homework. It was a little challenging to teach three children who were each at a different point in a subject, but the older boys were happy to help Joanna or each other. The house had a good library and a fine grand piano on which Rachel started teaching Joanna piano lessons. The children were well behaved and conscientious in their studies.

Sometimes when the weather was bad outside and the children were busy with homework inside, Rachel played the piano just for herself. She had played since she was seven; she was quite accomplished and knew a fair amount of music by heart. She played Debussy or Brahms or, when she was feeling wistful, Chopin, which had a special place in her repertoire. Before the war, Jacob had learned Rachel was studying Chopin's nocturnes. She could recall the conversation well.

"Do you know the nocturnes?" she asked.

"Oh, yes; I like them very much, although there are other pieces by Chopin I like more. The nocturnes are perfect when I want to be alone in my thoughts."

"What are your favorite pieces by Chopin?" Rachel asked.

"For sheer virtuosity and passion, I don't see how you can beat the ballades, especially when Artur Rubenstein is playing. You get the sense the music flows directly from Chopin's mind to Rubenstein's fingers, with no score in between."

"I have heard that said before, although I've never actually heard Rubenstein play."

"You haven't heard Rubenstein? Where did you say you come from? Did they have a school there?" he teased, causing Rachel to

smile. "Well, we'll need to fix that. Could I hear you play the nocturnes sometime?"

Now she played for herself and for Jacob. She hoped he was listening.

Chapter 18: Joanna
Rachel, Western Poland, Fall 1942

Joanna was a thoughtful child, not given to shouting or passionate outbursts. There was a quiet intensity about her—she was very diligent in her lessons, and she practiced a piano piece over and over until she could play it perfectly. She was attentive to her mother, always dropping whatever she was doing to obey any request from her.

As a result of many hours spent together in tutoring or playing the piano, an intimacy grew between Rachel and Joanna. They often held hands as they walked the grounds, sometimes talking in hushed tones but sometimes not saying anything at all. They read a story nearly every evening, right before bed. As they sat snuggled together in a rocking chair in Joanna's room, they each took a turn reading a page. This human contact was like a healing balm for Rachel. She felt herself become more whole in body and spirit.

But there was more than this. When she looked at Joanna with her olive complexion and dark hair, she couldn't help but think of another little girl, a little girl she had lost. As she hugged Joanna, kissed her goodnight, or read with her, she imagined that somehow these expressions of love were being extended to and felt by Esther as well. Joanna came to represent two little girls to Rachel, and in loving one, she felt she was loving both. *Dear God,* she prayed, *let Esther know I haven't forgotten her.* Even as she healed, there was a place in her heart that hurt for Esther.

One night, after reading together, Rachel was taken aback by something Joanna said. Usually as the story time ended, Joanna looked up at Rachel and said something like, "I liked that story," or "That rabbit was very silly." This night she looked up at Rachel and said, "We love you."

Rachel wondered if she had heard Joanna correctly. "What did you say?" she asked.

"I said, 'we love you.'"

"I love you too. But what do you mean by 'we'?" asked Rachel.

"I mean all of us."

"You mean all of your family?"

"I mean all of us who know you," Joanna said and gave her a hug.

Rachel was susceptible to anything that offered hope about Esther or Jacob, and she couldn't help but wonder if the "we" mentioned by Joanna included them. It was a small thing, and perhaps it was nonsense, but she grabbed on to it nonetheless.

***

It was now November, and Rachel marveled that she was in a place that was warm and dry, where she had enough food to eat, and where she was loved. The children were doing well at their lessons. The boys liked her. They were still at an age where they liked being hugged, especially by a pretty governess. *Frau* Kohler noticed the closeness developing between Rachel and Joanna but did not seem to mind.

Chapter 19: An Invitation
Rachel, Western Poland, Fall 1942

This period of relative tranquility in Rachel's life was broken in an unexpected way one evening. As she came back to her room to retire for the night, she found a note on her bed from *Frau* Kohler. *Julia*, it said, *we are so pleased to have you here with us. We appreciate your efforts to educate our children and feel you and they are doing splendidly. We need to ask a favor of you. Robert is having some German officers over for dinner in a week, and we feel a need for more female company, which we know the officers would appreciate. Would you join us? You will not need to do anything but converse with them during dinner. When it comes time for us to separate, you may return to your room. We would so appreciate your presence.* It was signed, *Sofia*.

My, Rachel thought. *A Jew among Germans, and not as a servant, but as a companion for dinner*. She took a deep breath. This would be hard for her on several levels, not the least of which was that she felt completely inexperienced in this type of role. She also wondered, given the destruction and misery inflicted by the Germans on her people, how she would manage to be good company. But she also realized she could not refuse. She must do what was asked of her by her employers if at all possible.

The next day she took an opportunity to speak with her mistress. "I will gladly comply with your request," she said, lying about being glad, "but I wonder how suitable I will be. I don't know a lot about entertaining." Suppressing what she really wanted to say, she added, "particularly with German officers. And, as I am sure you know, I have nothing suitable to wear."

"You only need to be yourself. Frankly, once the drinking begins, it is not too hard to keep a conversation going. And as for your gown, I will lend you one of my own. We are about the same size. Also, my hairdresser is coming here the day of the dinner, and she will do your hair as well as mine."

"I will do as you wish," said Rachel. "I only hope I can meet your expectations."

"I am sure you will do fine," Sofia responded confidently.

This conversation about the dinner made her wonder about *Herr* Kohler. She rarely saw him. When he was in town, he left early in the morning and didn't get back until late at night, unless they were entertaining. What was his life like, working for the Nazis? He was obviously allied to Germany more than to Poland. What was it like to be married to him? He seemed to love his children, so Rachel had to give him credit for that. But she was perplexed by the contradiction of working for the Nazis on the one hand and being married to a native Polish woman on the other.

The day for the dinner arrived, and Rachel dreaded it. First, she needed to get her hair done. Her hair had not been taken care of for a long time. The hairdresser took a look and said, "We'd better get started; we have a lot of work to do." It was washed, combed, cut, and styled. Rachel knew the hairdresser was essentially starting from scratch, but she still recoiled as she saw several inches of hair fall to the floor, victim of the hairdresser's scissors. By the time she was done, two hours had elapsed.

Rachel retired to her room where she looked in a mirror and for a split second didn't recognize herself. She looked like a lady. Her upswept and curled hair showed her graceful neck to advantage. It had been a long time since she had felt feminine and beautiful.

Rachel *was* a beautiful young woman. Slender in figure, she had dark-brown hair that flowed below her shoulders and was set off by her fair skin. Her brown eyes were darker toward the pupils, making her eyes seem especially large. Although she was pretty enough, she was beautiful in more of a classic sense—in the proportion and form of her features.

She had an expressive face. When she smiled or laughed, her whole face seemed to light up. When she was angry, her countenance glared. She had a contemplative side, and when she was lost in thought, she resembled a marble statue.

Despite her misgivings about the evening, she had to admit the dress her mistress provided was like something out of a fairy tale. The gown was made of cream-colored silk, with short sleeves, a pleated blouse with a high collar, and a gathered skirt. The elegant simplicity of the dress was completed by a dark-brown, velvet belt, some long white gloves, and diamond pendant earrings. Set against Rachel's brown eyes and brown hair, the overall effect was stunning.

Sofia had asked her to come downstairs as soon as she was dressed. Rachel joined her in the library. "Julia," Sofia said, "you look lovely. I wish we could just enjoy this evening without worry, but I need to impress some things upon you. The officers coming to dinner tonight are very important to my husband's future—" and here she corrected herself to say, "to our future. If they wished, they could take over the factory; they could take over this house. It is important that we keep them happy. This may not be easy for you, or," she added, "for me. Please remember that what we say and do tonight may have far-reaching effects."

"I understand," Rachel replied. "But," she asked, "what shall I talk about? I despise the Germans for what they have done to our country."

"Admire their military prowess; talk to them about what a great leader Hitler is. Toast to their success in Russia. Ask about their families. Ask about their girlfriends. Perhaps that will help them take their eyes off you."

Rachel blushed. "Yes, ma'am." This wasn't going to be easy. She was to praise the man who had destroyed her family and her country? Surely her feelings would seep through into her tone of voice—she would have to stay on other topics.

As a final comment, Sofia noted, "We will be speaking only German this evening. I have also invited Trudy, a German neighbor who is about your age. Hopefully she'll provide some distraction as well."

Chapter 20: The Dinner
Rachel, Western Poland, Fall 1942

The evening registered as a series of impressions for Rachel. Her first impression was of light, conveyed as she walked into the dining room, which was still empty. Everything in the room seemed to be caught in a reflection of light: the chandelier, the china, the glassware, the mirrors. Even Rachel was part of the scene when she looked in the mirror and saw her earrings sparkle with light.

Her second impression was of darkness. As their guests arrived, Rachel shuddered to see they were SS, not regular army. The three officers wore black SS uniforms, with the lightning SS insignia on their lapels, the skull and crossbones on their hats, and the blood-red swastika on their arms. They radiated darkness just as surely as the chandelier radiated light.

The evening started well enough, with one awkward exception, which seemed to be overlooked by everyone. As the officers entered, one after another, they said, "*Heil* Hitler" and gave the Nazi salute. What did they expect the hosts to do? *Herr* Kohler responded "*Heil* Hitler" with alacrity. Trudy also gave an enthusiastic response. Sofia and Rachel just stayed in the background, saying nothing. As Rachel saw and heard these Nazi salutes so close to her, a wave of anxiety came over her. Standing a few feet from her were men who would imprison or kill her if they knew who she was. She recalled the feelings she had in Marynka's barn, when she was only moments from discovery. Like then, she wanted to flee, but she willed herself to carry on.

Everyone tried to be polite. The soldiers introduced themselves, took *Frau* Kohler by the hand, and bowed. They were handsome—blond and blue-eyed, tall and athletic looking. The captain, who must have been in his early thirties, was particularly polite and respectful. His lieutenants were clearly some years younger. Klaus still looked like something of a boy. He was friendly and open; it wasn't too long before he was quite attentive to Trudy, who, Rachel could tell, liked to flirt. But Henrich's manner, though proper, was accompanied by a demeanor that brought a chill to Rachel's heart. There was a hardness about him, a coldness. *He,* she thought, *has been a killer.*

A third impression for Rachel was alarm. Not just alarm, but fear. She was seated next to Heinrich, and before the evening had progressed very far, she realized he had taken an interest in her. At first, she noticed his elbow graze her arm. Then a few minutes later his elbow didn't just graze her arm but pressed against it. She withdrew it and put it in her lap. There was a smile at the corner of his lips, but otherwise he acted as if nothing had happened. Then his foot rested next to hers. She quickly moved it. He was quite brazen, and Rachel surmised he was used to getting what he wanted. Then his hand rested lightly on her thigh, under the tablecloth where it wasn't seen. Rachel picked it up and moved it. He smiled again. Rachel's mind was racing. *How am I going to manage this? What is going to happen next? How is this evening going to end?*

She didn't have to wait long to find out. As these thoughts occupied her, he dropped his napkin to the floor. "Pardon me," he said almost inaudibly and bent down to pick it up. As he did so, he touched Rachel's ankle and began to slowly move his hand up her leg.

Rachel did not take time to think. She felt she had to do something—now. Before she could analyze her actions, she abruptly stood up. With indignation blazing in her eyes, she snapped, "How dare you take such liberties! I expected you to be a gentleman."

Then she slapped him hard across the face.

Chapter 21: Aftermath
Rachel, Western Poland, Fall 1942

The room was instantly silent. Everything stopped. *Frau* Kohler inhaled sharply. In the interval that followed, it dawned on Rachel what she had just done. She dropped her napkin to the table and ran from the room.

Her final impression was of despair. She had cost her hosts their future. She knew it, and she could not stem the floodtide of despair that came over her. Bitter tears came. She needed to leave tonight. She reflected that her actions had cost Marynka, who had befriended her as a stranger, her life, and now she likely had endangered this family, whom she loved. How could she even face them? But she must, if only to apologize. She took off her gown, put on her regular clothes, and waited for the dinner party to end, which would surely be soon. She decided to sleep in the stables and then make her way back to Father Sobieski. Hopefully he would still help her after the mess she had made of things.

But the party did not break up soon. It was after eleven before she perceived the guests were taking their leave. The voices did not sound angry, but cordial. Rachel had been so caught up in the awfulness of it all she hadn't noticed that after she left the room there had been laughter—led by the captain and joined in by others. Presently she heard footsteps coming up the stairs and down to her room. Both *Herr* and *Frau* Kohler were there as she opened the door.

Facing them both, she said, "I am so sorry. I knew this was a mistake." Rachel was wringing her hands.

"Julia," Sofia replied with unexpected kindness, "it is all right. Everything seemed to turn out all right."

Herr Kohler was not as forgiving. "Although the officer was out of line, you shouldn't have exploded like that. You need to learn to control yourself." Rachel began to sob, and *Herr* Kohler's tone softened. "You are a little too hot-blooded, I think, and you do need to work on that. But I don't believe any lasting harm was done. The SS pride themselves on their chivalry. I know it doesn't make much sense, given how cruel they can be. But when you mentioned the officer being a gentleman, I think it struck a chord. They weren't really embarrassed, for they are, after all, SS officers—the privileged few of the German army. In Germany women throw themselves at them. Now here they are in the company of a pretty woman, and what did one expect?"

Herr Kohler continued. "I'm guessing they felt that you, as the governess, were out of your depth socially, so your behavior was excusable."

Of course, Rachel thought ironically, *I wasn't the one making advances.*

"The captain briefly apologized with a wink toward the offending junior officer, and the dinner continued. Let's just make sure it doesn't happen again," he said seriously, "for slapping SS officers doesn't usually turn out well."

Consistent with the comments about chivalry, a note came the next day for the lady of the house, thanking her for the dinner. With the note came two vases of flowers: one for Sofia and one for Rachel.

Chapter 22: The New Ghetto
Jacob, Eastern Poland, Summer 1942

The morning after the *Aktion*, everyone assembled outside the shops for roll call. They shared a feeling of dread and anxiety. The commandant spoke. "From now on, this will be your home. You will live in the barracks and stables within the walls of this compound. The ghetto has been closed. As of this morning, it is empty, *kaputt*. All the inhabitants have been taken to other locations. This is the new ghetto, and the only place Jews will live. If you work hard, you will survive. That is all." As if to underscore his words, a black plume of smoke rose in the sky from a fire burning in the ghetto.

This announcement meant their families were gone. They had suspected something terrible was going to happen when they were not allowed to return to the ghetto the night before. They had heard the trucks and dogs during the night, muted and far away. But they hoped their own families were still safe because they carried the special identification cards indicating they were protected.

Now they knew their loved ones were gone. As this realization sank in, several of the inmates collapsed. Those standing next to them helped drag them up again to prevent them from being beaten. The normally quiet roll call was interrupted by cries of despair and pain. A few could do nothing more than stand senselessly, numb from shock.

There are losses so great they cannot be fully understood nor described. Jacob's father, mother, and sister were gone. Samuel, having already lost his father, had now lost the rest of his family—two sisters and his mother. Jacob felt as if he were teetering on the edge of an abyss, or being pulled into the vortex of a whirlpool. He wanted to give in, to surrender, to be gone. A vast emptiness stretched before him. Their families had been torn from them, and they were now alone. It was as if they had been taken to a different world.

***

One of Jacob's barrack mates, Yitzkhok, had lost his wife and two sons. Over the next few nights Jacob saw him writing something while weeping. Though words cannot express the inexpressible, his sentiments captured some of the ache and despair Jacob also felt. A few of the lines included,

> Hanna my Hanna my only one you!
> Where are my boys, my Benzion? My Benjamin?
> Their bright eyes, their beautiful heads
> Hanna tell me where you've been taken
> I cannot stand not to know where you are . . .
> I cannot rest day or night
> One call and I come, just a call
> With tears of happiness in my eyes
> …
> Oh tell me where you are—I ask though I know
>   that asking is no use . . .
> And if someone called out to me the place where you
>   are
> I could not come to you—oh my darkened world
> The roads are all blocked, fenced and hidden
> Don't disappear! O Hanna if I only knew where you are
> If I could find you, I would pay with my broken life for
>   a look at you all, just one look[*]

***

As they were dismissed, Samuel silently walked along with his head bowed. Although Jacob was struggling himself, he wanted to comfort his friend who had done so much for him. "Samuel, somehow we will get through this. We will be family to each other. We must try to survive."

"I suppose," said Samuel quietly, "we will do that. I just have two wishes."

"What are those?" asked Jacob.

"I wish God would choose another people. I don't want to be chosen anymore. God did not even grant that I could die with my family." Jacob could hear the bitterness in Samuel's voice. It was true: they had not been given the chance to die with their families. "I would

---

[*] By Yitzkhok Katzenelson. See the Notes.

have liked to have been with them and faced our last moments together. I could have comforted my mother and sisters."

"I have felt that way too," Jacob replied. "I can't help but think my father knew or suspected something was going to happen, so he stayed home, so he could be with them. I suppose he wanted me to live. I will need to live for all of them now." Jacob's voice trailed off. Then he said, "You mentioned another wish."

"Before I die, I am going to take at least one German with me. Hopefully more than one." Samuel's voice was steeled with resolve.

"I'll be right next to you," Jacob replied.

Jacob lay awake that night, too overwhelmed to sleep. The room was dark and silent, except for some stifled sobs.

Jacob thought how the Germans were the masters of the false promise. Each of the *Aktions* had been followed by a declaration that the remaining Jews would be spared if they followed orders and worked hard. The Jews clutched desperately to this sliver of hope. But it was all a ruse. It was now clear that from the very beginning the German objective was total annihilation of the Jews. Those who remained could no longer deceive themselves that they would not be included. In considering the choices before them, the one clear certainty was that the Germans would eventually execute them, usefulness be damned.

As an understanding of their true state unfolded upon them, they were seized, like Samuel, with a fierce determination. *They would act.* Those who remained formed a committee to look at possibilities for escape. The committee recommended that they attempt a breakout as soon as possible. They would fight with anything they could get their hands on—clubs, knives, rocks. Hopefully some would make it out of the camp to the forest; the others would at least die heroically.

Although Jacob was in favor of doing something, he knew what they were proposing did not offer a very good chance of success. The defenses of the camp had been fortified in the last few months. The compound was encircled with two rows of barbed wire and the wooden pole fence the Jews had moved there with their own hands. At each end was a guard tower with sentries equipped with machine guns. At night, a searchlight played over the compound. Given the difficulties of getting through the wire and over the fence, it appeared they would have to rely on storming the gate. If they failed, they would be trapped and killed.

Some vigorous discussion ensued at a secret meeting held a few nights later. Some people wanted to try to find another way. *Pani Azrylewicz*, the doctor's wife, said rather forcefully, "My husband has always done what he could to help others, including some in this room. Now he is recovering from broken ribs, thanks to a beating he received while helping an injured woman. He can barely walk. How is he supposed to escape? This will be a death sentence for him." Several people in the group nodded in sympathy. The doctor was highly respected. Most people would gladly adopt a plan that would help him. But what could they do?

Henryk Beck, a tailor, echoed the sentiment. "I agree with *Pani Azrylewicz*. I am an old man. What could I do to fight the Germans? How can I storm the gates and escape? Even if my chances of survival are small if I stay here, they seem better than trying to storm the gates."

Leah Shepetinski reminded them that they still had several teenagers in their midst. "If anyone deserves a chance to live, they do. Their lives are still in front of them. Any plan we adopt must give them a fighting chance."

The head of the breakout committee countered these arguments. "May I remind you of what the Nazis have already done? Everyone in the ghetto except us has been murdered. Lined up and shot. No mercy shown. We are next. We don't have many options."

Here was a dilemma. Jacob whispered to Samuel, "How can we escape with the young and the old? It seems impossible to me."

At some point, someone suggested they dig a tunnel out of the camp. At first, Jacob thought the idea was crazy. *Dig a tunnel? It would need to be at least fifty yards long to reach the fields outside. How could they complete such a major undertaking without it being discovered by the Germans? Where would they put the dirt? Were they going to do this after working long days with little food? It would take at least a month, maybe longer. Did they have that much time?*

Before they adjourned, to Jacob's surprise, a majority had agreed.

They would dig a tunnel.

Chapter 23: The Tunnel
Jacob, Eastern Poland, Summer 1942

The next day Jacob wondered how they would even get started on this improbable venture. He was pleased to hear that Adam Horowitz had been asked by the Breakout committee to head the tunnel project. One of the oldest among them, Adam was in his sixties and survived the recent *Aktion* because he was an expert leather worker. He had made or repaired saddles for several Nazi officers. Quiet and thoughtful, he had a steady manner that inspired confidence. He was the kind of leader Jacob liked—a man more of action than of words. He chose two lieutenants, and together they began to organize the tasks before them and designate work crews. Having seen that Jacob and Samuel worked well together, Adam paired them up and assigned them to Team 3. They would dig together.

Attached to Jacob's barracks was a shed used for storage. It was a small building—only about six by eight feet, with wooden walls, a corrugated metal roof, and a wooden plank floor. It contained odds and ends such as pieces of pipe, rope, a few bricks, and scrap lumber. There was a door to the outside that was jammed shut, so the only entrance was through the barracks. No one paid much attention to the building; the Germans had never tried or wanted to enter it. If the Germans unexpectedly entered the barracks, it would be possible for some warning to be given to those working inside the shed. It was here they decided the tunnel entrance would be.

The digging of the tunnel commenced the night of July 23. Jacob stood on a chair at the back of a group huddled around the entrance spot, so he could see what was going on. First Nachum and Levi, carpenters, carefully removed floor planks, exposing the bare earth below, until they had uncovered a space about one-yard square. The planks and nails were carefully stacked in a pile—they would be reused. Lots had been drawn to see who would have the honor of being on the first shift. Marek and Isaac won. Everyone sensed this was an auspicious moment. They knew they were starting something that would either lead to their deaths or their freedom.

They had little time for ceremony. Adam merely bowed his head and reverently said, "Hear, O Israel, the Lord our God; the Lord is One," and then nodded for them to start. Marek plunged the sharpened end of a steel bar into the ground. He moved it back and forth to loosen the earth. He stabbed it into the loosened earth several times more. Then Isaac shoveled out the loose earth and put it into sacks the tailors had made. After only a few minutes, they fell into a steady rhythm.

While Marek and Isaac were working, the "disposal detail" was getting rid of the dirt. They carried the sacks up a ladder to the shallow attic where Jacob could hear them be dumped and the dirt spread around until it was distributed across the ceiling.

Jacob was familiar with the overall tunnel plan. The idea was to go down vertically about six feet before they began to dig the horizontal shaft. They got about halfway down the first night. As they cleaned up, the carpenters fitted some boards into the sides of the freshly dug shaft, forming a frame to prevent the sides from collapsing. The carpenters replaced the floorboards and covered the opening with dirt and debris to hide it.

Although it was late, many of the group, including Jacob, waited for Marek and Isaac to enter the barracks with the others who had helped. Quietly their little community formed a circle around them. It seemed fitting to mark the occasion somehow—the occasion of their resistance. Adam asked Levi, who had studied to be a rabbi, to offer a prayer of thanksgiving and deliverance.

> Blessed are You, O Lord our God, King of the Universe,
> Author of all good things,
> We ask for Your blessing in this great endeavor,
> That we may escape the power of our enemies,
> That we may honor Your name and be Your people.

Then they quietly crept to their beds. They were tired, and in a few hours the dawn would break and they would have to be ready to face another day. As they fell into their bunks, Jacob heard Samuel say, "I feel good. I feel better than I have in a long time. We are doing something. God help us." He had touched on something Jacob felt that first night as well. There was a lightness of spirit and exhilaration he had not felt for a long time. They had forgotten what it felt like to lift up their heads and assert their will as free men and women. If nothing else came of it, this was some reward.

The next day Jacob was tired but also keyed up. Would their work from the night before be discovered? All during the day he waited for whistles to blow and for the SS guards to round them up for execution. But it didn't happen. Life went on as usual—the Germans had not noticed.

Jacob was excited that he and Samuel had been picked to be diggers. It was an honor to represent their fellow prisoners in this way. Yet Jacob wondered how he would do. He did not like confined spaces. He wanted to take part in creating the tunnel, but at the same time, he felt a pit in his stomach. He thought about what Rachel would say: "The only way out is through." You face the thing you are afraid of, and in so doing, conquer it.

On the third night, Jacob and Samuel reported for their inaugural tunneling shift. The horizontal shaft had just been started. The tunnel would be about thirty inches wide and twenty-four inches high, large enough for an adult to crawl through. The horizontal section would have to be at least fifty yards long to reach the wheat field on the outside of the camp. They expected the tunnel to be finished in August, when the wheat would be more than three feet high and could shield the escapees from the eyes of the sentries.

Jacob picked up a digging bar. He noted its heft and substance as he balanced it in his hand. It was black, except for the tapered end, which was shiny and polished from digging.

"Well, Samuel, are you ready for this?" Jacob asked.

"I've been ready for this for a long time," he replied.

"Then let's get at it."

Kneeling in the vertical shaft, Jacob plunged the bar into the dirt face. It penetrated a few inches. Clumps of dirt fell down as he worked the bar back and forth. Each stab in the earth inched them closer to freedom. It was satisfying work.

They gradually developed a routine. The digger crawled to the face of the tunnel with the digging bar and a small shovel. While leaning on one elbow, he stabbed the bar into the face of the earth until he had loosened a few inches of earth across the entire face. Then with the small shovel, he scooted the dirt back to the disposer, who shoveled the dirt into a sack. When the sack was full, the disposer crawled back to the vertical shaft and handed it to a person in the shaft, who hoisted it up to the floor and handed it off to be dumped in the attic. After about an hour, the digger and disposer changed places, as the digging job took a fair amount of effort and sometimes caused cramps.

Jacob and Samuel were glad to be doing something to resist the Nazis, and that feeling was reflected in some good-natured teasing that first night. They hadn't realized how dirty they would get digging. After their shift was over and they returned to the barracks, Jacob looked at himself and at Samuel and couldn't help but laugh. White eyes peered out from two muddy faces. "Samuel, what have you been doing? It looks like you've been down in a coal mine."

"Yes, *Mein Grabenführer**," replied Samuel, "I am working nights digging coal."

"We should honor you with an award—The Distinguished Cross of the Twenty-Four-Hour Slave Laborer. After they pin it on your chest, they shoot you in the back of the neck."

"If you don't mind, I think I will forgo the awards ceremony."

"Because of your coal, our *Führer* will be warm this winter."

"I doubt he will need it, *Mein Grabenführer*."

"Oh, why is that?"

"Because he will be in hell, *Mein Grabenführer*."

It felt good to laugh for a moment. It did take a while for them to get reasonably clean for the next day's work. They would have to figure out something better. Eventually they tunneled wearing only some shorts, which was convenient and cooler.

By the time they had extended the horizontal shaft twenty feet—after about a week of digging—Jacob was struggling to keep his feelings in check. For one thing, at twenty feet in, the face was almost in complete darkness. This was due both to the length of the tunnel and the fact it wasn't completely straight but wandered a little to the left and right. Digging at the face had to be done mostly through touch. While working in this near black-out, Jacob would talk to himself in a quiet voice to try to tamp down his anxiety. *You are all right. You are fine. Take a deep breath. You can do this.* He would focus on the dirt wall in front of him and not think about all the dirt above him or the long tunnel behind him. Sometimes he recited Psalms or talked with

---

* Digging leader

Samuel to keep from giving in to panic. There was something soothing about hearing another person's voice in this narrow, dark cave.

Without Jacob saying anything directly, Samuel seemed to pick up on his feelings. He occasionally asked, "How are you doing?" or grab Jacob's calf and say, "I'm with you."

Fortunately for Jacob, it became clear to everyone that they needed some light, if for no other reason than to see what they were doing. They experimented with making small lamps with wicks soaked in oil. But these were awkward to handle, they sometimes blew out, and worst of all, they used up precious oxygen.

Eli the electrician came to the rescue regarding the lighting problem. He was able to rig up a set of electric lights they could hang down the length of the tunnel. Shortly afterward, Jacob expressed his heart-felt appreciation. "Eli, I'm not sure how you were able to pull this off, but I, for one, am very grateful to no longer be working in the dark. How did you find enough wire? And all the lights?"

"I have my secrets. Let's just say the Germans were unusually generous."

"Is that so? The Germans aren't exactly known for their generosity to the Jews."

"Well, I must confess they don't know about it yet. And by the time they find out, I hope all of us are long gone."

They also realized that at some point they would eventually need a source of fresh air. As they dug, they inhaled oxygen and exhaled carbon dioxide, and the further they were from the entrance, the fouler the air became. One night, when Jacob couldn't sleep, he heard some low voices coming from the tunnel entrance. Curious, he quietly made his way over to the tunnel shed. He saw Adam bending over someone who was kneeling on all fours on the floor, panting.

"What happened?" Jacob whispered. Now that he was next to them, he could make out that the person gasping for air was Natan, one of the diggers.

"Not enough oxygen," Adam said. "He got dizzy and had to back out. Emil, his partner, told me the rope lamps won't even burn. We're going to have to do something." Inwardly Jacob was glad for this—he also was getting dizzy when he dug, and it didn't help his claustrophobia to feel like he was slowly suffocating.

To address the oxygen problem, they figured the easiest thing to do was to periodically make some airholes. They spent one day carefully digging up to the surface to try this out. They had to be very careful not to initiate a cave-in, and just to be safe they shored up the ceiling around the perimeter of the hole. When their measurements said they were within a few inches of the surface, they carefully pushed a stick up, angling it some so no light would seep through, until they could feel no more resistance. To their satisfaction, as they removed the stick, cool air tumbled down on them. How sweet it was compared to the stale air they were used to! By observing the sticks from the attic, they could also confirm or correct the direction of the tunnel.

However, they were in for a surprise. The next morning, members of the digging team casually walked over to the location of the airhole. It was, in fact, quite unobtrusive. However, there was a little column of steam rising from it, like a miniature volcanic vent. They had forgotten that the tunnel air was both warm and humid, and when it hit the cool air outside, the moisture condensed. This would not do. Quietly they used their shoes to fill the hole with rocks and dirt. They learned to camouflage the vent holes by day and open them only at night.

After digging in near darkness, having the electric lights was a godsend for Jacob—as long as the power stayed on. But occasionally, for various reasons, the power went out. Then the digging crew had two choices: they could try to back out of the tunnel, which took a while, or they could just lie there and wait for the lights to come back on. This was the worst time for Jacob. This was darkness as he had never before experienced—complete, inky blackness. It was like an opaque vapor he could feel and taste. On bad days, when the walls seemed to close in around him, he felt as if he was being buried alive. Besides keeping up a conversation with Samuel, he softly recited psalms.

Except when the power went out, working underground gradually became easier for Jacob, if not easy. In fact, Jacob liked the fresh smell of the earth. Above ground was an atmosphere of hate. Here the crumbling earth smelled of hope.

Sometimes while digging Jacob talked to Rachel and facetiously blamed her for his strange predicament. "Rachel," he whispered, "it is your fault I am down here lying in this black vault. If not for you, I would be up in our 'luxurious' barracks getting some sleep, not digging underground like a mole. So, 'the only way out is through,' is it? I didn't realize how literally that saying could be taken."

At other times, however, he lost himself in non-facetious thoughts about Rachel. There was one scene in particular he played over and over in his mind. He had arranged to meet her at a bookstore to tell her his family was moving to the east, to the Russian-occupied zone. They both knew this meant they might not see each other again, or at least not for a long time. He remembered how her face was upturned to his, and how beautiful her brown eyes were. He hadn't planned what happened next, but it just felt right: he pulled her gently behind a bookcase and kissed her. It was the first "boyfriend-girlfriend" kiss for both of them. What it lacked in finesse, it made up for in ardor. "I've wanted to do that for a long time," he told her.

He would not forget her reply. "I've wanted you to do that for a long time," she said, smiling.

Now, as he wielded a digging bar, he thought, *Too bad I wasn't a little bolder earlier*. With determination, he added, "Rachel, when I come back, if by the grace of God I survive, I'm going to make up for lost time. I'm just giving you fair warning." Then, with a surge of energy, he stabbed the bar into the face of the tunnel.

Sometimes as Jacob dug he felt just fine, and then a few seconds later a wave of grief washed over him and he began to weep. "Mama and Papa," he said through tear-blurred eyes, "I miss you. Mira, I miss you too. How is it you are gone? I keep hoping I will wake up and find you here, but each day I am disappointed. Every Sabbath I think of being with you, of blessing the wine and eating the challah and singing together. Now there is only emptiness. How am I still alive? Why should I live instead of you? I think of you. I miss you."

***

Jacob liked to solve problems. He would see something that wasn't as efficient or well-organized as it could be and he would begin to think about how it could be improved, just for the satisfaction of doing so. Now he began to think about the tunnel. After they had set up lights and provided for some fresh air, he considered ways they could make excavation more efficient. For example, rather than having the disposer crawl back and forth with sacks loaded with dirt, it made sense to pull a basket with some rope. After filling the basket, the disposer gave two yanks on the rope and the person at the entrance pulled the basket to the entrance, where it was emptied. The disposer then pulled the basket back with some rope on his end. Jacob further improved the disposal process by suggesting they lay a crude track in the tunnel and make the basket a wagon that could roll along the track.

By experimenting with Samuel, he also found it was most effective for the disposer and the digger to lie down with their feet together, the digger facing the dirt face and the disposer facing the entrance of the tunnel. As the digger advanced, the disposer backed up, pulling the loosened earth up toward the wagon and filling it. With these improvements the digging teams were able to increase their progress from one to two yards per day to two to three yards per day.

They worked with an earnestness borne from their resolve. Jacob became aware of a mental tally he was keeping. By day, the Germans were masters and added marks on their side of the ledger. Every humiliation, every beating, every cruelty was a mark. But by night, the Jews could add marks to their side with each shovelful of dirt removed. They never caught up, but it felt good to balance things out a little. And as the earth yielded to their efforts and the tunnel gained depth and length, it became a physical representation of throwing off the yoke of their tormentors and moving towards freedom.

***

It was a great day when the white stick creating an airhole could no longer be seen because it was beyond the wooden fence and into the wheat field. They had made it. The little group of 250—in the most unlikely of circumstances—had accomplished what seemed impossible.

They began to think of the actual escape. They made a list giving the order of line-up to enter the tunnel. Generally, the people who were the most fit were put at the beginning of the line, and those less fit were put toward the end. The leaders felt this gave the best chance for the greatest number of people to make it to the woods. They also decided to wait for a late-rising moon and a stormy night. Eli found a way to cut power to the searchlight; he turned it off for a few minutes every now and then so the Germans got used to it being unreliable.

There was a mood of great excitement. They were leaving! Then their plans were disrupted by something they hadn't expected.

The wheat field was harvested.

Chapter 24: The Little Hill
Jacob, Eastern Poland, Late Summer 1942

No longer would the wheat field offer concealment. They would be escaping right next to the compound. Could 250 people manage this without being detected? It seemed unlikely. What should they do now?

As before, they held a secret meeting to discuss options. As the meeting started, Jacob recalled a similar meeting four weeks earlier. Then the tunnel was nothing but an unlikely pipe dream. Now it existed. It was an amazing achievement.

Adam called the meeting to order. "As you all know, we have completed our original plans for the tunnel. It is now five yards outside the wall of the camp. But we no longer have cover, as the wheat has been harvested. It is the third week of August. We have only about two more months of good weather. We need to decide what we should do."

Pani Azrylewicz, the doctor's wife, asked to speak. "My husband and I wish to acknowledge what you have done. We will never forget what has happened here in the past four weeks, nor will we ever forget you. We see a glimmer of hope in the midst of darkness. We see it is possible to stand up against evil. No matter what happens, we will not forget how we came together to help each other." Her remarks were met by a chorus of agreement.

"What are the choices before us?" someone asked.

Adam answered, "We try to make an escape as soon as we can, in the next few days, or we extend the tunnel farther."

"How much farther?"

"There is a little hill a hundred yards farther on. If we were to tunnel past it, we would not be seen when we exit the tunnel." At the mention of one hundred yards, a murmur went through the room.

"One hundred yards farther? Are you serious? How long would it take? Can we even get rid of that much dirt?"

"A good question," responded Adam. "We have an idea for getting rid of the dirt. The attics are nearly full. We are beginning to worry they might collapse. We can remove some dirt when we do camp maintenance on Sunday as part of filling in old latrines."

Jacob was caught off guard when Samuel—who rarely spoke up in a group—said, "I think we should tunnel to the little hill. I know it is far, but it gives everyone here the best chance of escaping. There is no sign of an imminent *Aktion*. We can do it in four weeks if we press hard."

Not everyone agreed. *Pan* Saks advocated leaving now. "I am amazed we have gotten this far without the Nazis discovering what we are doing. We are pushing our luck. I say we make the escape attempt now. Let's wait for a dark night, turn off the searchlight, and get out." Quite a few agreed with him.

After much discussion, and contrary to Jacob's expectations, the group voted to keep digging. This was a bitter pill for many to swallow, but they could afford only a day's discouragement. The next day they began again.

Jacob and Samuel took their regular rotation. Their team of four now worked together like a well-oiled machine. They made good progress through the first week of September.

Then it began to rain.

Chapter 25: The Cave-In
Jacob, Eastern Poland, Fall 1942

It rained steadily for five days. The top of the tunnel became moist, and clumps of earth began to fall down. Things came to a crisis during Jacob and Samuel's shift. Jacob was working at the face and Samuel was filling the wagon. The lights, which needed to be extended, cast the face in shadows. Jacob was lost in thought, mechanically loosening soil and pushing it back behind him. Samuel was facing the other direction, scooping up the loose dirt and dumping it in the wagon. Suddenly there was a soft thump that vibrated the ground, like heavy snow sliding off a roof. The ceiling over Jacob had collapsed, burying him.

Samuel knew instantly what had happened, as he was partially buried too. As he craned his neck to look behind him, he saw the entire tunnel was filled with dirt. Jacob's feet and lower legs were sticking out, but that was all. They were not moving.

Samuel knew he had to act quickly, before the tunnel collapsed further and before Jacob suffocated. Reaching behind him, he grabbed Jacob's ankles. He was able to pull his own feet up. Wedging his feet against the walls of the tunnel, he pulled with all his might. Jacob barely moved. With adrenalin coursing through him, Samuel pulled again as hard as he could. Jacob moved an inch or two. Again and again he pulled, gradually moving them both to uncovered ground. When he finally pulled him free, Jacob had been buried for several minutes.

By rolling onto his side, Samuel was able to pull Jacob up beside him in the narrow width of the tunnel. Jacob, his eyes shut, appeared lifeless. His mud-caked face was ashen, and his lips were blue. "Breathe," Samuel said in a low but intense voice. He shook him by the shoulders. "Breathe!" he yelled. Not knowing what else to do, Samuel slapped Jacob hard, hoping this would shock him into response. Then, on impulse, he cleaned the dirt from around Jacob's mouth and breathed into it. After some long seconds, Jacob moaned. He began to breathe in irregular gasps as he struggled to get air into his lungs. Gradually his spasmodic gasping smoothed out into more regular breaths.

After a few minutes he opened his eyes and whispered hoarsely, "Am I alive? I was sure I was dead. I felt like I was encased in concrete. What happened? How did I get out?"

"I grabbed on and pulled for all I was worth, and then some. But it was a close call. For a while, I thought I'd lost you. Your legs, by the way, might be sore tomorrow."

Jacob flashed a weak smile. "I need to get another line of work. This is killing me. Although I've said it before, I don't know how I would manage without you."

"Me either," joked Samuel. "It's practically a full-time job keeping you out of trouble. Let's get above ground before something else happens."

They crawled back to the mouth of the tunnel without further mishap. But during the night, another section of the roof gave way.

The carpenters spent several days shoring up sections of the ceiling that were suspect or had partially collapsed. They were stealing wood from everywhere, including from all the bunks. This didn't help their sleeping, but things could always be worse. For one, the Germans didn't seem to notice several sections of ground in the wheat field that had slumped down, oddly in a straight line directly away from the camp.

During the last week of September, they reached the other side of the hill, and they were ready to try again. About this time, Samuel approached Jacob as they were cleaning up after their shift.

"I have a proposal for you."

"Go ahead."

"I am aware of a boy, a friend's cousin's son, who froze his feet badly last winter. Eventually all his toes had to be amputated. This was done without any anesthetic. The healing process has been long and painful, and he can still barely walk. He's only fourteen. He has no more family left."

Jacob could see where this was going, and it was typical Samuel. "And?"

"And I'd like to bring him with us."

"What is your plan if he can't walk?"

"We'd need to carry him."

"Really?" asked Jacob, taken aback by Samuel's rather blithe reply. It was twenty miles to the partisans. This was no small thing he was proposing.

"We can do it. We can't just leave him behind."

Jacob knew Samuel well enough by now to know he'd somehow make this work. Samuel didn't know the meaning of the phrase *It can't be done*. They would figure something out. Besides, Jacob knew himself well enough to know he would regret it if they left this boy behind.

"I think," Jacob said, after a long pause, "we should do it. Let's figure out how we can bring him along." And then, in a nice turnabout for Jacob, he put his hand on Samuel's shoulder and added, "I'm with you."

Samuel beamed back at him. "I'm glad to hear that."

Chapter 26: The Escape
Jacob, Eastern Poland, Fall 1942

The night of September 26 was cold and rainy. It was one of those nights that seem especially dark, a night when a person just wants to stay inside. This was the night they would leave. Everyone already had their number. Starting at 11 p.m., Numbers 1–120 lined up quietly in the barracks, waiting for the go-ahead to enter the tunnel. Digging Team 1 was just punching through the exit. As soon as the exit was clear, people would begin crawling down into the tunnel, one behind another. Eli turned off the searchlight.

Most had never been in the tunnel before, and there was some concern a few would "freeze" when they got in the tiny, enclosed space. A few, in fact, elected to stay behind and hide in the attic spaces, either because of their fear of the tunnel, or because they didn't believe they could survive in the woods over the winter. If anyone expressed misgivings about being in the tunnel and wanted help, a number of young men volunteered to accompany them. This meant they would go immediately behind and try to calm them if they began to panic or push them forward if they had to. The pushers would make sure no one held up the whole operation. There could be no backing up once they entered; it was forward to the end.

Samuel came into the barracks with his arm around Alex, the young man who'd had his toes amputated. Jacob had seen Alex limping around in the workshops and had wondered what had happened but had never asked. "Hello, Alex," Jacob said, offering the boy his hand. "I am Jacob, and I am glad we will share this journey together."

"Alex has some thoughts about what we should do," Samuel volunteered. "He grew up nearby and he knows someone he thinks would shelter us for the night. I think this is a good idea. We will not be able to travel very far tonight, and if we lay low for a day or two, we could leave for the forest after things have quieted down some." This made sense to Jacob.

Alex, Jacob, and Samuel entered the tunnel as numbers 81, 82, and 83, about one-third of the way back. Jacob had never been in the tunnel before in these conditions. It was a singular sight—a chain of people lined up in this earthen passageway, head to toe, for as far one could see in the constrained space. The scene was made all the more moving when he considered how many of these intrepid fellow travelers had become like family. They were now brothers and sisters, fathers and mothers. Recalling his own experience, he suspected that not a few were suppressing their own dread of small spaces. He knew of one person, in fact, who had taken a small stick with him so he could bite down on it if he felt the need to scream. But regardless of their fears, there they were, in all shapes and sizes, crawling determinedly towards freedom.

The lights in the tunnel were kept on, as it would have been terrifying for those escaping to proceed in complete darkness for 150 yards. But the lights had an unexpected effect: when some of the Jews exited the tunnel, their eyes were not accustomed to the darkness. In the low visibility of the rainy night, they became disoriented and inadvertently wandered back toward the compound. The guards, sensing that someone they couldn't see was approaching, probably assumed partisans were coming to attack.

They opened fire.

Chapter 27: In the Crossfire
Jacob, Eastern Poland, Fall 1942

Everyone froze. They must have been discovered. Were they going to get out only to be mowed down? Fortunately, Adam, the captain, surmised what had happened. He was stationed at the exit, helping people get out. He could see where the guards were aiming by their tracer bullets, which gave off streaks of light. He could see they were shooting randomly around the perimeter of the camp and not toward the tunnel. "Keep coming!" he shouted down the exit shaft. When people hesitated, he reached down and pulled them forward. "Go!" he said, pointing them to the forest. "They are not aiming at us, but hurry!" With bullets peppering the wheat field, they didn't need any more encouragement.

***

Jacob, Samuel, and Alex were only about thirty feet from reaching the exit when they heard the shooting. "Oh, dear God," someone cried out, "they've found us." The alarming news quickly spread down the tunnel.

"This could be the end," muttered Jacob. "And after all this work. Damn. Our luck couldn't hold forever, but we only needed one more night."

Then voices in front of him said, "We're supposed to keep going." With fear in their hearts, they started moving forward again. The gunfire got louder.

Jacob thought, *If we have to run, this is going to be difficult with Alex. We'll just have to take whatever comes.* They seemed to be crawling toward chaos. At the exit, Adam helped Alex out and wished him good luck, and he hugged both Jacob and Samuel. "Now," he said, "get on your way." Alex climbed piggyback onto Samuel's back and they ran toward the forest.

As soon as they reached some woods, they began to circle around away from the direction to the partisans, which was the direction most people were heading. They went behind the camp and down some backroads toward a farmhouse known by Alex. Weakened by their subsistence diet, they did not have a lot of endurance, and a slow walking pace was all they could manage.

It was quiet as Jacob, Samuel, and Alex walked alone down a narrow cart path. The rain had stopped, and as the sky cleared, the stars shone brilliantly, helping to light their way. They shivered in their rain-soaked clothes. The excitement had worn off some, and they realized they were worn out. Every twenty minutes or so Jacob and Samuel traded off carrying Alex. After about an hour, Alex told them to enter a meadow on their right. It was enclosed by a rail fence. They followed the fence to a clearing in which stood a wooden clapboard house with a tin roof and a small, weathered barn that leaned a bit crookedly. An old wagon stood in front of the barn, and they could hear a horse neigh at their approach. Alex knocked at the door. They saw an attic light go on; a window opened, and voice asked, "Who is there?"

Alex said softy, "Jurek, it is Alex Zirinski. My father is Zelik Zirinski."

"You are Zelik's son?"

"Yes."

"And who is with you?"

"We are Jews who need help," Jacob replied.

"Come closer so I can see you." They stepped forward. "What is your mother's name?"

"It is Natalia."

"Wait there." They heard the door being unbarred and then opened. "Come in," Jurek said. "It is not a good night to be out and about. I see you are very wet. Sabina, fetch some towels please."

Sabina was a step ahead of her husband. "Here are some towels and blankets. Take off your wet things and give them to me. I will hang them up to dry." After what they had been through, no one was embarrassed to strip down to their underwear and hand over their shirts and pants. Meanwhile, Jurek rekindled the fire, which had burned down to embers. Presently flames sprung up, casting the room in a warm, welcoming light.

They wrapped themselves in blankets, sitting around the fire on stools or the floor, and rehearsed the events of the night to their hosts, who were somewhat amazed. Jurek looked at Alex. "I take it your father and mother are no longer living."

Alex nodded. "Killed in the last *Aktion*. Shot on the edge of a pit and buried there with hundreds of others."

"How far is it to the partisans?" Jurek asked.

"We believe it is around twenty miles, maybe a little farther," answered Jacob.

"And you are going to carry Alex that far? That is a long way. Maybe he should stay here for a while."

But Alex wouldn't hear of it. "I am going to the partisans, even if I have to walk there myself. I want to kill Germans. I want to seek revenge for my family."

Everyone in the room exchanged glances. There was no denying the determination in Alex's voice. "We understand, Alex. We feel the same," Samuel said softly.

Jacob hesitated to make his next request. "We do not want to put you in any more danger than is necessary. But we wondered if we could stay two days, until things quiet down in the forest."

"Mother, what do you think?" Sabina nodded her approval. "Stay by the fire tonight so you don't get pneumonia. We'll have you sleep in the barn tomorrow. If anything happens, you'll be safer there."

"Thank you for your hospitality," Jacob said, feeling how totally inadequate his words were for people risking their lives to help them.

***

The escape was not discovered until 4:30 that morning, when guards found the barracks empty. By that time the escape was complete—more than 230 had gotten away. Search parties with dogs were immediately sent out. All through the day the stillness of the forest was broken with the staccato sounds of guns firing. Tragically more than eighty were tracked down and killed. They died as free men and women.

Chapter 28: A Step into the Unknown
Rachel, Western Poland, Winter 1942

The year was drawing to a close, and winter had come. Rachel realized she was extremely fortunate to be where she was. Yet this fact discomfited her. Poland was at war, and she was sitting comfortably on the sidelines. Her country and her people were under a yoke of great oppression. She wanted to help, even if it meant leaving these surroundings. Her conscience and her belief that God had something for her to do impelled her to act. But what could she do? The only person she felt might be able to help was Father Sobieski. She resolved that the next time she went to town, she would pass a message to him through Maria.

A week later, she had a warm but brief reunion with Maria when she stopped by the church. Maria was in the kitchen. Rachel poked her head through the door. "Hello," she said. "I hoped to find you here."

"Julia!" Maria exclaimed. "Come in. How nice to see you! How are things going for you with the Kohler family?"

Rachel stepped in and shut the door. "The children are wonderful, and I am treated well."

"I knew you would make a success of things."

"I suppose things are a success, if you don't include dinner parties." Maria gave her a puzzled look but said nothing. "How are you and the Father doing? Is everything going well for you?" They both understood this question implied more than it sounded like on the surface.

"Yes," she said, "we are surviving. The Father is always busy ministering to his flock."

Rachel cast a glance at the door to make sure it was shut tight. She lowered her voice. "Actually, that is why I am here. I want to help. I want to help my people and I want to help Poland. Can you ask the Father what I can do?"

"Are you sure about this?" questioned Maria. "It will put you in danger again." She paused and then added, "Very great danger."

"I am quite sure. I cannot just stand idly by. I want to help."

"Come back in a week. I'll make sure the Father is here, and you two can talk."

A week later, Rachel and Father Sobieski met in the kitchen. He suggested they go for a walk. "Maria has told me of your desire. I must also ask you if you are sure about this. You understand the SS has no reluctance to torture and kill members of the resistance?"

"Yes, I know that. I have lived a good part of the past two years with that kind of threat hanging over me."

"We have a need for couriers to carry items to Warsaw. With your Polish looks, your ability to think and act quickly, and as a woman, I believe you would be ideal for this. Do you want the job?" he asked.

"Yes," she replied without hesitation, feeling that tiny word could not begin to capture all she felt or what she had just agreed to.

"If my memory serves me correctly, I recall the Kohler estate has a large set of stables. I am assuming most of the horses are gone?"

"Most were lost when they were requisitioned by the Polish army at the start of the war."

"Ah, as I thought. Can you talk to *Frau* Kohler and arrange some time off?"

"I am sure I can. I am given one day off a week, in addition to Sunday, and I haven't yet taken any days. Also, for much of the time in the next two weeks, the children will be on holiday, and we won't be having lessons."

"Next Friday morning around ten a.m. you should retrieve a suitcase that will be left in the back of the stables under some hay. Don't look for it any earlier. Take the suitcase on the 12:20 p.m. train to Warsaw. The journey should last about four hours, if you are lucky and the train is not delayed for some reason. When you arrive, go to the streetcar plaza, platform six. A woman will meet you there. She will find you, but just so you know, she will be wearing a green dress under a dark coat. Within a sentence she will give you the passphrase, *a coming storm*. You will give her the suitcase—there will be lots of people around, and this will not look out of place—and then you will take another streetcar to a location where you can spend the night. Your contact will give you the address. Is this clear?"

"Yes. I am glad you feel you can give me this responsibility. It means a lot to me."

"It will mean a lot to those you help," he replied. "Many thousands were killed over the summer. Some thousands remain. They are brave, but bravery is not enough. They need guns."

Then he added, "Although you will still carry your identification papers with you, you will operate under a code name in communication with others. Your code name will be *Teresa*."

A new phase of her life was about to begin.

Chapter 29: The Train to Warsaw
Rachel, Western Poland and Warsaw, Winter 1942–1943

Rachel was afraid, but she was also exhilarated. The suitcase she had retrieved was very heavy. Judging from its weight, she presumed it contained weapons or explosives. There were rumors of an uprising being planned in the ghetto. Although she couldn't help but be anxious, she was also buoyant, even joyous about helping her brothers and sisters in arms. Theirs was a fight against the most uneven of odds. She was proud to be able to contribute a tiny bit to their cause.

She had decided to board the last car of the train. Then, if she saw the train was being searched, she could always try to jump from the back. This didn't console her much, however. She already knew the violent effects of jumping from a train, and if the Germans found the contraband, they would hunt her down. If she were found out, her chances of survival were almost nil. She just hoped the train would not be searched.

She chose not to board until the train was almost ready to depart. By waiting, she had a better chance of picking an open row and being left by herself. She didn't really want to get into a long chat with a friendly seatmate. The more she talked, she felt, the more she put herself at risk. She wanted to close her eyes and be invisible until the train pulled into the Warsaw station.

She was in luck. As she walked down the last car, she found a bench that was empty. The car was only about two-thirds full with a mix of Poles and Germans. Behind her were some regular German soldiers—*Wehrmacht*. Casually she asked one of them if he would help her put her suitcase up in the rack above her.

His accommodating smile changed to a look of surprise as he hefted the heavy suitcase. "Good heavens, what do you have in here?" he asked.

"I'm so sorry, it is some books for my father," she explained.

"Well," he said, as he shoved it on the overhead shelf, "we will try to make sure it doesn't fall on you."

"Thank you," she replied. She was pleased with her boldness. *Sometimes the best way to hide is in plain sight*, she thought.

Then, however, her luck changed. Entering the car, duffel bag in hand, was an SS officer. He looked familiar. Rachel blanched as she realized it was Heinrich from the disastrous dinner of weeks earlier. He looked at the open seat beside her and brusquely told her to move over. He threw his duffel bag up against her suitcase. She was now trapped between him and the window.

Rachel understood he hadn't picked this seat at random, but because it offered the prospect of female company. Knowing what had happened at the dinner, Rachel sat with a pit in her stomach, steeling herself against the advances that were sure to come. If he was aggressive at a dinner party with guests, in the presence of his commanding officer, she could only imagine how he would be here, when he could essentially do what he pleased. She also wondered how things would escalate if he recognized her. She told herself she would endure whatever humiliation might come as long as she could escape with her life and fulfill her mission.

He smelled of alcohol. Fortunately, his apparent drinking had made him sleepy, and for a while he seemed to doze off. Rachel closed her eyes and pretended to be asleep, hoping he would leave her alone. After a few minutes she felt the hair on the back of her neck stand up. Although her eyes were closed, she felt his gaze upon her. Suddenly his hand went around the back of her head. Grabbing her hair, he yanked her toward him. "For a Polish girl, you're not bad looking, do you know that? How about a little kiss?"

Rachel didn't know what to do or say. She was afraid if she resisted it would make the situation worse. His breath almost made her sick. He kissed her hard on the mouth; after a few seconds she broke away in disgust.

"Ah, you didn't like that? I think you need to learn to have more fun. How about you come with me when we get to Warsaw?" he suggested. "We'll have a real good time together." He laughed and ran his hand down her leg.

"I will be meeting my family," Rachel countered, hoping that bringing other people into the picture might discourage him.

"Oh, that's all right," he replied, "they won't miss you for a day or two. After all, there is a war on."

"They'll be waiting for me at the station," she insisted.

"You know, you look familiar to me. Where are you from?" he asked.

"The countryside," she answered evasively while avoiding his eyes.

He got up and went to the lavatory. As he wandered back, he stopped and visited with the soldiers behind her seat for a minute. Rachel could hear them laughing as he said something crude about Polish Jews. She pretended not to hear. If she could just get to Warsaw, she felt she would be all right. In his semi-drunken state, she knew she could escape in the crowds, as long as she didn't have to go very far with the suitcase.

He settled in again next to her. He said something, but his words were slurred. *Good,* she thought, *maybe he will just fall asleep.* The rocking of the train helped. After a few minutes she saw his eyes were closed, and he slumped down next to her. For the moment she felt out of danger.

Rachel stared out the window, wishing for the minutes to rush by and bring her to Warsaw. Although she appeared to be lost in thought, her senses were on high alert. About an hour into the journey, her subconscious mind registered that something was not normal in the car. A mental alarm went off and brought her abruptly upright. What was wrong? What was happening? At the front of the car she saw two policemen checking papers.

But they were not only checking papers, they were checking luggage.

Chapter 30: The Search
Rachel, Western Poland and Warsaw, Winter 1942–1943

In their German thoroughness, there were no exceptions. The police required everyone to open their luggage. It was embarrassing to see these men rifle through people's personal belongings. She thought of her suitcase sitting above her. What would happen when it was opened to display an assortment of guns or explosives?

Rachel had policemen in front of her, *Wehrmacht* soldiers behind her, and an SS officer sprawled asleep next to her. She would have to climb over him just to get access to the aisle. There was no way she could try to run and make it. She had only a few minutes before the policemen would demand her papers and open her luggage. For one of the few times in her life, she panicked. Her mind and heart were racing, but she couldn't get herself to focus. What could she do? Usually she could figure out some sort of plan. Now all was confusion.

As a measure of her desperation, she briefly considered trying to break the window and leap from the train. But she had no means to do this, and the idea of squeezing through the small opening while the other passengers looked on was ludicrous. She felt like she was caught in a cavern with water inching up higher and higher. The water was at her chin, and she saw no path of escape.

Somehow, she had to go on the offensive. A wild idea came to her. It wasn't much, but it was the only thing she could think of. She kicked the officer's foot. He lurched up out of his stupor, his eyes blinking wide, wondering what was going on. He looked over at her.

"I'm sorry my first kiss wasn't very good," she said as she put *her* hand on *his* leg. "Let me see if I can do better." For a moment Heinrich was confused, but it didn't take long for him to catch on. He grabbed her hair and pulled her over to him, and holding her tightly, began to kiss her.

Rachel didn't have much experience kissing men. Her only romantic kiss was with Jacob. This wasn't like that. Besides his awful breath, he was rough with her. He held her hair so tightly it hurt her. His mouth pressed forcefully on hers. He obviously didn't care about her—she was only an expendable Polish girl. Although she was surprised at how violated she felt, still she forced herself to respond.

Thus, when the policemen got to her row, she was in an embrace with an SS officer. They knew better than to interrupt.

As soon as they passed, Rachel could take no more. She broke off the embrace, turned her head away, and said something about going with him when they arrived in Warsaw. Heinrich paused for a moment and stared at her. "Yes," he said, "all right, in Warsaw then." Then he noticed the policemen checking papers and opening the luggage of passengers behind them. He turned and looked again at Rachel, studying her. Rachel saw a puzzled look in his eyes. She could see he was trying to put these pieces together. She saw his expression change from a question to an answer, from uncertainty to certainty.

Rachel knew that he knew.

Chapter 31: Assault
Rachel, Western Poland and Warsaw, Winter 1942—1943

"I need some air," he announced. "I am going out on the platform at the back of the car, and I want you to come with me." He grabbed her wrist and pulled her up sharply. He pushed her in front of him to the back of the car. There he opened the door and shoved her out onto the exterior platform. The platform, as wide as the car and about five feet long, was covered by a roof but had open sides. A low railing ran all the way around, broken only by two metal poles, one on each side, which supported the roof. It was cold and windy and noisy. The platform shuddered back and forth with the movement of the train.

He pushed her up against the back wall of the car. "Now, my sweet little Polish girl, I know who you are, and I can guess what you're up to. You will regret playing an SS officer for a fool. First, though, we are going to have some fun. Didn't I say you needed to learn to have more fun? I don't think, though, I will worry about being a gentleman." Then he began to assault her.

Rachel realized it wasn't just rape that was on his mind; it was murder.

Chapter 32: Shattered Glass
Rachel, Western Poland and Warsaw, Winter 1942–1943

In the next moment they were both startled by the sound of gunshots, and a glass lamp near the door shattered. Heinrich instinctively ducked while drawing out his sidearm. In the terrain behind them there was a flash of light—a reflection perhaps—in the forest to their right. Grabbing a pole with his left hand, Heinrich leaned out over the railing to get a better line of sight and fired, cursing the whole time.

Rachel saw her chance and didn't hesitate. Only his left hand kept him secure. With all her might she slammed into him from behind. His arm buckled, and his hand came free. For a moment he grasped wildly at anything behind him, and she had to jerk her head back to prevent him from catching her hair. Then he toppled over the railing headfirst onto the tracks.

As she snapped her head away from his grasp, Rachel fell backward to the floor. Having heard the shots, soldiers entered from the car with their pistols drawn. Rachel lay sprawled on the floor, her clothes and hair disheveled. She appeared dazed and in a state of shock. "What happened?" they demanded.

"I don't know," she answered weakly in German, "I think they shot him, and he fell over." After seeing their comrade was gone, they went back inside to try to stop the train, paying no further attention to her.

Rachel crawled to the back wall of the car, and, resting against it, pulled her knees up tight against her chest. She was shaking. Events had happened so quickly and altered so drastically she was having a hard time comprehending them. Only seconds before she was being assaulted—she could still feel his hands on her and smell his breath, stinking of schnapps. Then *she* had been the one to strike out—her hands were on him as she pushed him over the railing. The wind and the noise and the rocking of the train remained, but that was all. There was no *him*. Was this real? She tried to replay in her mind what had happened, but her thoughts seemed to swirl about her. She couldn't quite put all the moments together. Gradually, though, reality settled on her: *he was gone*. After some minutes, still shivering from cold and shock, she made her way back into the car.

***

The train could not stop without risking collision with trains following behind. This was a route to the east, and rail lines to the east were heavily used to transport military supplies to the Russian front. A search party was sent out later for the SS officer, but no body was found. Perhaps he had only been injured and had made his way to safety. There was a rumor, however, that partisans had gotten there first.

To her relief, Rachel was ignored for the rest of the journey, although seeing her shivering, one passenger kindly lent her a blanket.

Chapter 33: The Hand-off
Rachel, Western Poland and Warsaw, December 1942

When the train pulled into the station, Rachel waited for the other passengers to get off the train before gathering her things. The *Wehrmacht* soldier who had helped her before offered to get her suitcase down for her, and she thanked him politely. As she stepped out of the car, she tried to unobtrusively check to see if anyone was watching her. No one seemed to be paying her any attention.

The train station was next to a large streetcar terminal where streetcars from all over the city converged. Rachel would have to leave the train station and cross a busy street to get to the streetcar terminal. As she exited the station, she was met by a city in twilight. The streets were slushy from snow that had fallen earlier in the day; the sky was still overcast and threatening. Streetlamps were reflected in the snow that blanketed the sidewalks and trees.

Rachel lugged the heavy suitcase as far as she could and then stopped to rest. Crowds of people, heads bowed, hurried past her. *I'm sure they are anxious to get home,* she thought. Though there was only a light breeze blowing, the cold air seemed to slice through her coat.

With tired hands and aching arms, she made it to platform six with the suitcase. The terminal was crowded with people leaving work. With the congestion of the small space, she began to worry that her contact wouldn't be able to find her. Lacking any kind of backup plan, Rachel waited nervously, standing behind a bench with the suitcase between her and the back of the bench.

After a few minutes, a stout, grandmotherly-looking woman sidled up to her. "Hello. How are you this evening?" She seemed warm and friendly, much as a neighbor would be.

Rachel glanced at her and decided she couldn't possibly be the contact. Nonetheless, she responded courteously, "I am doing well, thank you, but it is cold, isn't it?"

"Yes," the grandmother replied. "I believe we have *a coming storm.*" Rachel was glad no one noticed how startled she was. This wasn't at all what she had imagined her hand-off would be like. But maybe that was the point. Rachel glanced again and noticed a green dress under a dark coat.

"I have heard that, yes," Rachel said as she listened intently.

"I am transferring over from platform eight. It is also very crowded over there," the grandmother explained. Rachel felt the woman's hand slip something into her coat pocket. "I hope you have a nice journey and will be warm tonight."

"Thank you; I wish you the same. I need to be going."

Rachel took a step back, leaving her suitcase and allowing the grandmother to take the spot where she had been standing. Then she walked toward platform eight. About halfway there, she stepped off the sidewalk and casually looked back to where she had been waiting. The grandmother and suitcase were gone.

Rachel retrieved the paper out of her coat pocket and read the instructions for getting to her room for the night. Then she slipped the paper inside her blouse.

A huge weight lifted from Rachel's shoulders, and she felt a great sense of accomplishment. She had fulfilled her first mission, although it had been by the slimmest of margins. She imagined the suitcase making its way into the ghetto, where it would be gladly received by Jews preparing to fight. *I wonder,* she thought, *if another courier, who looks more like a member of the resistance, will take it on its last leg?* She imagined someone tall and lean, with a beret and a heavy shadow of beard. But you never knew. Who would suspect a grandmother?

Rachel felt she was living on a heightened, more intense level of consciousness, brought on by the danger she had been under. Never before had she felt she was doing something so worthwhile.

Chapter 34: Helmuth
Helmuth, Warsaw, Spring 1942

Helmuth sometimes reflected on how he ended up in Warsaw. Just a few months earlier, he was in the *Waffen SS*[*] as a gunner on a machine gun, fighting through the bitter cold of Russia in February 1942. He had just come off guard duty at midnight and was looking forward to falling asleep in his unit's dugout when the sentry sounded the alarm and he could hear flares going off. They were under attack! Everyone jumped up, yanked on their boots, grabbed their helmets and weapons, and rushed to their posts.

Helmuth ripped the cover off his machine gun and began firing, sweeping the gun in an arc at targets he could only vaguely see through the smoke and flickering light of the flares. Before long, the first ammo belt was gone. The second gunner loaded a new belt within seconds. The noise of the battle was deafening, yet somehow through the din Helmuth heard his sergeant yell, "Grenade!" He and the other gunner dived into their trench.

He wasn't quite fast enough. There was an explosion just a few feet in front of them, and Helmuth felt hot metal tear into his right shoulder.

In the morning he found himself in the back of a truck bouncing along frozen roads with a heavily bandaged shoulder. With every rut and bump it felt like someone was stabbing him with a hot knife. After a journey of two hours, Helmuth was relieved to arrive at an army medical unit. Since he had a non-life-threatening injury, he waited hours for a doctor to operate, extracting from his shoulder as many pieces of metal as he could find. Fortunately, a medic took pity on him while he waited for surgery and gave him a shot of morphine.

His shoulder was mangled to the extent he would likely not be able to fully use it again. At a minimum, he would have a long convalescent and rehabilitation period. That meant he would no longer be able to carry an extra machine gun barrel and belts of ammunition—along with all his personal gear—on long marches.

---

[*] Combat units of the SS. These were elite units that fought alongside the regular army (*Wehrmacht*). Other branches of the SS ran the concentration camps and were responsible for security in occupied areas.

Because of his disability, Helmuth was transferred to the branch of the SS responsible for security in the occupied territories. His new assignment was Warsaw, where he would help implement the Reich's policies for the Poles and the Jews.

Chapter 35: Joining the SS
Helmuth, Warsaw, Spring 1942

Helmuth thought back to when he had volunteered to join the *Waffen SS*. The SS was the living embodiment of the Nazi doctrine of the superiority of Aryan blood. It was a racial, physical, and intellectual elite, a ruling class that would provide leadership to establish a new order throughout Europe when the war was over.

The genetic lottery had been kind to Helmuth: at nineteen years of age, he stood six feet tall and was a muscular 185 pounds, with broad shoulders and strong arms. He looked like the child of a Nordic god with his light-brown hair and blue eyes. As part of his application to the *Waffen SS*, he had to prove his Aryan ancestry back to 1800 and meet special physical requirements, including having no fillings in his teeth and 20/20 vision. As part of the SS, his training was more extensive than that of the regular soldier, and even included such things as the proper etiquette at a formal dinner. The *Waffen SS* were to represent the best of the German soldier: strong, brave, smart, indefatigable, unstoppable.

Helmuth had learned about Darwin's theories in school. In many respects, the mission of the SS was Darwinian in nature. As the superior race, they would implement survival of the fittest by wiping out inferior races, especially the Jews and the Slavs—Poles, Serbs, Russians. Sometimes these were combined, as when Heinrich Himmler, their leader, stated the main enemy was the "Jewish-Bolshevik revolution of subhumans."

Helmuth especially agreed with the war against Russia. He was convinced that Bolshevism and National Socialism were diametrically opposed—that Bolshevism threatened the survival of the German nation; indeed, that it threatened the survival of western civilization. He joined the *Waffen SS* specifically so he could fight on the eastern front. For him, it was akin to a holy war.

Because of his injury, he was now stationed in Poland, where the enemy was both the Poles, as a Slavic people, and the Polish Jews. Poland had more Jews than any other country in Europe. Helmuth grew up in a city in northern Germany where there weren't many Jews. Nevertheless, he was relentlessly taught—in school, in Hitler Youth, and in countless speeches, newspaper articles, and movies—

that the Jew is filthy; the Jew is evil and a swindler; the Jew is the enemy of Germany and undermines its existence; the Jew was the force behind the Versailles Treaty; the Jew was the cause of the worldwide depression; the Jew is Satan, who sows dissension among nations in order to gain profit; the Jew transmits typhus but is immune to it; and the Jew defiles the Aryan race. He recalled a song they had sung in Hitler Youth that started out, "The Jews' blood spurting from the knife makes us feel especially good."

These teachings were reinforced in the SS, where it was pounded into them that Germans had the moral right, *they had the duty*, to destroy this people who wanted to destroy them.

Helmuth didn't have much first-hand knowledge of the perfidy of the Jews, but he accepted it on faith. He had heard rumors of SS units—not the *Waffen SS*, as far as he knew—executing Jews in mass shootings. He had taken an oath of unconditional obedience and wondered if he would have to be part of such a thing. Every SS soldier had to be prepared to blindly carry out any order given by his superior, regardless of the sacrifice involved. He remembered one day in training when this was tested in an off-hand sort of way. His company was marching in formation. When they approached a lake, the drill instructor said nothing, so they marched into the water and continued marching until it was up to their necks. Just as they were about to go under, the instructor ordered an about-face.

Helmuth remembered no one had faltered. They would march into hell if asked to, so a lake was nothing.

Chapter 36: Sitting on the Porch
Helmuth, Northern Germany, 1934-1939

As Helmuth grew up, his mind was fertile ground for the seeds of the Nazi ideology. His father's family owned a spacious vacation home on the Baltic Sea, and every summer Helmuth and his aunts and uncles and cousins gathered to spend the summer at the seashore. At night they sat on the large porch in a circle where the adults talked and the children listened. They often talked about what had happened since the Great War. Helmuth's family had sacrificed much in the war—his father had fought, and he had lost two uncles in the war, one on each side of the family.

They didn't talk much about the actual fighting—that was still too painful. But they did talk about how it ended. The soldiers, who had fought bravely, felt betrayed and stunned by the armistice. The home front had also made great sacrifices, to the extent there was mass hunger and even starvation. Then suddenly everything collapsed. They were defeated. There had been no fighting on German soil, so how could they have lost the war?

Everyone Helmuth knew in his parent's generation felt the Versailles Treaty was a humiliation for Germany. He had heard the terms of the treaty many times, always expressed with great resentment: "We were forced to accept full responsibility for the war and make huge payments to the victors. We lost territory populated with German-speaking peoples. It gutted our army and navy. We couldn't have an air force. The French could occupy the Ruhr and take our coal whenever they wanted. It was shameful. We were second-class citizens in our own country."

As a cool breeze came off the sea during those nights on the porch, they also spoke about the aftermath of the war. The "olden days" could be spellbinding. There were tales of runaway inflation. Aunt Lilly recounted, "As soon as Fred was paid, I rushed to the grocery store to buy food, knowing tomorrow it might cost twice as much. In 1922, a loaf of bread cost 150 marks. I thought that was a lot. But a year later, it cost 1,500,000 marks! You had to have a wheelbarrow of cash to buy a loaf of bread! Everyone's savings were wiped out. The only ones making money were the rich Jews."

They also discussed the politics of the time. The Kaiser abdicated, leaving a political vacuum. The Communists attempted a coup that was beaten back by the Social Democrats and members of the army. Each political party had its own security force, and when these clashed, there were brawls and battles in the streets. Helmuth remembered the night his father came home bruised and bloody. Helmuth always enjoyed hearing this story.

"*Meine Güte**, what happened to you?" his mother had cried out.

"I got caught in a clash between the Bolsheviks and the Social Democrats. They were going at it with clubs, rocks, bottles, brass knuckles—you name it. Knocking men down, kicking them senseless."

"Couldn't you escape? Couldn't you take a different way home?"

At this point in the story his father sheepishly grinned. "Well," he said, "it looked to me like the Social Democrats were losing, and we couldn't have that, could we? You know how I feel about the Bolsheviks. So, I figured I'd join in. I think in the end we whipped them." Helmuth's male cousins heartily approved of this story; his female cousins, not so much.

Then came the Depression. American banks called in their loans, plunging the German economy into turmoil. Unemployment hit 30 percent. Helmuth's father still had a job, but he worked fewer hours so the company could keep more workers. Aunt Ilse and her family came to live with Helmuth's family because they could no longer afford to pay rent. People were weary—weary of political upheaval, weary of hardship, weary of not having enough to feed their families.

When Hitler came to power in 1933, promising strong leadership, stability, economic growth, a rejection of the Versailles Treaty, and the restoration of German honor and respect among the nations of the world, he found a receptive populace—including Helmuth's family. Now when they sat on the porch at night, they talked of Hitler's achievements. "I don't think I would have believed, five years ago, where we are today," his uncle Richard said. "Think of

---

* My goodness.

135

it—Austria and Germany united! The Sudetenland* made part of Germany! It is a dream come true." Helmuth's father added, "And we are rid of the Bolsheviks. The army has been rebuilt, and we have the strongest air force in the world."

Hitler seemed able to do no wrong. Perhaps he was a little excessive when it came to the Jews, but Helmuth didn't really know. With the enthusiasm of youth, Helmuth enrolled in the *Waffen SS*. He wanted to play his part; he wanted to contribute to the defeat of Bolshevism and to the rise of Germany.

---

* A part of Czechoslovakia adjacent to Germany and populated with ethnic Germans.

Chapter 37: The Aryan Side of Warsaw
Helmuth, Warsaw, April 1942

Following two months of rest and recuperation from his shoulder injury, Helmuth began his service in Warsaw in April 1942. He found a friend in Paul Bauer, who had also come from the *Waffen SS*. Paul had been wounded when a comrade six feet away stepped on a landmine. His comrade lost a leg; Paul injured his knee and now walked with a limp. They were an interesting pair—one with a gimpy shoulder and one with a gimpy leg—and they laughed that they'd have a pretty good soldier if they could just take the good parts of each other.

During Helmuth's first week on duty, he and Paul were part of a team canvassing apartments on the Aryan side of Warsaw, looking for members of the resistance or Jews in hiding. Addresses had been provided by the Gestapo, which in turn had received them from informers or from interrogations. They started at two a.m., arriving at a fourth-floor apartment and pounding on the door.

"Open up," the captain yelled, continuing to pound on the door.

After a few moments, they heard, "Wait, we are coming." The voice sounded terrified.

The door was opened by a middle-aged Polish man in a nightshirt. "What is the matter? What do you want? We have done nothing wrong."

As the SS captain pushed past him, he ordered, "Gather everyone in the front room. Bring your papers." Then turning to his men, he said, "Search the apartment." The soldiers began tearing the apartment apart, spilling drawers on the floor, stabbing bayonets into mattresses, pulling clothes out of closets.

"We are looking for a man named Jan Brodzki. Do you know him?"

"No, I have never heard that name. You can see it is just my wife and me and our two children."

The captain seemed unconvinced. "Let me see your papers." He looked these over and then handed them back. "Is there anyone else staying here? Are you hiding someone?" he asked.

"No, you can see, no one." *Of course,* Helmuth thought, *he will deny it. Maybe the captain is just trying to see how he reacts.*

Helmuth and the other SS soldiers had finished their search and found nothing. But the captain wasn't done. "I want each of you to stand in front of a window with your flashlight on. Keep them on until I return. I am going down into the street. Hoffman, come with me."

Helmuth wondered what was going on but dutifully followed the captain down into the street. There they looked up at the windows on the fourth floor. There were ten windows across the side of the building. "Hoffman," his captain said, "let's assume there are two apartments of the same size on this side of the building. How many windows would you expect to be lit?"

"Five, sir."

"That is what I would think also. Yet as you can see, there are only four windows with flashlights. Why do you suppose that is?"

"We have missed a window, sir."

"So, either you men cannot follow instructions very well, or we can't get into where that window is."

"Yes, sir," Helmuth answered, "I believe that is true."

"Go up to the apartment on the opposite side and tell me how many windows you find."

Helmuth did as he was told. Fifteen minutes later he reported back to the captain. "I found five windows in the apartment, sir."

"All right. That's as I suspected. Grab a couple of sledgehammers from the truck and follow me back upstairs. Wait, I forgot about your shoulder. Can you grab two sledgehammers okay?"

"Yes, sir, I will be fine."

As they re-entered the apartment, the captain addressed the Pole in the nightshirt. "Do you want to change your story at all?" he asked.

"No," the man said with decidedly less conviction and a look of dread in his eyes.

"If you are lying, it will go hard for you," the captain warned.

The captain directed two men to take the sledgehammers and go into the room with the fourth window. "Punch a hole in the furthest side wall. The rest of you cover them. Let's see what we find."

It took only ten minutes. They found a room eight feet wide with four men hiding inside. Two of them had pistols and put up a fight; they were shot dead in seconds. One of the SS men was wounded. The two surviving fugitives were led away in handcuffs for questioning.

The captain approached the Pole, who was sitting with his head bowed. "Stand up," he said. He then pistol-whipped him until he fell to the floor, his face a bloody mess. The captain ignored the cries of his wife and children while he repeatedly kicked him with his steel-toed boots. When he no longer moved, the captain told his men to pick him up and carry him to the truck. "You have seen your father for the last time," he told the children. "Be glad I don't take all of you away."

The Pole got what he deserved, Helmuth thought. *After all, he was sheltering the enemy.* Nevertheless, this was a different side of the war for Helmuth. He understood it was necessary, but he was not used to killing civilians.

Chapter 38: The Warsaw Ghetto
Helmuth, Warsaw, Summer 1942

When it came to the Jews in Warsaw, a lot of what Helmuth did involved the ghetto. Paul, who had been there a few weeks longer, gave him a tour. Helmuth immediately noticed how crowded it was. "How many people live here?" he asked.

"I think we are up to 450,000 in an area of 1.5 square miles," Paul said. "You'll find people sleeping in stairwells or on the streets; in some places there are ten to a room. It can't go on this way indefinitely. When winter comes, there will be an epidemic if something isn't done. There are rumors that sometime this summer there will be deportations."

"Deportations to where?" Helmuth asked.

"Supposedly to the east," Paul said. Helmuth had the impression he should leave things at that.

As they walked through the ghetto, Helmuth noticed the Jews doffed their caps to them. They also stepped down into the street to leave plenty of room for Paul and Helmuth on the sidewalk. The ghetto was completely enclosed by a nine-foot-high wall with entrances and exits that were carefully controlled. Helmuth saw in some places that "Aryan streets" bisected the ghetto. Pedestrian bridges had been built over the streets so the Jews could cross without entering Aryan territory.

Sometimes he patrolled the perimeter in an attempt to control smuggling. It was forbidden to bring food into the ghetto. When he was inside the wall, Helmuth saw evidence of great hunger—people collapsed or dying on the sidewalks, scrawny children begging for food. To survive, he realized, they *had* to smuggle.

Many of the best smugglers were children. They could squeeze through small holes underneath the ghetto wall or through sewer grates. Sometimes they were given money to buy food on the black market; sometimes they stole food and raced off before they could be caught. Helmuth suspected that in many cases they were their family's lifeline to survival. But smuggling was illegal, and the SS, along with the Polish and Jewish police, was charged with catching and punishing smugglers.

One day he was standing right outside the ghetto wall when he heard a commotion about forty yards away. He saw a German policeman beating something with a club. People were shouting from inside the wall, and he could hear screaming. As he walked over, he saw the policeman was beating a child who had tried to get back into the ghetto through a small drain and had become stuck.

"What is going on?" Helmuth asked. Although he was quite calloused to violence from the war, he was still shocked to see a child being beaten—the policeman's club striking the half-exposed back, the small legs, the bare feet.

"This little brat is a smuggler. He's stuck because he has some potatoes in his pockets. Serves him right."

The little boy was screaming. People on the Jewish side were yelling, "Get him out; pull harder!"

The scene conjured up a memory from Helmuth's youth when he saw hunters club seals to death on an island in the Baltic Sea. He remembered how the clubs struck their bodies with a dull thud, just like now. It wasn't too long before the policeman won—the little boy stopped screaming, his body crushed and broken.

In justification the policeman said, "If you show any mercy, they multiply like rats. The Jews know the rules. They must be punished."

Still, Helmuth thought, *clubbing a child to death?* It made him sick.

Smuggling also took place at the gates to the ghetto. Many of the policemen, including the SS, accepted bribes. For the right amount of money, they turned a blind eye to smuggling. It was just an accepted way of doing business. From there it was not a big step to extortion of valuables from the Jews. Many of his fellow SS soldiers were getting rich from the war.

One day he asked Paul a question that had been forming in his mind for some time: "How do the soldiers we're with now compare to the men in your old *Waffen SS* unit?"

Paul answered candidly. "There are a few good men here, but for the most part they are a bunch of sadists and thugs." The answer, while disturbing, struck a chord in Helmuth, although he hadn't recognized his feelings until that moment. These were supposed to be the elite soldiers of Germany. What had happened? Helmuth recalled a talk given by Himmler where he said of the Jews, "We have carried out this most difficult of tasks in a spirit of love for our people. And we have suffered no harm to our inner being, our soul, our character." The reality, Helmuth thought, indicated otherwise.

***

In July Helmuth witnessed the *Grossaktion*—the great deportation. From July 22 to September 21, between five and six thousand people a day were deported from the Warsaw ghetto. They were told they were being taken to labor camps in the east, where food would be plentiful. Instead, they were taken sixty miles away to Treblinka, where they were executed in gas chambers. At first, people believed the German lies, but as evidence of the truth mounted, they began to go into hiding.

They slipped into holes they had dug under foundations, behind false walls in apartments, in the crawl space under floors, or in secret attic rooms. They crawled into sewers; they inhabited the hidden space between buildings. There they lived like moles in small, dirty, dark places until the day's search was over.

Helmuth became an expert at discovering hiding places. He became adept at noticing floorboards that didn't quite fit. He learned how to tap the butt of his rifle against a wall and listen for a change in sound that indicated a hollow space. After rather loudly inspecting a set of rooms and finding nothing, he walked down the stairs and then quietly waited. If he waited long enough, he often heard something—a creak or a cough or a baby's cry. Then he homed in on the noise.

One time he stabbed his bayonet into a plaster wall, expecting the point to strike brick, but instead feeling it slip easily on through. He heard a groan and a cry, and when he withdrew his bayonet, it was covered in blood. While he stared at his bloody bayonet, the soldier with him stabbed into the wall. Helmuth stood back while he stabbed again and again.

Chapter 39: The Orphanage
Helmuth, Warsaw Ghetto, August 1942

In the first week of August 1942, the order came down that all orphanages in the ghetto were to be emptied. Helmuth had been promoted to SS Unterscharführer*. He was assigned to bring the children from the orphanage on Sienna Street, at the south end of the ghetto, to the *Umschlagplatz*, the deportation assembly area, at the northernmost tip of the ghetto.

Helmuth and a contingent of six SS men began the walk from their entrance gate to the orphanage, about a mile away. Their black boots gleamed as they walked down the street, and their uniforms, with the skull and crossbones on their caps, were clean and smartly pressed. They projected an air of dark efficiency. They were joined by a dozen Jewish policemen.

Arriving at the orphanage, an SS soldier pounded on the door and demanded that the children immediately assemble outside in rows of four.

Helmuth heard an older man inside the doorway call out to the children. "Children, it is time. Do just as we did when we practiced. Run and put on your best clothes. Bring your bag. Hurry! Please assemble outside with your traveling partner—younger children in the front, older children in the rear. I will be going with you out to the countryside. It will be nice to be in the fresh air."

Surely the old man knows what is really going on, Helmuth thought, *and it is far from a field trip to the country.*

Within a few minutes, the nearly two hundred children had assembled outside. Despite the warmth of the day, the children looked clean and fresh. They gathered in two pairs of children per row, each holding the hand of a companion. An older boy at the front held a green flag with a blue Star of David set against a field of white. The animated chatter among the children hinted at their excitement. *Where have I seen that flag before*? Helmuth wondered.

Helmuth strolled slowly down the rows. Each child held a pillowcase with something inside. "What is in the bags?" Helmuth asked an attendant.

---

* Similar to a senior corporal or lance sergeant.

"A favorite book or toy. That was all they were allowed to bring."

Helmuth stopped in front of a girl who looked no older than five, her dark hair in barrettes. "What is in your bag?" he asked.

"My dolly. Would you like to see her?"

"Thank you, perhaps another time." He felt a stab in his heart.

About halfway down the fifty rows, Helmuth paused. The young boy in front of him looked just like his nephew, from his blonde hair with a cowlick in back to his dark-brown eyes and eager expression. When he saw Helmuth looking at him, he asked, "Am I standing up straight enough, Uncle*?"

"Yes. You are doing just fine." Helmuth patted the boy's shoulder.

Helmuth had been involved in the deaths of many people. But today, the little girl's and the little boy's voices spoke more loudly and forcefully than all the voices that had gone before. He tried to ignore them; he tried to brush them aside; he tried to bury them, but he could not. Rising through all the layers of his training and indoctrination, through all the irrational accusations and propaganda and hate, they penetrated his consciousness. *How could these children be considered enemies of the Reich? How can I march them to their deaths?*

A bald, older man with a neatly trimmed, salt-and-pepper beard walked out of the house. Dressed in a faded Polish army uniform, his pants tucked into his boots, he took his place at the head of the procession. His appearance was a study in contrasts: behind his wire-rimmed glasses, his eyes were bright but puffy and red-rimmed. His forehead was smooth, but there were deep wrinkles around his eyes and mouth. He was stooped and walked slowly, but there was something distinguished about him.

One of the Jewish policemen approached Helmuth. "I am authorized by the head of the *Judenrat* to offer this man sanctuary. Do I have your permission?"

"Yes." *It's not going to matter much. If the old man isn't deported today, he will be within a few days. Everyone is going.*

---

* In this context, the word Uncle is used in a familiar sense to mean an older, friendly man, not just a relative.

Helmuth watched as the policeman approached the man and talked to him. In response, the older man shook his head. "I will stay with my children," Helmuth heard him say.

I will stay with my children. I will die rather than abandon them. These words lingered in Helmuth's mind and heart.

They started off on their walk of more than two miles, Helmuth and the old man at the front, the SS and Jewish police fanned out on both sides. As the children walked down the cobblestone streets, their wooden-soled shoes created a racket of clip-clops. With the streets empty, the drab buildings flanking the sides seemed taller. There was not a patch of green anywhere. Pieces of wood and glass from smashed doors and windows littered the sidewalk, evidence of the forced deportations of the previous weeks. A few residents peered cautiously from their windows, being careful to avoid detection. There was always a risk of being taken during an *Aktion*. The children walked slowly but steadily. There was no breeze to ruffle the flag they followed.

One of the women who watched from a window was named Halinka. She would never forget what she saw. She had seen people beaten to death, and she had seen people executed. Every day she was approached on the street by people who were starving. But she had never been as moved as she was this day to see children—in their best clothes, their leader at the front—walk to their deaths.

Some of the smaller children struggled to mount the steps of the pedestrian bridge at Chlodna Street, forcing the group to slow down. The old man at the front turned around. "Older children, please help the younger ones. Giena and Leon, would you help Mietek and Hanna?" Helmuth watched the older children grab hands, pulling the smaller children up the steps and steadying them on the way down. *They are clearly devoted to one another and to their leader.*

The excitement initially shown by the children soon evaporated. The heat was oppressive—even the birds refused to chirp. Block after block they continued to walk. Some complained that their feet hurt. Some needed to use the bathroom. Despite it all, the SS and Jewish policemen kept the children moving.

More than two hours later, the little parade reached the *Umschlagplatz*, a large dirt field hemmed in by buildings and a high fence. Thousands of people already sat on the dusty ground, waiting to board cattle cars standing on the train tracks. There was no food or water or toilets. The people were herded roughly by SS with whips, guns, and dogs.

There seemed nowhere for the children to sit. One of the orphanage staff noticed an area at the back that looked unoccupied. "Why not sit over there?" she asked. As they approached the area, she saw why. Half a dozen bodies lay in pools of blood on the ground, covered in black flies.

As the attendants tried to comfort the children, a young boy of about seven years ran to the old man. "Yes, Jakub, what is wrong?" the old man asked kindly.

"I am scared, *Pan* Doctor. The men with the guns and the dogs. The people who are crying. Everything here scares me. When will we get to the countryside?"

"It will be a while yet, but I am here, and I will stay with you."

Shortly after they entered the *Umschlagplatz*, the Jewish policemen posted there came to attention and saluted. Helmuth motioned one of them over to him. "What are you doing?"

"We are saluting the head of the orphanage."

"Why salute him? Who is this man?"

"He is Janusz Korczak, a doctor and noted author of children's books."

"I know this man," Helmuth exclaimed. "I read some of his books as a boy. That's where I remember the flag—it was in one of his books." Helmuth approached him. "Are you sure you would not like to have sanctuary?"

"And the children? Do they receive sanctuary too?"

Helmuth knew there was no choice. "I am afraid they must go."

"Then I must go with them. I will not leave them."

I will not leave them. The words pierced his heart.

Several hours later, Helmuth watched as the children were led up a ramp into a cattle car, faithfully following their beloved leader. *They think that as long as their leader is with them, everything will be alright. What a scene! Beautiful children lined up and marching to their deaths!* He didn't know it yet, but something inside him had changed.

***

    It wasn't just children who were herded into the cattle car while Helmuth watched. Ten orphanage staff members accompanied *Pan* Doctor, including Madame Stefania Wilczuńska, who had worked with the doctor for thirty years and who also turned down an opportunity for sanctuary to be with the children of the orphanage.

    Among the children who filed into the cattle car was Giena, who would have grown up to be a writer; and Jakub, who would have become a businessman; and Leon, who would have been a father of four. There was Mietek, who would have become a rabbi; and Zygmus and Ruzha, who would have become doctors; and Hanna, who would have become a grandmother of ten; and Hanka and Paulina, who would have become teachers. Then there was the boy who looked like Helmuth's nephew—he would have changed the world.

Chapter 40: Halinka
Rachel, Warsaw, December 1942

Rachel was anxious to get to a place where she felt protected. After riding the crowded streetcar for several stops, she got off in a poorer section of the city and followed the instructions on the paper, making her way to the safe house on the Aryan side of Warsaw. She climbed a dirty set of stairs to the third floor of an old brick apartment building that was located on a back street. The linoleum flooring in the hallway was peeling, and the ceiling was stained and sagging in places, but she didn't care. All she wanted was a little food and somewhere she could sleep. Her host should be expecting her. Just below the apartment number, on the right side of the door, Rachel saw two nails sticking out, about a half inch apart. She took a coin from her pocket and touched them both simultaneously. She could not hear the buzzer that went off inside. Then, as instructed, she gave only one knock.

She was pleased when the door opened to reveal a smiling face and brightly lit interior. Her host introduced herself as Halinka, a woman Rachel assumed was a member of the resistance. Halinka was petite, but it didn't take long for Rachel to realize her small body was home to an outsized personality. She was friendly and warm, with an infectious smile and short, blond hair. Rachel's first impression was of someone who could be your best friend. Halinka greeted Rachel with a big hug and asked about her journey. Rachel paused before she said, "It was my first time and I didn't know what to expect. It wasn't easy. In fact, I nearly didn't make it." She lifted her hand to show Halinka it was still trembling.

"Here, sit down and have a mug of tea . . . or what passes for tea these days, anyway. You'll feel better. Then, while we have some beet soup, you can tell me about your trip. I'd like to hear everything."

Rachel gratefully accepted the invitation for food and drink and a listening ear. While they ate, she recounted all the details of her journey. After she finished her story, Halinka squeezed her hand and said, "Very few people could have done what you did today. You handled things superbly. I'm sure your next trip will be easier."

"I certainly hope so," Rachel replied. "If it's any worse, I won't be here."

Halinka smiled. "It may have been a close call, but you *are* here. You *did* make it," she said as she touched Rachel's shoulders. "And I fully expect to see you many times in the future!" Halinka's enthusiasm was catching. Rachel could feel some of the knots in her insides begin to loosen.

Rachel was intrigued by Halinka, a woman who seemed a lot like her. "I don't want to ask about anything I shouldn't know," Rachel said. "And I'm sure you wouldn't tell me anyway. But tell me something about yourself that I *can* know."

Halinka smiled as she responded, "I am a hairdresser, which happens to be a very useful occupation for someone in my position. Not many people would suspect a hairdresser of being in the resistance. It's just not glamorous enough, I suppose. But I learn a lot from my clients, some of whom are German. Husbands are not always very discreet when it comes to talking to their wives about what is going on, and many women view their hairdresser as something of a confidant. Besides collecting information, however, I am also called on quite often to turn black hair blond."

Such a thing had never occurred to Rachel, but she could immediately see the value of someone who could dye hair professionally. "Did you ever live in the Warsaw ghetto?" she asked.

"I lived in the ghetto from its creation until a few months ago, when I came over to the Aryan side. If it wasn't for Żegota[*], which provided me with papers, I would be there still. That, or I would have already perished."

"What was it like for your family?"

Halinka was thoughtful for a moment; Rachel assumed she was having to navigate through a sea of difficult memories. "The ghetto didn't exist until about a year after the occupation. We had to sell our apartment on the Aryan side and move to the ghetto in November 1940. Because the ghetto was very crowded, we shared our apartment—which was small compared to our old one—with another family. But we had two bedrooms, a sitting area, and a small kitchen. Better than most, so we couldn't complain.

"The ghetto was enclosed, by Jews of course, with a nine-foot wall topped with barbed wire or broken glass. Almost immediately the

---

[*] Żegota was the Polish Council to Aid Jews, an underground resistance organization.

ghetto was sealed. Entrances and exits were carefully controlled, and we were essentially prisoners. The Nazis kept drawing the noose tighter. It was forbidden for Jews or Poles to bring food into the ghetto, and food supplies were gradually reduced while the population increased. The black market flourished—only the rich got enough to eat. We were beset with relentless hunger. Many people starved or became ill and died. And many were executed."

Halinka then digressed. "Have you ever been *really* cold? One winter evening years ago, before we moved to the city, my father and I were caught in a snowstorm on the way back from my school and had to wait it out through the night. I had on nothing more than my dressy coat for warmth with thin gloves and regular socks and shoes. Even huddled with my father under a quilt in the wagon, I had never been so cold. Every minute seemed like hours. That was the longest night of my life. I was miserable, but at least I knew morning would come. In the ghetto, there was little hope of morning; there was only delaying the night.

"The ghetto was slow starvation, disease, terror, and death. Time seemed to slow down. We could count the number of people who died each day, but we couldn't count or measure the suffering they endured, or the suffering of those who continued to live.

"The worst for me was to see the children. Before God and heaven, it is one of the vilest of sins to starve a child, to intentionally make a child suffer, to ignore a child's cries." Halinka's voice broke, and she had to pause to bring her emotions under control. "I am sorry; I cannot talk any more about this. But I have resolved to give my life to help my people. If I can save one child, that is enough for me."

Rachel understood this. She thought of her own experiences, especially the children herded onto the train to Auschwitz—including, of course, Esther. She thought of the little girl in the shabby dress who clutched a doll in one hand while clinging in terror to her mother. Halinka, she thought, was a kindred spirit.

"I have heard there was a large *Aktion* in the ghetto over the summer," Rachel said.

"Yes, to add to the misery, the Germans kept relocating Jews from surrounding areas into the ghetto. At one point we had five families living in our small apartment. No wonder we had outbreaks of typhus. But that didn't last long. In the middle of the summer, the *Grossaktion* began.

"Over the course of two months, thousands of Jews were deported every day, including all my family. At first, we believed they were being resettled in the east. We even received postcards encouraging us to follow. Now we know the postcards were fake, and everyone was killed at the Treblinka extermination camp.

"In two months, the population of the ghetto was reduced by ninety percent. Rarely has killing been so efficient. Most of the Jews that remain have papers to work in German shops, the word *shops* being used loosely to describe places of slave labor. But thousands without papers managed to escape deportation; they live in the 'wild' ghetto—sections of the ghetto that are officially closed. Many are building bunkers to hide in against the time of the next *Aktion*. At night you can hear the sounds of picks and shovels coming through the pipes. Some young men and women have banded together to form a Jewish army. They are preparing to fight. Your suitcase will make a difference."

Halinka's comment warmed Rachel's heart, making all the difficulty involved in getting the suitcase to her contact—even risking her life—worth it.

Rachel and Halinka talked until late into the night. Rachel shared some events from her own life, including about Jacob and Esther. When they finished talking, Halinka showed Rachel a space behind a false wall that concealed several narrow mattresses where Rachel could sleep in safety. Before they retired for the night, they fell into a hug of appreciation and friendship.

Chapter 41: A Courier and an Escort
Rachel, Warsaw, Winter 1942–1943

Early the next morning, as Rachel and Halinka were eating breakfast, the buzzer sounded and there was a knock at the door. In came a man who introduced himself as David; he was holding the hands of two children. He greeted Halinka and then addressed himself to Rachel. "Do I understand correctly that you are traveling southwest this morning?"

"Yes," replied Rachel.

"Then I wonder if you would accept an important assignment?" he asked.

"What is it?"

"We need an escort for these children. They have been brought over, at substantial risk, from the ghetto. We want to take them to a convent located a few miles from your destination. It is, of course, somewhat dangerous."

"Everything associated with being a Jew is dangerous," replied Rachel. "Of course, I will take them. I am willing to do whatever I can to help."

"The younger boy is seven. His new Christian name is Wiktor. His older brother is ten. His Christian name is Oskar. They both speak Polish and have birth certificates," the man said, handing the papers to Rachel. As he tucked some currency into her hand, he continued, "Here is money for the tickets. They have only a few belongings to take with them. I also have a sedative you can give them so they will sleep most of the way. You will be met at the station by some nuns from the convent, dressed in habits, so it won't be hard to spot them."

Rachel noticed both children were blond. *Halinka's work, perhaps?* The task seemed straightforward enough, but then she reflected on the journey from the day before that had been anything but straightforward. She was still drained from that experience. She hoped she could rest some on the return journey.

The trip with the children was blessedly uneventful. Fortunately, the sedative helped them sleep a good portion of the way. As they climbed off the car at the station, Rachel saw two nuns looking up and down the platform, obviously searching for someone.

They noticed her looking in their direction and began to walk toward her.

"You are looking for some children, I believe," said Rachel.

"We are, and these look like the ones. How are you boys?" the older sister asked.

The children looked up at the nuns from behind apprehensive eyes. Rachel knelt and tried to reassure them, saying, "These sisters will take good care of you. You don't need to worry. You'll have enough to eat and you will be safe." Turning to the sisters as she put her hands on the shoulders of the younger child, she said, "This is Wiktor. And this is his older brother, Oskar."

"Hello Wiktor, Oskar, I am sister Maria, and this is sister Sylwia. We are glad to meet you and have you come and live with us."

Rachel's curiosity was piqued. "Are there many children at the convent?"

"It is actually a combined convent and an orphanage," explained the older sister. "We have about ninety children. As you might imagine, it is not unusual during these times to have new children brought to us."

It suddenly occurred to Rachel that taking care of ninety children must be expensive. "Do you accept donations?" she asked.

"Absolutely."

"Then please accept this from me," Rachel said, handing them 50 złoty.

"Bless you," they both said in reply.

Turning to the children again, Rachel reinforced her previous comment. "You will be safe. You will be with other children. Oskar, you take care of your little brother, okay?" He nodded. The sisters led them off to a wagon that was waiting while Rachel made her way back to the estate.

***

Shortly after returning, Rachel had a chance to speak with her mistress. "I see you are back safe and sound," Sofia said. "How was your trip to Warsaw?"

"Memorable. I'd never been to Warsaw before. And I am worn out."

"Traveling makes me tired as well. Tomorrow is Sunday, so you should be able to rest."

"I was thinking I would try to have a quiet day and just recuperate. But," and here Rachel felt she should tread carefully, "I wanted to mention that I would like to go back again soon."

"Julia?" Sofia asked. Rachel turned to meet the eyes of her mistress, who was gazing intently at her. "Is it important that you return to visit your friend in Warsaw?"

"Yes, ma'am," she said slowly, "yes, it is."

"Then you should do it. I would suggest you go over a Saturday/Sunday, however, as this will be less disruptive to the children's lessons."

"That makes sense. I will try to arrange things that way for next time. Will *Herr* Kohler be upset at my absence?"

"Don't worry about *Herr* Kohler. I will take care of that side of things."

***

Rachel had adjusted over the past few months to the challenges of leading a double life as a Catholic governess and as a Jew in hiding. It occurred to her now that she was leading a triple life: she had also become a member of the resistance. The distinctiveness of each life was represented by her having a different name for each. Her real name was known only to Esther, Jacob, Maria, Father Sobieski, and God—an admittedly small group, but a group that she hoped loved her. She was Julia to almost everyone else, particularly to the Kohlers. In conversations with members of the resistance, she was Teresa.

Rachel was surprised at how easily she had slipped into this new role. She had asked, and Father Sobieski had accepted. He did grill her about her backstory—it was important there were no cracks or inconsistencies in case she was interrogated. But there was no induction ceremony or membership card for this organization that was shrouded in secrecy and fighting for the freedom of Poland. She might not ever meet more than a few of its members, and even then she wouldn't know their real names. But she was proud to join with these patriots, seen and unseen, and she felt buoyed up by their strength and courage.

In her "third" life as a courier Rachel traveled every two or three weeks to Warsaw with a heavy suitcase to deliver. She did not know where the suitcase came from, and that was just as well. Each time, she took the 12:20 p.m. train to Warsaw, spent the night at Halinka's, and escorted some children back to the convent on the return journey. The escort duty was the assignment she came to enjoy the most. Although she knew the suitcase she carried was important, as an escort she could hold the hands and touch the faces and look into the frightened eyes of the children she was helping to save. Rachel assumed after her first harrowing trip things would settle down and become less stressful.

She was wrong.

Chapter 42: The Streetcar
Rachel, Warsaw, January 1943

On a trip in the middle of January, Rachel was asked to take two children—a boy of five with the new name of Michał, and a girl of eight with the new name of Emilia—to the convent. Rachel introduced herself as Teresa and told the children she was excited to take them to their new home. She reminded them of their new names and told them it was best they not speak while they walked to the streetcar.

Rachel was careful to be aware of her surroundings, a habit she had developed out of necessity to stay alive. Thus, as she and the children started out, she did a brief check up and down the street. She mostly saw what she expected to see—a man walking a dog, a mother with children in hand, several teenagers dressed in school uniforms, and across the street, a scruffy-looking man leaning against a lightpole. With her powers of observation made more acute by her months of hiding, she noted the man was short of stature, with a dark beard, thick mustache, and slicked-back hair. He wore a gold chain around his neck. He seemed somewhat out of place to Rachel; yet she had no indication anything was wrong, and so she and the children began their walk to the streetcar stop.

As Rachel and her two charges walked down the sidewalk, Michał stumbled and fell, scraping his knee. He cried out and said his knee hurt.

"I'm sorry, Michał, but we need to keep going," Rachel said as she tried to comfort him. "When we get on the train, I'll have a look at it."

As Michał took a moment to get back up, Rachel turned and saw that the man who had been leaning agains the lightpole was now following behind them.

"Madam," he called out, "may I speak with you for a moment?"

"What do you want?"

"I couldn't help noticing your beautiful children."

"They are my niece and nephew, actually," Rachel replied cautiously. She didn't like strangers who were forward like this, and she was on her guard.

"I also couldn't help noticing they are Jewish."

"What are you talking about?"

"Come, my dear, let's not pretend. I heard your 'nephew' cry out in Yiddish when he fell." Now Rachel understood. He was a *schmaltzovnik*—a Pole who extorted money from Jews.

"He is only a child," Rachel replied, which she felt was all the explanation she needed to give. "Now leave us alone," she said firmly.

"Oh, I will leave you alone all right, but it will cost you 3000 złoty." His tone was menacing.

The streetcar had just pulled up, and Rachel moved the children into line. "I asked you to leave us alone, and I meant it."

"Well, we'll see about that. I think I will ride the streetcar as well." Since other people were now around, he said nothing more through his thin smile.

A ten-minute walk to the streetcar—something which a non-Jew would never have given a second thought—now threatened their lives. Poles did not have to worry about *schmaltzovniks*. Rachel's thoughts and concern were for the children. She could probably get enough money to pay the man off, but she knew he wouldn't leave them alone even if she paid him. He would just make another demand, and another—and, in the end, he would turn them in. How could she save the children? Could she somehow offer herself for ransom?

The streetcar was full, and it was standing room only. Rachel saw a spot open up just behind the conductor. Thinking that location might be of some advantage, she moved with the children there, Rachel holding on to an overhead strap and Michał and Emilia grabbing a pole behind the driver's seat. Their "friend" stood just behind them. Rachel turned her back to him, but she could feel his presence. He reminded her of the SS officer on the train. It had taken all her wits and some luck, but she had made it out of that situation. *There must be a way out now*, she thought. *I just need to focus.* The streetcar continued on its route. Its final stop was the train station.

Things were about to get worse.

Michał was a sensitive child, and he could tell the man standing behind them meant them harm. After a couple of stops, Michał became overwhelmed with a sense of peril. He grabbed on to Rachel and cried out in Yiddish, "I want my mother!" before beginning to cry. Now most of the streetcar knew Michał was Jewish. Everyone around them stopped talking. Passengers standing nearby carefully moved away, crowding up against others, as though the children had an infectious disease.

Rachel felt sick to her stomach. Her insides churned as they had when she realized she couldn't find Esther. She pulled Michał close; he buried his head in her skirt. She didn't even have a list of options in mind, but whatever they were, she was sure they had just narrowed considerably.

Rachel knew that as soon as they exited, they would be in grave danger. All it would take would be for one person to point them out to a policeman, and their lives would be over. And there was at least one person—their "friend"—ready to do that. "Please," she whispered to the conductor, "help us."

He seemed to ignore her.

Chapter 43: A Free Poland
Rachel, Warsaw, January 1943

Rachel didn't know what she should do. But if there was anything she had learned in the past few months of her life, it was this: she should go on the offensive. Jumping off the train, turning around to face the police at the train station, pushing the SS officer over the railing—these experiences taught her that her best chance for survival came when she wrested the initiative away from her attacker and took it upon herself. Somehow, she needed to do that now.

It dawned on her that there was something unique about the current situation: there were no Germans around. This was a streetcar full of Poles. She knew many Poles were anti-Semitic, but she didn't know any native Poles who weren't proud of their country and who didn't yearn for freedom from Nazi tyranny. Mentally she pulled herself up, and in a clear, strong voice she said to the conductor, "In the name of a free Poland, and as a member of the resistance, I ask for your help."

The conductor's body seemed to stiffen, as if he had been given an electric shock. A few moments went by, and then Rachel saw his hand yank on a lever. The streetcar gave a violent lurch and came to a halt. Several people yelled out as they lost their balance, and Rachel could hear some packages hit the floor. Then the streetcar started up again, went fifty yards, and lurched to a stop a second time. They were in the middle of a block.

The conductor got out of his seat and faced them all. He was a surprisingly big man. "This streetcar needs repair," he announced. "I am going back to the depot. Everyone needs to get off," he said loudly. Then he turned to Rachel and said, "You remain."

The doors opened and people began to exit. The *schmaltzovnik* could see his opportunity slipping away. "I'm with her," he said.

"Is he?" asked the conductor.

"No, he is not," Rachel answered angrily. She wanted to spit on the man.

"Then you get off too. Now." The conductor's manner brooked no nonsense.

When the streetcar was empty, the conductor closed the doors. He turned a crank over his seat that rotated the destination sign on the

159

front to say, *Out of Service*. He started the car up again. Then he turned to Rachel. "Now," he said, "where do you want me to take you?"

Rachel exploded into tears but managed to choke out, "To the train station, please."

Once they were on the train, the trip back to the convent was uneventful. As usual, Rachel gave the children a sedative so they would sleep. But not as usual, she took some of the sedative herself.

Chapter 44: On Their Way
Jacob, Eastern Poland, Fall 1942

After two days of rest and recuperation, Jacob, Samuel, and Alex were ready to go. Both Jacob and Samuel knew that carrying Alex was possible but not very practical. They had twenty miles to cover, and carrying more than one hundred pounds hour after hour would wear them down, especially in their weakened state. Although they didn't resent helping their friend, it was going to be a slow journey. If they were discovered by the Germans, it was unlikely they would be able to escape.

Jacob was thus intrigued when he saw Samuel and Jurek in a hushed conversation as they got ready to leave. He saw Jurek nod his head and then stride toward the barn. Presently he came out with…a wheelbarrow. It had obviously seen years of use—the grips were blackened from the sweat of many hands, the bed was brown with rust, and the front wheel was no more than a rusted iron rim with spokes.

"Here you go," said Jurek proudly. "She's all yours."

"*Monsieur*," Samuel said to Alex with a flourish, "your chariot awaits."

Everyone enjoyed a laugh as Alex sat down in the bed with his legs curled up. This, they hoped, would be much easier.

They started off as dusk fell, heading back up the cart path. They would leave the path in a few miles so they could skirt the camp by a wide margin. The wheelbarrow was a lot faster way to travel. Most of Alex's weight was on the wheel, and it was easy to navigate around obstacles such as rocks or tree roots.

Jacob and Samuel knew Alex felt he was a burden to them. Thinking of this and wanting to ease Alex's concern, Jacob said, "Alex, you likely saved our lives. If not for you, we would have had to spend the night in the forest or at some unknown peasant's house. Either one would have been very dangerous."

Samuel added, "With the forest crawling with SS, we probably had only a fifty-fifty chance of surviving. Thanks to you, we had two days of safety." Alex's eyes shone gratefully at their words.

As their little band made its way through the forest, Jacob thought of the friendship they felt for each other. He remarked, "This reminds me of *The Three Musketeers*. Have you ever read that book, Alex?"

It took only a moment for Alex to respond with gusto, "All for one, and one for all!" Getting into the spirit of things, Samuel stopped the wheelbarrow long enough so they could put their hands together.

They continued along the cart trail for two miles, then left it and started walking directly through the forest. The ground was covered in yellow leaves, which made it firm enough for the wheelbarrow to roll easily. Illuminated by starlight, the forest was full of deep shadows. They followed a serpentine path as they zigzagged around trees and fallen logs. Sometimes it was easier to just pick up the wheelbarrow and carry it over obstacles. It was a quiet journey as they kept talking to a minimum to avoid detection.

Samuel or Jacob—whichever one was not pushing the wheelbarrow—scouted ahead a few yards, keeping a lookout and trying to find the best path for the wheelbarrow. In the morning, they stopped for a brief breakfast of bread and cheese, supplied by their former host.

"How are you doing, Alex?" asked Samuel. "Sorry the ride is a little bumpy."

Alex was not one to complain. "I am doing great. My feet thank you. I can't wait until we get to the partisan camps." Both Samuel and Jacob noticed he winced in pain any time he tried to walk by himself. In the excitement of the escape, he had punished his feet. "How far do you think we have to go?" he asked.

"We'll know for sure when we hit the river," replied Jacob. "I would guess we've covered about six or seven miles during the night. What do you think, Samuel?"

"We've certainly covered that far in total distance, but our roundabout course makes it hard to know how far we've actually come toward the river. At least we can't miss it."

Although it made sense to stop and sleep for a few hours, everyone wanted to keep going.

In general, they traveled northeast toward the Naliboki forest, the home of several partisan groups. They knew that about halfway to the partisans, they would hit the Neman River, which ran along the entire southern boundary of the forest—a landmark they couldn't miss. Once they found the river, they would follow it west until they came to the confluence of the Neman and Berezina. Following directions they had received in the ghetto, they would make their way to the Kozlovsky farm. The Kozlovsky family was friendly to Jews, and, more important, they were in contact with the Bielski brothers. The Bielski brothers were famous in the ghettos of eastern Poland. They welcomed any Jew—regardless of fighting experience, age, gender, health, or resources—to their camp. Without them, many people escaping the ghettos would have no place to go.

The importance of the Bielski brothers could not be overestimated. It was not easy to feed a large group in the forest, especially over the winter. The elderly, the young, the sick, the inexperienced—these kinds of volunteers compromised fighting effectiveness, consumed resources, and hindered the partisans' ability to move quickly, which was a key to their survival. Other partisan groups refused to take such people.

After a night and a morning of traveling, Samuel, Jacob, and Alex reached the Neman River. The forest came almost up to its edge. It was about sixty yards wide and had slow-moving, quiet water. "There's a welcome sight," Samuel said, expressing the feelings of all three. After being in the dense forest for hours, it was nice to see a stretch of sky.

"At least we know we haven't been traveling in circles," Jacob added. "Let's stop and rest awhile."

"I'd like that," Alex said. Jacob knew Alex wouldn't complain, but he could imagine Alex's back was sore from riding in the wheelbarrow.

Jacob and Samuel removed their shoes and all three lay on the bank out of sight. There was a stillness in the forest that covered them like a blanket. They could only faintly hear the muffled rustle of leaves in the trees high above them, and the river flowed by noiselessly. "It feels," Jacob remarked, "like we are in a primeval forest." He glanced over at Samuel who was gazing out across the water. "What are you thinking?" asked Jacob.

Samuel propped himself up on his elbow, facing Jacob and Alex. "I'm thinking that I am ready. I'm ready for whatever comes next, whether I live or die."

They now followed the riverbank toward the Kozlovsky farm. That afternoon, after a tiring seven-hour march, they made it without incident to the farm, which sat next to a forest surrounded by open fields. They learned that partisans were expected there soon.

That evening, two partisans emerged from the forest and walked past them toward the farmhouse. They had not seen partisan soldiers before. Both wore calf-length boots into which their pants were tucked. Both wore berets and had on jackets. One carried a submachine gun with a circular clip of bullets. The other had a rifle slung over his shoulder, with several grenades and a long knife in a sheath hanging from his belt. A cigarette dangled carelessly from his mouth. They were caught up in a lively conversation.

"Hey," Samuel said to Jacob and Alex, nodding in the direction of the partisans, "Do you think we can be like that?"

Jacob noticed the partisans walked with an easy self-assurance. They looked every bit the equal of the vaunted German soldier. "I hope so. I envy them their confidence."

"Well," said Samuel, "I envy them their experience. I can't wait to get into battle."

Alex, wanting to say something, piped up, "Well I envy them their feet with toes." This elicited a laugh he appreciated.

Jacob pondered this moment on several occasions, wondering if he had fully made the transition from victim to fighter and whether it showed. He supposed it started when they decided to build the tunnel—they had resisted the Germans and they had escaped. They burned with a desire for revenge. He was sure their confidence and toughness would grow with experience, forged in the heat of battle. He thought of Rachel's words: "The only way out is through." He had faced and fought down his fears in the tunnel; he would do it again.

Chapter 45: The Camp
Jacob, Eastern Poland, Late Fall 1942

If meeting the partisans was a small revelation, then arriving at the Bielski camp was a big one. Here, to their amazement, was an entire village situated in the middle of the forest, a small Jewish *shtetl*[*] located in Nazi-occupied territory. One of the partisans who conducted them to the camp introduced them to Tuvia Bielski. Tuvia welcomed them warmly. They all felt like they were meeting a celebrity. He took a special interest in Alex.

"It looks like you received a ride like royalty, eh? These must be good friends," said Tuvia.

"Yes," answered Alex. "We are like the Three Musketeers," he said proudly.

"All for one and one for all, eh? Well, we must get you better so you can help us defeat the Germans."

"That is what I dream about," said Alex earnestly.

"Spoken like a true partisan. Would you like a quick tour?" Jacob and Samuel were flattered that he would suggest this. He was certainly a busy man, and they felt honored he would spend a little time with them.

"We would enjoy that very much," responded Samuel. They began a walk down the main path of the village, still pushing Alex in the wheelbarrow.

"We have here a group of about eight hundred. We are still rebuilding after the Nazis attacked us this summer. You were lucky that you didn't try to escape then. The woods would have been crawling with Nazis."

Jacob and Samuel were amazed by that number—it was enough to populate a little city. They also reflected on how having to tunnel past the wheat field to the little hill had been a blessing in disguise. Unknown to them, the Germans had mounted a major offensive against the partisans during the summer. As bad as it was when they did escape, it would have been even worse if they had gone earlier.

---

[*] Jewish Village

"First is the hospital. We have a good doctor and dentist but poor supplies. Our main anesthetic is vodka. Many patients don't complain, however.

"On both sides we have almost twenty dugouts. They can each sleep forty." They noticed how all the structures were half buried in the ground, with logs for sides and boughs and tarps for the roofs, which were covered with dirt and more branches. The dugouts would be hard to spot from the air.

"Here are the food storehouse and the kitchen," said Tuvia, gesturing. "We keep the fire going all the time. With eight hundred mouths to feed, as soon as we finish one meal, we start preparing another. Hello, Dolek," he said as he passed by. "Dolek is one of our cooks. You are making us a good dinner, eh?"

"Of course," said Dolek with a smile. "Potato soup."

"Well, we haven't had that for a while. Since yesterday, I believe," said Tuvia, grinning.

"Across the path from the kitchen is a school. And next to the school," said Tuvia, with a little pride in his voice, "is our biggest building. It is the workplace for more than a hundred people. It houses the tailor shop, where we have about thirty tailors or seamstresses. They modify clothes captured by the partisans or make cloth into garments. We have our leatherworks, where we make bridles and saddles and such. Then the shoemakers, hatmakers, watchmakers, and carpenters. You don't appreciate a shoemaker as much as you do in the winter when you have a hole in your boot—or you have no boot at all.

"Off in the forest is our tannery, where the leather is made for the leatherworks and the cobblers. We harvest resin from the trees to tan the hides." Motioning in front of them, he said, "Here we have a mill to grind wheat into flour. Across from the workshops are stables and a blacksmith shop. We have about thirty horses and sixty cows.

"Over here," he said, pointing to a small hut across from the mill, "is our sausage-making shop. Some of our men found a meat-grinding machine in one of the villages while gathering food supplies."

"Something smells pretty good," said Alex.

"That is our smokehouse, and the building just beyond is the soap-making shed.

"Then we have our metal shop. A lot of what we do there is repair weapons. We have people who can take a bunch of discarded parts and make a very fine firearm. They were even able to put together a small cannon. Unfortunately, we had to leave it behind when we were on the run.

"Beyond the workshop we have the bakery and bathhouse. I know a bathhouse seems like something of a luxury, but we must be careful about lice, because of typhus." Having much first-hand knowledge of lice, they understood.

Jacob, Samuel, and Alex were quite astonished at the amazing camp. "How have you been able to do this?" Jacob asked.

"It takes a lot of effort, as you will learn. We are constantly having to find supplies and food, as you will also learn. At the beginning, the other partisans wouldn't give us the time of day. They wanted nothing to do with people who didn't fight. But now they see the value in being able to get some clothes or boots, or have a gun repaired, or even get a haircut. We trade them services for supplies and guns."

Chapter 46: Training
Jacob, Eastern Poland, November 1942

All the new recruits capable of fighting underwent a training regimen. Most of the newcomers certainly needed training—most had not been in the armed forces, and some had never fired a gun. They were put under the direction of Yakov Fyodorovich. He welcomed the new recruits.

"Welcome to our little army," he told the group. "I am Yakov Fyodorovich, and I am honored to be the first commander of the 51st Partisan Brigade, the first all-Jewish brigade of partisans. I am Russian, but I am also Jewish. I am from Gomel. Since many of you are Polish, and I am Russian, we will talk in Yiddish." This drew smiles from the group. They would later learn he was an officer in the Red army and had been decorated with the Order of Lenin in the war against Finland.

"I need you to listen to what I will now tell you. This is the most important thing I can say. This is not a place to sit out the war. This is a place to fight. Our objective is to kill Germans. I expect you to be bold, to be aggressive, to fight like tigers. Many of us will die. You already know much about death. But it is not just about being willing to die—it is also about how we live until we die. We will live as men and women worthy to be called partisans. We will no longer bow before the German tyrant.

"We have some things to prove. The Russians are not convinced Jews can fight. If you want a doctor or a lawyer, then call a Jew. But if you want a fighter, call someone else. We need to show them differently. The same for the Polish partisans. They think you waste a weapon if you give it to a Jew.

"But it is not just Poles or Russians. As you know, German hatred runs deep. Being killed by a Jew is a disgrace. When they learn they are opposed by Jewish partisans, they will do anything, including bringing in hundreds of troops, to find and kill us. We must show the world, but especially the Germans, how Jews can fight."

Pointing to another man, Fyodorovich said, "This is my second-in-command, Zerach Bojarski. He is in charge of training. Learn everything he can teach you. Begin right now to strengthen your body, which is weak from the ghetto. Then practice every chance you get. Your reactions need to become automatic. I want you dreaming about killing Germans." Here there were some grins. "When we think you are ready, you will be allowed to go on expeditions to find food. From there, you will graduate to real raids to destroy trains or attack German outposts."

Zerach stepped forward and said, "We will not beat the Germans in a conventional fight. There are more of them than us; they are well trained, they have heavier weapons, and they have plenty of ammunition. We will lose if we play by their rules.

"To win, we must fight our kind of fight: take them by surprise, hit and run, stay on the move, melt into the forest. We must be like a small dog attacking a large one: sneaking up from behind, biting its heels, constantly worrying it, racing away before it can catch us in its jaws.

"Besides your weapon, the most important friend you have is the forest. The forest offers concealment. But we must be smart and take advantage of what it has to offer. Little things matter. Little things can save you or betray you." The men gave him their rapt attention.

"We don't want to be seen or heard. We don't want to give away our size or direction of travel. When we are on the move, do not talk except in a whisper, and then only if necessary. Many directions can be given without words." Zerach then taught them a half dozen of the most important hand signals.

"Remember, *little things matter*. When performing reconnaissance near the enemy, step heel first on soft ground, toe first on hard ground, and put your weight on your whole foot when walking on grass. Raise it above the level of the grass to make another step. This will prevent rustling. If we are on ground that leaves footprints, move in single file and step in the footprints of the person in front of you. This conceals our number and leaves the least visible trail. Take advantage of shadows. If you hear the drone of an airplane, immediately get into the shadow of a tree or boulder and don't move. You will be difficult to spot from above."

"Avoid entering meadows, roads, or cuts in the forest. If you must enter open country, scout it carefully first and move quickly. Learn to take advantage of anything the terrain gives you: every knoll, depression, or ravine may serve as protection from the enemy."

After some further instruction, they practiced. In the coming days they would learn about enemy tactics and enemy weapons. About their own weapons. About explosives. They would learn how to derail a train. How to attack an enemy tank. How to cross a river. How to throw a grenade. How to take out a bridge. There was a lot to learn, and it was both exciting and sobering, since they knew they would be using this knowledge to kill—or, if they failed, they would be killed.

They learned about hand-to-hand combat. Their rifles, Russian-made Mosins, had a bayonet. They practiced using it by stabbing bundles of branches. They learned to thrust upward into the vital organs from below the rib cage. If the bayonet was thrust through the rib cage, it could get stuck. They learned what a good weapon a shovel is. It could not only parry the enemy's thrusts but could inflict a mortal wound if slashed down onto the base of the neck. They learned how to use a hatchet to kill a sentry without a sound.

Hand-to-hand combat was not something Jacob did well. It was too primitive, too up-close, too brutal for someone with his temperament. Confiding in Samuel, Jacob said, "I don't have much confidence I could kill someone with a hatchet. If I'm locked into one-on-one combat with a German soldier, I doubt I'll be the winner. I'm not sure I could be vicious enough. I'm going to keep a pistol ready in case I'm about to be overrun. I'll save the last bullet for myself."

Samuel replied, "I can tell you haven't grown up on a farm. If you'd ever delivered a calf or slaughtered a hog, you'd be more comfortable fighting up close and bloody. I guess it's good, for some things at least, to be a farm boy."

Where Jacob did excel was in shooting. He became familiar with every part of his rifle, a Mosin 1891—1891 being the year it was first introduced into the Russian army. It was very basic and somewhat crudely made. He could see machining marks on some of the less important parts, and the stock was roughly finished. Nevertheless, he was proud to have it. It almost became an extension of his body, never leaving his side. He understood its peculiarities; he knew every way it could jam and what to do if that happened. He zeroed in the sight and then practiced until he could put a clip of five bullets into a six-inch diameter circle at a hundred yards, firing the entire clip in twenty seconds.

Using the Mosin was a gritty, hands-on experience. Weighing in at nine pounds, it felt substantial in his hands. Jacob liked the action of the bolt, of ejecting the fired shell and ramming the next one into the firing chamber. The trigger release was sometimes uneven from shot to shot, so he learned to pull smoothly through it. The recoil of the 7.6-millimeter shell punched his shoulder, and the bang deafened his ear. It felt like it was made for fighting.

This was also a time for the new recruits to rebuild their bodies and develop the mental and physical toughness of a partisan. They hiked several miles every day, regardless of the weather. They learned how to hike at night and during a snowstorm. They learned how to conserve food and how to live off the land if necessary. They felt ready.

Chapter 47: First Mission
Jacob, Eastern Poland, November 1942

After a few weeks of training, Jacob was excited when he was given his first assignment to go on a food-gathering mission. He traveled with a dozen other young men under leaders Yasha and Piotr, away from the forest and close to German garrisons. The partisan family village required an enormous amount of food, and the only way to get it was to take it from surrounding villages or farms. As the group silently approached the farmhouse of a family that had reportedly betrayed Jews, Jacob and the others scattered, taking up positions around the house while their two leaders approached the entrance.

Yasha pounded on the door.

"No need to be so loud. I'm coming." A grizzled and nearly toothless man pulled the door open. "What do you want?"

"We are from the forest, and we are looking for Jews. Do you have any Jews hiding here?"

Looking over his shoulder, the man shouted, "Daria, are we hiding any Jews?"

Laughter drifted from behind the door. "Not anymore."

"What does she mean?" asked Piotr.

"Didn't you hear about the tunnel breakout some weeks ago?" asked the peasant.

"Only vaguely. What happened?"

"The Germans," he said derisively, "supermen that they are, allowed the entire ghetto of Jews to escape under their noses. The Jews had dug a tunnel. Do you believe it? I'll bet someone was sent to the eastern front for *that*."

Yasha and Piotr laughed along with him. "So what happened?"

"Four of them showed up here, asking for help."

"What did you do?"

"What do you think I did? I told them they could stay in the barn and then I went for the police. The police shot them right here. Didn't even take them back to the village. They buried them out in the trees."

"Can we see where they are buried?"

"There's only one grave. Why do you want to see it?"

"So we know you are telling the truth."

"Look, if you knew me at all, you would know I am telling the truth. These aren't the first Jews I've turned in."

"Oh, how's that?"

"Two months back I came across a whole family—husband, wife, two children. While my son held them at gunpoint, I tied them up. Then we took them to the police station. I think we still have some of their clothes." Calling over his shoulder again, he asked, "Daria, do you still have that little jacket?"

A moment later, the peasant's wife handed him a small, blue coat. "Look, you can still see where the star was sewn on."

"Okay, I believe you. Still, how about you show us the grave?"

The peasant sighed with obvious annoyance. "It's not like I don't have anything else to do. And exactly who are you? AK, NSZ?" Stepping through the doorway, he walked a few steps into the courtyard. There he noticed the other partisans scattered about. Jacob could see fear come into his eyes.

"We are Jews from the 51st Partisan Brigade."

The peasant stumbled backward, his face a picture of complete surprise.

"That's right—we are Jews. In fact, some of us were in the tunnel escape. What do you say now?"

The peasant took another step back and eyed the weapons they were holding. "I . . . I had no choice," he stammered. "The Germans would have killed me if I hadn't done it."

"You had a choice. You chose to have them murdered. And we are going to make sure you learn that killing Jews comes at a price."

Two partisans grabbed the peasant and shoved him to the ground; Yasha pulled out his pistol, placed it at the back of his head and fired. A scream echoed from inside the house.

"Tie her up," Yasha ordered, "and search the house for others. Tell them this is what happens to people who betray the Jews. Tell her to warn her neighbors, or they will be next."

They looted the house of all its food and clothing. They took the horse and cow and chickens. Then they set fire to the house, leaving the wife tied up next to her husband in the courtyard for others to find.

Chapter 48: A Revelation
Helmuth, Warsaw, Fall 1942

The orphanage trek was one of a series of events that had given Helmuth much to think about. Every day they were taking thousands of men, women, and children—families—to the *Umschlagplatz* to be transported to their deaths. Their crime was being Jewish. He didn't know about the parents; most of them looked harmless. But the children—he *knew* the children were innocent. *How can I be an accomplice in the murder of children?* he asked himself. Gradually everything he had seen and felt over the past few months welled up inside him until he inescapably faced a conclusion that staggered him: the leaders of Nazi Germany were committing a great crime. *He* was participating in a great crime. His knees actually felt weak and he had to sit down. These were the leaders who had made his country great again, a country he loved. Could they lead Germany to greatness and commit a great crime, *a most evil crime*, at the same time?

He had sworn an oath of absolute obedience. What was he to do? Did he have a choice? He could be shot for failing to obey an order. He thought of the *Waffen SS* motto: "Loyalty is my Honor." It wasn't just loyalty to his comrades, but also loyalty to Adolf Hitler. Was it excusable for him to be part of a great crime if he was following orders?

Helmuth was a Lutheran. Many times in Sunday School he had heard the story of how Martin Luther was called before an assembly of the Holy Roman Empire and asked to recant his teachings regarding the Protestant reformation. Helmuth thought of Luther's reply: "I cannot and will not recant anything, since it is neither safe nor right to go against conscience." Luther would say a man's conscience is a higher authority than any other, that obedience to conscience is the most fundamental loyalty a man can have.

What was he to do?

Chapter 49: A Proposal
Rachel, Warsaw, February 1943

In February, the stakes got higher. The trip with the suitcase went fine. Rachel was always relieved and happy when she was able to hand it over to someone else. She also enjoyed ending the day by staying over at Halinka's.

"Come in." Halinka welcomed her warmly. "I have some tea ready and dinner will be ready in a few minutes." The rich aroma of *pierogi*—dumplings—filled the room. Rachel's stomach gave an embarrassing growl.

As they settled down to eat dinner, Rachel asked, "What has happened since my last trip?"

"I assume you know about the January *Aktion*?"

"No I haven't heard. Tell me about it."

"The Germans unleashed a surprise *Aktion* on January 18. There was a rumor the ghetto would be emptied—the final liquidation. Members of the Jewish fighters infiltrated a group of Jews being marched to the *Umschlagplatz* and attacked the SS guards. Over the next four days there was fighting at several locations. Several Germans and many Jews were killed. The deportations stopped, and the Germans withdrew. Now we are waiting to see what happens next."

"Oh, I am glad to hear this! We are finally standing up for ourselves—finally taking action. Oh, how I wish I could be there with them!"

"Hmm," Halinka replied. She looked long and carefully at Rachel. "Do you really mean what you just said?"

Rachel had to think for a moment. She hadn't expected that an off-the-cuff remark might represent a commitment. "Yes," she said slowly. "Yes, I do."

"Well, then, let me run something past you. There are hundreds—maybe thousands—of children still left in the ghetto. Many are orphans. I just learned about two who lost their parents today. If you are willing, I suggest we enter the ghetto tomorrow at dusk and bring them out. I know of several locations where children need help. The police do not like being in the ghetto now after dark. We could split up and check twice as many houses. The danger, of course, is the usual. If we are caught, we are killed."

"If there is an opportunity to save children, I would like to go with you. How do we get in and out?" Rachel asked.

"The same way the suitcase does. You've probably wondered how it makes the last leg of the journey."

"I have. I've also wondered who carries it." Rachel decided not to share her fantasies of the handsome resistance fighter.

"There are bombed-out buildings on the Aryan side of the ghetto that are adjacent to buildings on the Jewish side of the ghetto. Tunnels have been dug in the cellars to connect the two. Rubble obscures the entrances. We enter on the Aryan side and exit on the Jewish side, using the same procedure in reverse to come back. If it were only as easy to do as to say."

"Where do we take the children?" Rachel asked. She had noticed that all the children brought for her to escort were clean and had good clothes. Some of them had their hair dyed. There must be an intermediate stop for them.

"We have several 'protective readiness locations' that give the children shelter, food, clothing, and medical care, as well as birth or baptismal certificates."

Rachel was awed by the organization this implied. "I'm impressed. There must be a lot of people involved."

"There are a few, yes. We need more of them. I can understand it is difficult to risk your life for someone you haven't met. There is a saying, 'It takes ten Poles to save one Jew.' And unfortunately, every month we lose a few as the Germans close in."

"Remind me in the morning to telegram my mistress telling her I'll be delayed."

Chapter 50: Into the Ghetto
Rachel, Warsaw, February 1943

The time came to leave. Rachel's hands were clammy, and she felt her heart pounding in her chest. She had wanted to enter the ghetto for some time. She wanted to mingle with her people—to share, if even for a few minutes, the circumstances of their lives, to see where the suitcase went. And she wanted to help children. *Perhaps*, she thought, *someone somewhere is helping Esther*.

Both Rachel and Halinka carried knapsacks, and each of them had a flashlight. They brought some bread, which made sense, but Rachel was a little surprised that they took several pairs of shoes of different sizes. When Rachel asked, Halinka explained, "Many of the children have no shoes, even in winter. All they have are rags on their feet." The two also carried some jackets—not only to provide warmth for the children, but also help disguise them so they did not stand out as much.

"We'll take the streetcar on Leszno to Wronia Street, a block before the ghetto entrance," Halinka told her. "We'll then walk north to Żytnia. We follow Żytnia east to where it butts up against the ghetto. Then we cross over."

The ride to Wronia along Leszno took only a few minutes. At five p.m. it was dusk, but the sky was clear, and a half moon was already rising. The sidewalks were crowded with people hurrying to get home. Curfew was not until seven p.m. for the Jews and eleven p.m. for the Poles, so they should have plenty of time. They walked quickly along sidewalks hemmed in by four- and five-story buildings. Lights showed through the windows of the apartments on the upper floors.

As they got closer to the ghetto, the crowds thinned. They approached several bombed-out buildings like ones that existed all over Warsaw. Remnants of walls framed piles of rubble. Halinka did not hesitate but walked through the doorway of one such building into the interior. As soon as they entered what had been the inside, they moved behind a portion of wall where they couldn't be seen from the street. They waited for several minutes to make sure no one followed them. Then they carefully made their way toward the rear of the building, ducking underneath fallen beams or climbing over piles of bricks. Rachel had to walk carefully; in the growing darkness, she couldn't see all the obstacles in the way.

Rachel was surprised when they reached the back of the building, exited, and entered the building alongside. It seemed their roundabout path was taken to conceal the real entrance. They were in a large building that had not been completely destroyed—its walls were mostly standing, but the roof had caved in and all the windows were blown out. A few sections of the exterior walls were gone, revealing the inside, as if it were a grown-up doll house.

Eventually they reached a spot where Halinka cleared a pile of debris off the floor to uncover a trap door that led to the cellar. She and Rachel went down a wooden staircase, feeling their way along.

Only when the door was closed did they turn on their flashlights. Immediately a male voice called out, "Who goes there?"

Halinka answered, "Masada."

"Halinka, is that you?" the voice asked.

"Tis I," she replied, "with a friend, Teresa. We are on a hunt for children."

"Unfortunately, there are plenty to choose from. Any cargo I can help you with?"

"Not tonight, I am afraid."

They were caught in the beam of his flashlight. In response, Halinka shone her flashlight on him, and Rachel noticed he looked a lot like her imagined resistance fighter—relaxed, scruffy, dark, with a pistol in his hand. Next to him was a three-foot round opening in the wall. He leaned into the tunnel and said quietly, "Friendlies coming." He flashed his light twice.

Entering the tunnel, Rachel and Halinka crawled on their knees for some thirty feet, getting their coats dirty and their knees bruised. *Dresses and long coats weren't made for crawling,* Rachel thought. *I can see the advantages of wearing pants.* As they exited, they were helped up by the guard at the other end.

"How are things tonight?" Halinka asked the guard. "Anything happening?"

"Quiet. Too quiet. The calm before the storm. Where are you off to?"

"We are looking for children on the east end of Nowolipie. We have a good idea we'll find some."

"Good luck. We'll see you back here when?" the guard asked.

"In about an hour, maybe a little longer, and hopefully with children."

Halinka turned to Rachel. "Nowolipie is just a stone's throw from here. I'll show you where we enter. I brought this for you," she said, giving Rachel a white armband with the star of David on it. After fastening these to their right sleeves, they made their way out of the cellar of the intact Jewish building to a side street where they joined the crowd walking down the sidewalk on Nowolipie. They were in a shopping district, and quite a few people were out.

Rachel noticed the addresses here were in the sixties. Halinka had mentioned they needed to get to the twenties, so Rachel knew they had some blocks to go. In the dim light of the streetlamps, everything was in shades of gray—the buildings, the street, the people. No one looked at her. The eyes of passersby were dull and empty. *These are eyes that have seen too much*, she thought. *Too much cruelty, too much suffering.*

"Since the *Grossaktion*, there aren't as many beggars in the street," Halinka commented. Rachel noticed store windows that had an assortment of goods, but she didn't see any customers.

They were getting close. "Are you ready?" Halinka asked. "With luck you'll find two girls at Number 23. Check there first. There are no orphanages left, so there is nowhere for them to go. Also check Numbers 21 and 27. I'll take the other side of the street. If you hit Karmelicka, you have gone too far. I'm afraid we can only take four to five children between us. You may have to choose. I'll meet you back at the entrance of the tunnel in an hour."

Number 23 Nowolipie Street was a shop that bought and sold used cameras. The proprietor gave a nod to Rachel as she climbed the stairs to the apartments above. She knocked on the door of the first apartment—no answer. She twisted the knob; it was open. The apartment was dark and cold. She flipped on the light. It had not been ransacked, yet it seemed to be deserted. "Hello," she called out, "is anyone here? It is a friend. Don't be afraid. I've come to help."

She went into the bedroom and flipped the light switch, but nothing happened. She stood still and listened. She caught the faintest whisper of whimpering. "Children," she said in a soothing voice, "don't be afraid. I am a friend." A little more whimpering came from under the bed. Kneeling down, she turned on her flashlight. She saw two sets of eyes. *They must feel like trapped animals.* "Don't worry. I've come to help you. I've brought some food. And I'm going to take you out of here."

The oldest child began to cry. Rachel reached in and grabbed hands and gently pulled the littlest one over. "Here, let me help you," she said, as she put the child on the bed. Then she helped her older sister, who was sobbing and shaking. *What a responsibility she must've felt,* Rachel thought.

They were little more than rag dolls, but they still had beautiful, dark eyes. "My name is Teresa," Rachel said.

"My . . . My . . . My name is Hanna," the oldest choked out between sobs. "Th . . . Th . . . This is Alina. Wh . . . Wh . . . Where are our parents?"

"I don't know where your parents are. They have been taken away by the Germans. But I am going to help you. We are going to leave this bad place. Do you know if there are any more children here?" Hanna shook her head. "It is all right. Let me hold you for a minute." She gathered a child in each arm and began to rock them.

After a few minutes, when the children had calmed down some, she said, "I have some bread for you. Let's go to the other room where we can see better." Sitting on the sofa in the other room, she broke off a chunk for each of them.

"Now I want you girls to stay here while I check the upstairs. I brought some things for you in this knapsack. See if you can find a pair of shoes that fit and put on a jacket. If you have a good coat, put that on over the jacket." Rachel dumped several pairs of shoes and jackets out of her knapsack onto the floor. The girls were wide-eyed at this bounty. "I will be back in just a few minutes. I will leave my things here."

Rachel scouted out the upper floors. She found no one. Returning to where she left the children, she helped the girls try on some shoes and found some that fit. Alina mustered a weak smile. Rachel grabbed each by the hand. "We are going down to the street and up in the next apartment to see if we can find any more children like you. Don't worry, I won't leave you."

They tramped down and then up the stairs together and poked around in the empty apartments on both sides. They found nothing. In some ways Rachel was relieved; she didn't want to have to leave children behind. Then they began their trek back to the tunnel. Dusk had become darkness with a little moonshine showing the way, and they had no trouble getting to the entrance of the tunnel unseen. They were shortly joined by Halinka, who also had two children with her. When they got to the tunnel itself, Halinka went first, her children behind her.

Before leaving the cover of the bombed-out buildings, Halinka checked up and down the street for police. As best she could tell, they were in the clear. Halinka gave an okay nod to Rachel, and the two of them stepped out on the sidewalk with a child in each hand. Rachel noticed in her peripheral vision a dark shape emerge from a doorway to her left. She did not have time to figure out what the shape was before a flashlight blinded her, and the shadow stepped into the light of a streetlamp. Standing in front of her was an SS officer. His pistol was pointed right at her.

"Hello *Fräuleins*. I see you've been on a little trip."

Chapter 51: The SS Officer
Rachel and Helmuth, Warsaw, February 1943

Since the officer's light was shining on her, Rachel spoke. "A trip to save children," she said. Surprisingly, she felt perfectly calm. She expected to be shot in the next few seconds, but she was not afraid. Everything in her life seemed to fall away but this moment. She fixed her eyes on the officer and said in a steady voice, "We have no guns. We have no valuables. We only have children."

The SS officer hesitated, as if he were considering what Rachel said. Taking advantage of the pause, she boldly said, "May I ask you a question?" She knew she was being impertinent, but she didn't care.

"What is it?"

"Amidst all the killing, have you ever wanted to save a life, *Herr* . . . ?"

"Hoffman," he responded, "Helmuth Hoffman."

"Have you ever wanted to save the life of a child, *Herr* Hoffman?"

***

Helmuth didn't answer. He looked down at the ground and thought about when he saw a boy being beaten to death for smuggling food. He thought of the children six months ago at the orphanage, the girl with the doll in her pillowcase and the boy who looked like his nephew. The boy's words still rang in his ears. "Am I standing up straight enough, Uncle?" In his mind's eye he saw the children marching into the cattle car with their leader, who could have saved his own life but chose not to. In some vague way this woman reminded him of that man.

Noticing that Helmuth seemed to be pondering her question, Rachel said, "You have a chance to save a child right now."

Helmuth shined his light on the four children. He could see terror in their eyes. He could go down this road no longer. He looked at Rachel and lowered his gun. "You and your children may go."

It took a second for his words to sink in. "Come, children, let's be on our way," Rachel said, and she and Halinka began to quickly pull the children along. When she reached the halo of the next streetlamp, however, she stopped and turned around. Helmuth couldn't see her face, but he could see her bow her head. In acknowledgment, he touched his fingers to his cap.

Helmuth went back to his barracks and thought about what he had just done. Under his breath he said, "As God is my witness, I will not willingly kill another child."

A few days later he mentioned to Paul, "If part of being in the SS is sending children to their deaths, then I don't want to be one of the elite anymore. I don't want to be one of the chosen anymore."

Chapter 52: The Convent
Rachel, Warsaw, March 1943

On one late afternoon in March, Rachel arrived back home on the train from Warsaw with children in tow. The nun meeting her at the station greeted her by saying, "We are having a special dinner for the children tonight and thought you might like to come. In fact, I understand you know Father Sobieski. He especially asked if you would join us."

After a long train journey and two stressful days, Rachel felt wilted and in need of a bath. She wouldn't have picked this night for an evening with company. But it was Father Sobieski asking, and she would never turn him down if whatever he asked was physically possible. She also welcomed a chance to see "her" children. "I will be pleased to come if you will show me the way."

Rachel joined the children in the wagon, and they all started out on a leisurely hour-long ride to the convent, which was out in the countryside. As Rachel already knew, the convent had been built as a combination convent and orphanage. As such, it was a compound of several buildings surrounded by a wall on several acres of land. A sign on the front said *Congregation of the Sisters of Mary*.

The main building included the chapel and a meeting/dining hall. Two rows of long, low buildings extended from the back of the main building. Rachel learned they were dormitories for the sisters and for the children, along with some classrooms. Everything on the outside looked rundown: walls were cracked and flaking, paint was peeling, and wood was split and bleached by the sun.

The depressing scene was offset by the cheerfulness of the sisters and the presence of Father Sobieski. As the party drove up in the wagon, several sisters and the local priest came out to greet them. As they entered, Rachel glimpsed Father Sobieski, who was in conversation with the Mother Superior. Rachel saw him glance her way and then excuse himself from the conversation. He came up to Rachel, grasped her by the arms, and with evident pleasure said, "How good it is to see you! How was your journey?"

"Fortunately, it was uneventful. The kind I like these days."
"The children made it fine?"
"Yes, the children did well."

"I am so glad you could come tonight. I am sure you are tired. Let me show you where you can wash and rest for a few minutes. Then meet me in the dining room. I would like to speak with you before the dinner begins."

Rachel felt refreshed after washing her face and hands. And it was good to just sit and relax and not feel responsible for others' lives. After a few minutes, she found the Father. "You wanted to tell me something?"

"Please come with me." He took her out into the hall, past the chapel to the dormitory wing, and motioned toward a doorway. "Have you had a chance to see any of the children you brought down?"

"No, I haven't, but I'm looking forward to it tonight."

They entered a small room, perhaps eight feet square. Two sets of bunk beds stood kitty-corner to each other on the cement floor. A rope clothesline stretched diagonally across the room with a few articles of children's clothing hanging from it. A bare bulb dangled from the ceiling, illuminating the space in a yellow glow.

Standing in the middle of the room was a young girl. She was rocking back and forth on the balls of her feet in nervous anticipation. Father Sobieski stepped forward and took her by the hand. "Do you recognize this young lady?" he asked Rachel with an air of excitement.

Rachel didn't answer. She didn't remember the girl from any of her trips. She looked at the Father's face for a clue. Deep in her heart she felt some stirrings, but she had learned to protect herself by not expecting too much.

"This," he said softly, "is the girl you have been searching for. You know her by her Jewish name of Esther."

There she was, standing before Rachel like an angelic apparition. Her hair, neatly tied with pink ribbons, was now down to her shoulders. She had grown at least an inch. She still had freckles. She was beautiful.

The little girl volunteered, "You helped my mother when we were on the bad train."

Rachel stood stupefied as the words sank in. Then, as if in a trance, Rachel slowly knelt in front of the little girl. She reached out and stroked her face and hair. All she could say was, "Oh, my." It seemed as if she were in a dream. Presently she recovered enough to whisper, "Esther, is it really you?"

In answer, Esther fished out a ring tied around her neck. "Do you remember this?" she asked. Rachel took it and read the inscription on the inside. There was no doubt.

Rachel buried her face in her hands and quietly wept. After some moments she looked up at Father Sobieski and said in a halting voice, "Now I can keep my promise."

"I am very glad for both your sakes that you can keep your promise," he answered.

Esther put her arms around Rachel's neck and laid her head on her shoulder, just as she had on the train. But this time it was Esther comforting Rachel.

Chapter 53: Holiness
Rachel, Warsaw, March 1943

The dinner was simple: soup, bread, cabbage, and—thanks to the Father—a piece of candy for each child. Though simple, there was enough. A short program followed that included singing some Polish folk songs while a sister accompanied on a guitar. If anyone was paying attention to Rachel, they would have noticed she didn't let go of the hand of the little girl sitting next to her.

Later that evening, when they were alone, she asked the Father, "How did this happen?"

"She was found wandering along the tracks by a Polish railway worker. She told him how she came to be there. He took her home with the intention of taking care of her until he and his wife could decide what should be done. Although they had grown fond of her and had treated her like their own child, their neighbors became suspicious, and she wasn't safe. They also wanted her to be reunited with any family that survived and to be raised in the Jewish faith. For now, you are that family."

Rachel gave the Father a long, sustained hug. "I don't know what to say, except I will always be in your debt."

"There is nothing that needs to be said." He held her by her shoulders at arm's length. "I am glad to help, and to be working side by side with good and brave people. It isn't that often we have a happy event. It was a privilege to be here."

"I have been thinking," Rachel said, "tonight changes my life in many ways. I wonder if you would have a few minutes in the next few days I could talk to you. I need advice from someone wiser than myself."

"You flatter me. I would be pleased to visit. How would next Saturday be? As I recall, you won't be traveling this week. Would that work? Could you come by at noon, so we could break bread together?"

"That would be wonderful."

That night, though very tired, Rachel could not sleep. She kept picturing Esther standing before her. She again felt Esther's head on her shoulder and the warmth of her small hand as they walked to dinner. These feelings filled her heart and reassured her that it was all real.

But she also felt something else: she felt holiness around her.

Rachel had long been sensitive to holy and sacred things. She loved having holy writings that contained God's words, represented by the Torah scrolls. She felt holiness when she sang and prayed with her family during the Sabbath. Although she loved the mystery of candles and canopies and the mezuzah on the doorpost that she could touch when she walked into the house, it was the feeling of closeness to God that these engendered that most impressed her.

She often felt holiness during feasts and holidays. She felt a kinship with Jews of the past. Once during the Passover supper when her father opened the door for Elijah to enter, a breath of wind brushed by and opened it a few more inches. It was as though someone were entering and needed a bit more room. She gasped and felt goosebumps on her arms. She almost expected the empty chair to push back from the table.

Tonight she felt holiness in her room. Several times she slipped out of bed and, facing Jerusalem, said a simple prayer. "Dear God, thank You for this miracle."

***

That Saturday, Rachel entered the church kitchen at noon. She found Maria and the Father there, conversing. "Hello everyone," she said.

"Come in, come in, Julia," the Father said enthusiastically. "Maria and I were just finishing our conversation." Maria got up from the table, gave Rachel a hug, and excused herself.

"How are you, Julia?" the Father asked.

"I'm still a little bit in shock, actually."

"Ah, I don't wonder. But at least it was a pleasant shock."

"Pleasant is an understatement. It was breathtaking."

"So, how can I help you?"

"I wanted to ask your advice about some things. They center around Esther. It is like a miracle to me that she is here. I don't want to forget that, ever. I'm trying to understand the changes I should make in my life because of this. You remember at the convent, when I was convinced it was her, I said, 'Now I can keep my promise.'"

"Yes, I remember," the Father replied.

"What I meant by that was, I promised Eva that if Esther and I survived, I would treat her as my own daughter, at least until the end of the war when we might reunite her with her family." Rachel spoke with some intensity. "Now I am pondering what that means, particularly in terms of being in the resistance. Does my commitment to Eva and Esther outweigh my desire to serve my people and countrymen? Should I keep myself as safe as possible for Esther's sake?" Rachel was clearly troubled.

"As an aside," the Father answered, "there is little question in my mind that Eva has been killed. If she did not have the little baby with her, she might have survived at Auschwitz, but with a small child, she had virtually no chance. So, if I understand it, you are asking what it means for you to be her surrogate mother."

"That is one question I am asking. I am not sure I even know what other questions to ask."

"And what do you think, at least so far?"

"I *want* to be like a mother to her. I want her to know she is loved. I want her to be safe and well and have enough to eat," Rachel replied. "I also want her to be proud of her Jewish heritage, difficult though that may be right now. But I am struggling some, because I don't see how she can live with me, and I don't think she would be safer living with me."

"Ah, this is an important point," the Father replied. "I agree. I think she is better off staying at the convent. I'm not sure we really have a choice, since it seems farfetched to think the Kohlers would allow you to take her in. You would have to move, and then what? I know the convent would appreciate it, however, if you could help with Esther's expenses."

"Of course. But you agree it is better if she stays at the convent?" Rachel repeated, just to make sure.

"Yes, I do. I think she is quite safe there."

"Something else. Can I be a good mother to Esther and continue in the resistance? Is it right for me to put myself in danger when I have a little girl to look out for? I want to continue, but given all that has happened, should I continue? I do feel I am doing something to help my people."

"Only you can answer that question. I will understand either way, and I mean that. You *are*, by the way, doing something to help your people. But there is a little girl now that enters the equation. I understand that."

"I apologize for asking so many questions," Rachel continued, "but it is helpful for me to talk with you. When you found me in the church and listened to my story, you told me you thought God had something for me to do. How do I find out what that is? Is taking care of Esther the answer? Or is there more to it? How do I know?"

"I do not mind your questions. They are good ones. We must answer many questions for ourselves. The only advice I can give is this: listen to your heart. Try to hear God speaking inside you." The Father glanced at his watch. "As much as I am enjoying our lunch, I need to be going soon. Sometime we need to discuss something else."

"What is that?" Rachel asked.

"It can wait for now. You have enough on your mind."

Chapter 54: Clarity
Rachel, Warsaw, March 1943

That night Rachel tossed and turned until the small hours of the morning. How could she know what God wanted her to do? She felt like she was mentally running in circles. Esther, of course, was at the center of her thoughts. Rachel had referred to Esther's survival and return as a miracle, and indeed it was so overwhelming and so unexpected that it seemed like a miracle.

What was a miracle? Did a miracle require some sort of supernatural manifestation, like parting the Red Sea, or could a miracle be the result of ordinary people doing extraordinary things? If so, then it was not an exaggeration to say it was a miracle made possible by the railway worker who found Esther and took her home.

As she mulled this over, everything seemed to rise or fall with the railway worker. Where would they be without him? What if he had decided it was too risky to pick up Esther? What if he had decided he couldn't get involved? Esther would have perished.

These thoughts provided some insight for her. *Most of the time*, she thought, *miracles don't happen without someone choosing to be involved, without someone acting.* If she stayed in the resistance, she could conceivably be the means of bringing other children like Esther home, of facilitating miracles for someone else. She thought of Hanna and Alina. Where would they be without Rachel or Halinka? It broke her heart to think of them hiding under the bed and no one ever coming to their rescue.

She began to feel some clarity. Still she struggled. Was she being selfish with her own life *by wanting to risk it?* Was she being fair to Esther? She resolved to talk it over with Esther. She may be only a little girl, but she had seen a lot in her life, and she was wise beyond her years. Rachel would have to keep things very general to protect both Esther and her companions in the resistance.

***

The next day, Sunday, Rachel made the nearly ninety-minute journey from the estate to the convent. She was greeted by the Mother

Superior. "We are grateful for your efforts in helping children. We are, however, greatly in need of funds. Can you help out?"

"Father Sobieski mentioned this to me. What would you suggest?" Rachel asked.

"For one Jewish child, 7000 złoty per year." Rachel gulped. That was more than she had expected and much more than she had. "You realize if we were discovered, we would all be in mortal danger. And we have many children for whom we have no support."

"I will do what I can. Here is 300 złoty to start."

Rachel and Esther's greeting was infused with the lingering joy of reunion. Rachel hugged Esther, lifting the little girl off her feet and swinging her around. "Oh, I am glad to see you. I still can't believe I get to hold you," Rachel said, smiling.

As they passed the chapel, Rachel saw that it was empty. "Let's go in here for a minute. I have something I want to show you. Do you have a place where you can keep something special, where you can make sure it won't get lost or taken?"

"I have a drawer I can lock."

"I have brought something for you that I have kept safe. On many nights I held it close to me to remind me of you, especially when I was discouraged." As she spoke, Rachel produced the small sack of Esther's belongings that had been thrown out the window from the train.

"Oh, yes, I remember this! Show me what is inside," Esther said eagerly. Rachel opened the sack and spread the contents on the pew. There was a pink sweater (missing the ribbon at its neck), a dress, a change of underwear, and some shoes. There was the note written by her mother asking her to be a good girl. There was even a small crust of dried-out bread.

"Everything here was touched by your mother. If, like me, you ever feel discouraged, you can hold this and feel she is near, watching over you."

They walked outside where they had more privacy. The grounds were brown and drab-looking, but the sky was a cerulean blue—just gazing at it made Rachel's heart beat faster. They could still see traces of their breath in the air. "How are things here? Do you feel like you are getting to know the other children? Are they nice to you?"

"I've been here only a few days, but the girls in my room seem nice. I am glad I can go to school."

"Father Sobieski and I have discussed the situation, and both of us feel you are safer staying here at the convent. I don't have a way to take you in, at least not right now. The sisters will be good to you, and you will have other children to play with. I will come to see you as often as I can. I wish I could be with you all the time. Do you understand?"

"I think so. Please come as much as you can."

"I need to ask you something. Before you came here, I decided to try to help other people who are Jews, like you and me, so they wouldn't be put on bad trains, like we were. I need to know if you are okay with me still doing that. It can be dangerous. If I were caught, I would be killed."

Esther asked, "Would you be helping other little girls like me?"

Rachel was astonished at her perceptiveness, "Yes," she said, "I would. I have brought several girls already to this very orphanage. It is better I don't say their names."

Esther clutched her mother's bag to her. It was clear she was trying to be brave, but her face betrayed her anguish. With quivering lips, she said, "I don't want you to leave me. I don't want to be alone again. You have to come back!" Tears slid down her cheek.

Rachel's heart melted and she pulled Esther close.

Chapter 55: The Bridge
Jacob, Eastern Poland, March 1943

In the beginning of March, all the partisans were called to a meeting. Fyodorovich conducted. "My superiors," he said, "have decided to attack the ghetto at Kosovo for two reasons. First, to free the Jews that remain. There have already been several *Aktions*, so there are only a few hundred left. And second, to capture weapons. It is a strange thing," and here he fingered his beard, as if to emphasize the strangeness, "but the Germans have the Jews there repairing Russian weapons that were discarded when the Germans advanced. There is a warehouse of these weapons a block or two from the ghetto. Other brigades will have the responsibility of capturing these. In all, we will have a force of more than three hundred."

"As the only all-Jewish brigade, we will have the honor of opening the gate to the ghetto." Jacob was elated to hear this. "But," and here Fyodorovich paused, anticipating their excitement, "only after we have captured the bridge across the Oginski canal." Jacob gave a questioning glance to Samuel, who only shrugged. "For those of you still learning your geography, the Oginski connects the Dneiper and Neman rivers, making a waterway between the Black and Baltic seas. It is not a large bridge, but it is crucial to the operation. It is the only way we can get several hundred people, and wagonfuls of weapons, across the canal."

"The first objective will be for us to take out the house of the bridge watchman, which is adjacent to the bridge, on the near side of the canal. Several SS officers are billeted there. We will sneak up at first light and storm the house. From there we will take out the bridge. I have selected a dozen of our best fighters to lead the bridge assault. Once the bridge is secured, we will proceed to the ghetto. It shouldn't take long, as the main gate is only fifty yards away. It all depends, however, on what level of resistance we meet."

***

The day for assault arrived. Jacob and Samuel and the rest of their brigade had hiked through the night to arrive at the canal just before dawn. They approached the bridge watchman's house cautiously, crouching down among the bushes. Though the morning air was cool, Jacob's hands were sweating, and his heart was beating rapidly. As he had been taught, he stepped carefully, making sure not to break any twigs or branches, and he gripped his rifle firmly. All his senses were on high alert. He noticed the smoke from the chimney dissipating in the early-morning breeze. He could hear the dark canal water flowing gently downstream, burbling as it went around the bridge abutments. He could smell the smoke, mixed with earthy odors of soil and wet hay. As they approached the house, the bushes gave way to a grassy bank. Fyodorovich motioned for them to stay back where they could remain hidden. Four of them stealthily moved toward the house.

Without warning, shots echoed from the second story, and Fyodorovich fell to the ground. The Nazis had been waiting for them. "Keep going," he shouted to the others. Within moments a firefight broke out, with shots from the house answered many times over by the partisans concealed in the bushes. Jacob saw the house sprout mushrooms of cement dust as bullets struck the walls; the shutters splintered and fell to the ground. He saw a familiar figure run to Fyodorovich and drag him under the porch. Of course—it was Samuel. Now joined by several others, Samuel stepped back and threw grenades into the second-story windows. Soon the first floor crackled with red and orange flames, and smoke poured from the windows. There was no more shooting from the inside.

Fyodorovich, badly wounded, was carried behind their lines on a stretcher. A doctor examined him and pronounced his wounds to be mortal. Fyodorovich confirmed that Zerach, his second-in-command, was now in charge of the attack. He then said, "Comrades, there is no chance of me surviving, but as Jews we must demonstrate courage and a strong spirit and fall in battle without fear as Jewish heroes." Then he added, "I ask for one of you to put me out of my misery. I can no longer fight. I am in agony. Please." They drew lots, but the person selected refused. "I cannot shoot my commander," he said. Fyodorovich, in great pain, asked again.

Fyodorovich was taken behind a haystack; soon everyone heard a gunshot. A close friend had carried out this most difficult of requests.

***

The action at the watchman's house had forewarned the Germans of the attack, and they were now digging in along the far side of the canal. Zerach gathered the assault team, each with a submachine gun. At his command, they would sprint to the base of the bridge, where they could take cover behind the concrete abutments. Meanwhile, everyone still in hiding would lay down covering fire.

Zerach raised his hand and then dropped it. A dozen men rushed forward, running a zigzag course. Both sides of the canal erupted with fire, and it wasn't long before two of the twelve men dropped. The rest made it to the base of the bridge.

Zerach glanced across the bridge from where he was kneeling. It wasn't a long span, perhaps thirty yards in length, with a web of girders on both sides. At the far end was a sentry box, about five feet wide, and a flimsy crossing gate. In front were some waist-high wooden barriers; he could see several gun barrels protruding.

He glanced behind him and saw his men crouching at the back of the bridge below the deck, where bullets could not reach them. They were waiting for his order. This wasn't going to be anything fancy—they would storm the bridge in a frontal assault. The Germans enjoyed a good defensive position, and they would no doubt make use of it.

"Okay, everyone, let's show them what it means for Jews to fight," Zerach said. Waving his hand forward, he leapt up on the deck and began racing over the span, his submachine gun blazing. The men followed in twos and threes, sprinting forward while firing to answer the half dozen guns shooting directly back at them.

Two, then three, then four went down; then Zerach was hit and collapsed. Although the Jews inflicted some casualties on the German defenders, they did not prevail. All the Jewish fighters were wounded or killed. The bridge was littered with the fallen bodies.

Jacob winced. *Oh, no; this is awful.* He looked out over the ground where the brave men had fallen. The smoke cleared, and all was quiet. *What do we do now?* His spirits sank. *Will we have to retreat?*

Then he heard a voice, a female voice, shout, "Comrades, have courage! Avenge these brave soldiers! Forward, forward!" A young woman burst from the foliage thirty yards to his right. A thrill went through Jacob. *The only way out*, he said to himself, *is through*, and he stood and added his might to that of the others who were emerging from their hiding places. Soon three hundred partisans were rushing the bridge. He could feel bullets flying around him; he could hear them ring as they hit the girders of the bridge. Spouts of dirt were shooting up like geysers at his feet.

He ran past a fallen comrade and noticed his submachine gun next to him. He picked it up and kept running. The Germans guarding the exit of the bridge fell back and then ran. A torrent of partisans, Jacob among them, swept over the bridge and began attacking the Germans on their flanks. Jacob knelt and fired bursts of ten rounds each. He loved the feeling of being profligate with bullets, of laying down a hose of fire. The German line began to crumble and then collapse.

Having taken the bridge, the 51st battalion was to help free the ghetto. The bridge was almost kitty-corner to the main entrance of the ghetto. Jacob had the great satisfaction of swinging the gates open, revealing a familiar scene—ragged bodies with sunken eyes. But there were smiles among them as they realized what was happening. Samuel showed up at his side; Jacob knew Samuel had been busy pressing the attack. Soon they had a stream of ill-clad refugees making their way back across the bridge to freedom. They would become part of the Bielski family camp. Thousands had once been there; now they were bringing only a few hundred to safety. Still, it was something.

Chapter 56: Another Conversation with Father Sobieski
Rachel, Western Poland, April 1943

Rachel visited Esther every week she wasn't traveling, but she wrote to Esther every day. She gave Esther the letters when she visited and asked her to wait and open one per day. Rachel's letters were short and always started off with, "Your mother and father love you, and I love you too." She didn't think it would be helpful to talk about her duties as a governess, as this would emphasize the contrast between the lives of the Kohler children and Esther's life. In fact, Rachel felt guilty about the relative luxury in which she lived compared to the conditions at the convent. But while conditions at the convent were very spartan, it was safe—and safety was Rachel's top priority.

In her letters, Rachel always talked about something she and Esther could share. She might write, "I love the sky, with its puffy white clouds and the dark blue at the horizon." Or, "I see the trees are beginning to have leaves. Spring always gives me hope for the future." Sometimes she enclosed a leaf, a small piece of candy, or a lock of her hair—something Esther could touch or taste or smell to be reminded that Rachel was real.

She was torn between this little girl and the misery of the Warsaw ghetto, where there were many little girls. Rachel could tell the situation there was deteriorating, and she wanted to talk to Father Sobieski about it. When she remembered that the Father had mentioned he had something to speak to her about, she set up a visit through Maria.

***

"Thank you, Father, for meeting with me."

"It is always a pleasure. Please, sit down," he said, motioning to the empty chair across from him. It was the first time Rachel had been in his office at the church. There was a sort of friendly clutter about the place. Some old birthday cards with lots of hearts drawn on them were taped to the wall. "I believe Maria will bring us some tea. What can I do for you?"

"You mentioned when we last met that you had something you wished to speak to me about. Is it something you can discuss now? Then I have some other things—"

"I think so. It is not really a surprise. As you know, Esther is at a Catholic orphanage. The sisters there have dedicated their lives to Christ, and they have also incurred significant risk by taking in Jewish children. You are aware that Esther will be taught and will need to practice the principles of the Catholic faith. This understandably is of great concern to many Jews. They worry that by placing their children in convents they may save them physically but lose them spiritually."

The Father continued. "I think I can see both sides of this issue. You know I told you that in my eyes and in God's eyes, you will always be Jewish. That is also true for Esther and for all the other Jewish children there. But you are an adult, and Esther is a child. Children are very impressionable. What would happen if Esther eventually wished to convert to Catholicism?"

"From my point of view, that would be a catastrophe," Rachel answered. "How would her parents feel if that happened? What did they die for, if not for their Jewish faith?"

The Father gave a slight nod, as if he expected Rachel's response. "Among many other things, you are a person of conviction, and I appreciate that about you. My suggestion, for Esther at least, is that you be something of a counterweight. Without disparaging the sisters, help Esther understand the importance of her Jewish faith. Share your conviction with her whenever you can. I caution you not to mention this subject in writing, such as in letters, because that would entail danger for everyone. I believe in the end things will turn out all right."

"I will do as you suggest," Rachel said. Then as an aside, she added, "There is always a lot for me to think about."

The Father smiled and said, "I know the feeling. Now, what else is on your mind?"

"What do you think will happen in Warsaw?"

"As I think you can also see, Warsaw is on a collision course. The Germans will liquidate the ghetto soon. The Jews will fight, and though they will fight the best they can, I fear it will be a very lopsided fight. The time for the battle is coming soon."

"I think the same thing," Rachel replied. "Father, we talked before about what I should do now that Esther has been found. I want to tell you what I decided. I love Esther, something I tell her every time I see her. I am so grateful for her, and I would do anything I could for her. But as I have struggled over what God wants me to do, I can't help but feel that while I am able, I should help save other children like her."

She continued. "The reason I have Esther is because the railway worker did not turn away. He reached out to help her. Now I feel I must do the same—I must reach out and help those I can. I would gladly live only for Esther if there were no others, but there *are* others. Last month I helped save two little girls just like Esther. I feel I would be ungrateful to God and unworthy of Esther if I did not do everything I can."

The Father was quiet. "I believe I understand your feelings. I have also wrestled with these questions. At what point do you protect what you have already won and not risk any more by trying to add to it? If we weren't talking about human life, it would be an easier question to answer."

The Father continued, "This may soon become a moot point as far as Warsaw is concerned. As I mentioned, I believe the Warsaw ghetto will be destroyed in the near future. In all your pondering, I ask you to remember one thing."

"Which is?"

"You are very dear to me."

It took a moment for Rachel to reply, for these few unexpected words meant a lot to her. "Thank you, Father," she said with a catch in her voice. "I will remember. The feeling is mutual."

Chapter 57: Again to the Ghetto
Rachel, Western Poland, April 1943

Rachel was back in the Father's office. "Father, I believe the Germans are planning to begin something on the first day of Passover, April 19th. It would be just like them. The *Grossaktion* last summer started on the day of Tisha B'av* and ended on Yom Kippur*. I would like to take a suitcase, if you can pull it together, a day or two before. Then I want to bring some children to safety. I believe it will be the last time I can help. Can you have a suitcase ready?"

"I will see what I can do. If you are correct in your prediction, then you will be visiting very close to when the *Aktion* begins. Are you sure that's wise?"

"If I can save a life, it is worth the risk," Rachel answered.

Rachel explained that she wanted to try to go on Saturday, April 17, two days before Passover, and return Sunday, April 18. She could tell the Father was concerned.

"Things there are changing rapidly," he said, "and they may quickly spiral out of control. Please be especially careful. If you need to abort the trip, do so. Dump the suitcase in the wreckage of some building and get out."

***

Rachel noticed the suitcase was somewhat lighter than normal. She supposed it was the best the Father could do with the relatively short notice. She didn't know that pistols, the least desirable weapon for the resistance but the most affordable, were now selling for upwards of 7000* złoty. Acquiring weapons was getting harder.

She arrived without incident in Warsaw. It was a gray day, but warmer than her last visit two weeks earlier. The lighter suitcase did make for easier traveling. She arrived a little early at the streetcar platform, where she was to make the hand-off. It was five p.m. on Saturday.

---

* Tish B'av is a day of fasting for the Jews.

* Yom Kippur, also known as the Day of Atonement, is the holiest day of the year in Judaism.

* In 1939 exchange rates, this would be about $1400, more than the cost of an average car.

Rachel waited for more than an hour, but her contact never showed up. She had no idea what had happened. Was this just a communication mix-up, or did it signify something more serious? If need be, she could take the suitcase into the ghetto herself. But after a little thought, she decided to stop by the safe house and talk with Halinka about how to proceed. Perhaps she could leave the suitcase at Halinka's in the hiding place where she slept, and Halinka could arrange for its transport into the ghetto.

After she lugged the suitcase up three flights of stairs, she began to have second thoughts. *Maybe this wasn't such a good idea.* She gave one knock and fitted a coin between the two nail heads. No answer. Nothing. She could wait, with no guarantee when Halinka might return, or she could take the suitcase into the ghetto herself. She needed to get in tonight so she could catch the train tomorrow; she could not risk staying over another day. If her prediction was correct, the next *Aktion* would start by then.

Rachel determined to go into the ghetto the same way she did when they rescued Hanna and Alina. It was the only way she knew. The SS officer who had confronted them during that rescue surely understood there was an entrance nearby. Had he discovered it? She didn't know, but it was a chance she'd have to take.

She caught the streetcar for Leszno Street. As she got off the streetcar in the twilight, she felt conspicuous and vulnerable and alone. She missed Halinka and her infectious confidence. A few people walked by—she imagined they were staring at her. She noticed several policemen half a block away. *Are they looking in my direction?*

At that moment Rachel hated the suitcase. She felt twice as noticeable and half as mobile walking with it. As soon as she could, she ducked into a doorway on Wronia Street. Panic rose inside her. *Why am I so nervous?* She felt her stomach cramp and tasted a bitterness in her mouth. She tried to talk herself down off the ledge of her anxiety. *You are all right. Nothing has happened. Stay calm. Focus on what you can do.* Thoughts of Jacob went through her mind—she used to say the same things to him.

As she began walking again, she noticed a horse-drawn wagon coming her way. She flagged down the driver. "Can you take me to the intersection of Żytnia and Nowolipie? I'll make it worth your while—say 20 złoty?"

The driver looked her over for a moment. "Put your suitcase in the back. You can climb up next to me." He helped her up onto the seat. Rachel felt less vulnerable sitting in the wagon—less conspicuous—and she was able to calm herself somewhat.

She paid the driver and retrieved her suitcase. After walking a short distance off the street, she walked into the rubble of the same bombed-out building she had entered with Halinka. She waited out of sight; no one followed. She was beginning to recover some confidence, but it nosedived again when she realized she had no flashlight. *Can I find the entrance without one?* She doubted the nearly full moon would help her much in the enclosed space where the trap door was located—a realization that again filled her with doubt and fear.

She made it out of the first building and into the second. She thought she could recall the layout of the rooms, but it was quite dark inside, and everything seemed mixed up. The room with the trap door had apparently been in some sort of maintenance closet—she remembered a row of cabinets along one side that had fallen over, as well as some brooms and mops on the floor. As she felt her way along, rats scurried around her and made her jump. This trip had been exciting when she was with Halinka; now it was frightening.

When she could not find the room with the trap door, she decided she must be in a different part of the building. She sat quietly on a chair that was still upright in the wreckage and said a prayer. At the conclusion of her prayer, she simply listened. After a few minutes, she heard hushed voices and saw a flicker of light coming through cracks in the wall. Someone was leaving. She waited until they had moved beyond where she was, and then she crawled toward where the light had been.

When Rachel realized she had found the room with the trap door, a tremendous sense of relief came over her. She lifted the door and carefully felt her way down the staircase. As she expected, she met a challenge. "Who goes there?" A flashlight shone on her.

"I am a friend of Halinka's," she replied. "I don't know what the password is today, but two months ago when I came with Halinka, it was *Masada*. I have brought a suitcase of supplies."

"Stay there and don't move." A man she couldn't see took the suitcase and, while holding a pistol aimed at her, shined his flashlight on the stairs so she could find her way down.

At the bottom of the stairs, two Jewish fighters took her by the arm and led her to a chair next to the tunnel. "Who are you?" they demanded.

"My name is Teresa. I am a courier. I bring suitcases to Warsaw, which I assume are full of weapons, and I escort Jewish children out of Warsaw to a convent in the countryside. After I drop off a suitcase, I spend the night at a safe house run by Halinka. In fact, we came here together two months ago to rescue some children."

"That should be easy enough for us to check out, since Halinka isn't too far from here."

"Halinka is here?" Rachel asked with surprise.

"Halinka is getting ready for battle. She is one of our group commanders."

Chapter 58: The Nowolipki Hotel
Rachel, Western Poland, April 1943

"Can you take me to Halinka?" Rachel asked. "She will confirm what I just told you."

"First, let's get through the tunnel to the Jewish side," one of the men said as he motioned to the tunnel. "That's a safer place to have a conversation."

Rachel crawled through the tunnel, again wishing she was wearing pants. After they emerged from the tunnel, she sat at a table with several others. A few lights illuminated the large, dirty cellar. Her interrogators seemed to believe her story; Rachel suspected they were just being careful.

The men broke the latches off the suitcase and opened it to reveal six pistols wrapped in cloth, several boxes of ammunition, and several grenades. Although it was no surprise for Rachel to see what was in the suitcase, it was gratifying for her to see what was there with her own eyes.

They were joined by another comrade. "Antek," one of the fighters said, "this woman says she knows Halinka. Says she came here with her two months ago. To her credit, she just entered with a suitcase full of arms."

Antek looked Rachel over. "Ah, yes, I remember you. I was there the night you and Halinka were rescuing children. In fact, I heard you were nearly murdered by an SS officer. It was quite a story. You were apparently very persuasive in convincing him not to shoot. Everything is fine here—she's one of us." Turning to Rachel, he said, "Remind me of your name."

"Teresa."

"Teresa, I am Antek, as you have heard," he said, offering his hand to her. "You and Halinka are friends, I take it."

"Yes, good friends."

"Then you are lucky. Halinka is one of our leaders. Her post, though, is about a half mile from here. We can take you over in the morning if you like. You can sleep in the bunker here tonight. You will be quite safe."

Rachel weighed the offer. She wanted to see Halinka, but the safe house wasn't an option. And she wanted to try to find a child to

205

take to safety. These reasons argued in favor of accepting. "Thank you; I would like to take you up on your offer. What time can we go over to see Halinka?"

"Since it will be a Sunday, I would suggest around eight a.m. That is when the ghetto starts to wake up, and it's better for us to travel when we aren't the only ones in the street. We could go via underground tunnels or through attics, but it will be faster to walk outside."

"When do you anticipate the next *Aktion* will be?" she asked.

"Soon. Within a day or two."

"Are you ready?"

"We will find out, I suppose. We are ready to fight, and we are ready to die. I just hope we can inflict some pain on the Germans. It is truly a case of David fighting Goliath—we have pistols; they have machine guns. You risk getting caught in all of this by coming into the ghetto right now. What are your plans?"

"I'd like to find a child to bring out, and I want to leave tomorrow morning. I wish I could stay and fight with you, but I have a little girl I am caring for, and I need to be with her."

"I understand. We will try to be of assistance. Let's hope nothing unexpected happens. I assume you are catching a train?"

"Yes. It leaves at either ten a.m. or two p.m. I'm guessing that trying to catch the earlier train is not realistic."

"If you want to visit with Halinka and find a child to bring out, I would agree—it won't be possible. Here," Antek said with some passion, "let me show you our bunker."

Antek opened a door to what might have been some sort of cold storage room before the war. He shone a flashlight around. The walls were lined with broken shelves, stained brown by former contents. Old meat and vegetable boxes were scattered about. Pieces of broken glass lay on the floor and made walking hazardous. The ground crunched under their steps. The place was a mess.

"Well," Antek said, as he raised his arms around him, "what do you think?" He saw Rachel's confused look. "I admit," he said with a smile, "we could have used the decorating sense of a woman." Then, with a laugh, he put his hand under a broken shelf and lifted it up. The back of the shelf swung away and revealed a passageway. They stepped through.

They walked down the dirt-walled passageway, which was illuminated by electric lights, and entered a room to their left. Rachel was astonished: the room held forty beds. The beds had clearly been scavenged from various places, since they were different heights, colors, and styles. A few men looked up as she and Antek entered, and they nodded their heads in greeting. None of them seemed surprised to see a woman enter. They were more interested in their card game.

"Let me put you in a bed away from the entrance; you'll have less chance of being disturbed. How does this look?" Antek said as he patted a white frame bed on one side of the room. Two worn blankets were on the bed.

"It will be fine," Rachel answered. "I am not taking anyone's bed, am I?"

"No, we have lots of vacancies at 'Hotel Nowolipki' tonight. When the *Aktion* begins, however, we will be full. In fact, when the *Aktion* begins, bunkers will be full all across the ghetto. Virtually no one will be living above ground. There's an entire underground city here."

Antek pointed to a door on the far side of the room. "The toilets are over there. Across the passageway is the kitchen, where we have running water. You can get a bowl of soup and some bread there. We also have a separate air supply, and there is an emergency exit at the other end of the passageway. It comes out on Smocza Street. We could hold out down here for weeks if we had enough food."

Chapter 59: Commander Halinka
Rachel, Western Poland, April 1943

Rachel didn't sleep well that night; she was in a strange place and in a strange bed. She also wasn't used to being in a large room sleeping with a bunch of men, some of whom snored loudly. But more than that, it seemed that nothing that day had gone according to plan. She recalled Halinka's words when she barely escaped the SS officer on the train: "But you *did* make it, and you *are* here." Rachel did have a place to lay her head and she was safe, but she wondered what the morrow would bring. She felt as if she were inexorably being pulled into the coming fight, as if a silken web of circumstances was weaving itself around her, making it harder and harder for her to leave. A part of her heart wanted to stand with her people, but another part of her heart was deeply committed to Esther. Esther, she knew, had to win out.

After a breakfast of bread and ersatz coffee, Rachel and Antek set out for Halinka's location. She learned there were three main areas where fighters had gathered: the "productive ghetto," which is where she had spent the night and where many factories were located; the "central ghetto," where Halinka was and where many Jews lived; and the "brushmakers' ghetto" at the northeast end of the ghetto boundaries, where there was a large brushmaking operation. Each of these areas was near a major entrance and crossroads of the ghetto. The Jews believed the Germans would of necessity have to use these entryways.

The Jews positioned groups of twenty fighters each at all four corners of major intersections; they took refuge in the upper floors of buildings, where they enjoyed excellent visibility. Halinka was apparently in charge of one of these groups.

As Rachel and Antek climbed the stairs to the top level, Rachel noticed people moving things out of their apartments—eating utensils, mattresses, food. A few doors hung open, and Rachel could see that no one was inside. She suddenly understood: *These people are moving into bunkers.*

Upon approaching Halinka's location, they were stopped by a sentry, who asked for the password. Antek answered, "Maccabee." They entered a building that was situated at the corner of an intersection and climbed the stairs to the fourth floor. The door was opened by a fighter, pistol in hand. The fighter flashed a smile as soon as he saw Antek.

"Antek, good to see you! It's been a while. What brings you over this way?"

"I have a friend who wants to see Halinka."

"Come in," he said, motioning for them to enter.

As she entered, Rachel could see it was a spacious corner apartment furnished with tables, chairs, and two sofas. Piles of belongings lay scattered about, evidence of the fighters' recent arrival.

"Let me get Halinka," he said. Then turning, he said somewhat loudly, "Halinka, someone here to see you."

There was a pause as Halinka walked over. Her eyes grew wide as she asked with surprise, "Teresa? Is that you? What are you doing here?" Before Rachel could answer, Halinka gave Rachel one of her well-known hugs. "Everyone," she said, facing the group, "this is Teresa. Many of you have weapons and ammunition because of her. She is one of the bravest women I know." The fighters erupted into spontaneous applause, and Rachel blushed.

"It is wonderful to see you, but how did you get here?" Halinka asked, this time waiting for a reply. After Rachel gave her an abbreviated version of the previous day's events, Halinka said, "I am so sorry I wasn't at the safe house. Some wires obviously got crossed. Things are mixed up right now—you can see we are getting ready to fight."

"What am I doing here is a good question," Rachel said. "I wanted to bring in one last suitcase. I wanted," and here she bit her lip, "to see you one last time and say goodbye. And I wanted to take out one last child before the next *Aktion* begins. I can see now I underestimated what this would entail, but I hope it might still be possible."

"We'll do what we can. As you are aware, we don't have much time." Halinka glanced at Antek. "Antek, I don't want to keep you. I can have someone escort Teresa back. I am sure you have plenty to do."

Antek looked at Rachel. "Don't stay too long. We don't know when things will begin, but we expect them to start soon." He started to leave, then stopped and turned around to face her. "I almost forgot. I

209

have something for you. You may need these before your time with us is over," he said, reaching into his pockets and pulling out a pistol and some bullets. "It seems appropriate that they came from your suitcase."

Rachel was taken aback. "Are you sure about this? Aren't there other fighters who need them more than me? After all, I will be leaving."

Halinka looked at her and merely said, "Everyone up here needs a weapon." Rachel accepted the pistol and bullets awkwardly, carefully taking the bullets in one hand and the pistol in the other. She had never held a gun before.

"Now," Antek said to Rachel, "you are like one of us."

Another silken thread was added.

Chapter 60: Rebeka
Rachel, Western Poland, April 1943

"You wanted to bring a child over," Halinka said to Rachel. "Now that an *Aktion* is imminent, we will have many takers. The problem will be in choosing just one. I'm afraid, by the way, it will be too risky to try to take more than one. In fact, even that will be difficult. Dolek," she said, and a young man got up from where he was talking with others and came over to her. "We need to find a child to take out of the ghetto. I would suggest a female with Polish looks. Can you locate one? People will be down in the bunkers. You will have to be discreet, or we may cause chaos."

"I think I can find one. Give me an hour or so."

"Excellent. In the meantime," Halinka said, speaking now to Rachel, "I want you to learn how to use this," referring to the pistol in Rachel's hand. "Julian," she said, and another young man got to his feet. "Show Teresa how to use this, but obviously don't fire it. We are going to need all the bullets we have."

Rachel subsequently received a crash course in how to use a pistol. It was an old, World War I, six-shot revolver from the Polish army. With the gun empty, they picked out a target—a shop door across the street. "Now," Julian said, "you hold it with both hands, your arms straight and close to your body, and slowly lower it onto the target, lining up the sight. Pull the trigger with smooth pressure, using your index finger positioned halfway between the end of your finger and the first knuckle." Rachel practiced this. "Remember, there will be recoil, which will be stronger than you think." After Rachel had practiced a few more times, Julian showed her how to load the pistol and put on the safety.

"In reality," Julian told her, "a pistol is a short-range weapon—thirty feet or so, and that's if you've practiced. It is difficult to shoot a pistol accurately down five stories, especially at a moving target, like we are trying to do here. We really need rifles. But we make do with what we have. Remember, you have only a few bullets, so make them count. If you fire from this distance, try to aim at a group of soldiers—you're more likely to hit something."

Just then Dolek walked in the door holding the hand of a young girl. She had fine features, with blond hair and blue eyes, and was holding a book in her other hand. "This," he told everyone, "is Rebeka. Rebeka is nine years old, loves reading fairy tales, and her favorite color is yellow. She will be leaving with Teresa."

Rachel smiled. "How do you know all that about Rebeka?"

"Because," he replied, "she is my sister."

Dear God, Rachel thought, *another witness. Probably the only one of her family who will be left.* And then she caught herself. As she looked at the fighters around her and thought of where she was, she was impressed with the feeling, *assuming she and I survive.* Her thoughts were interrupted by a phone ringing.

"You have a phone here?" Rachel asked no one in particular.

"For now. Once the fighting starts, it will surely be cut off," a fighter answered. "But we have several backup methods, including this young man here," he said, and he ruffled the hair of a boy about twelve years old. "He is what we call a 'runner.' He knows how to move through the ghetto without being seen."

Halinka took the call and quickly became immersed in conversation. At one point, Rachel heard her mention the name of Antek, the fighter who had brought her over this morning.

Halinka turned to Rachel as soon as she hung up the phone. "I have some bad news. The western side of the ghetto is now surrounded by policemen. The entrance you used to get here is no longer open. We'll have to rely on the tunnel at Muranowska Street, near the brushmakers' ghetto, on the northeast side. But it will take a while before we can arrange to get you there. Until then, welcome to our little army."

The web was closing around Rachel.

Chapter 61: The Train
Jacob, Eastern Poland, April 1943

Jacob had been on a dozen sabotage missions, but this was the first one he had led. He was to take a group of thirty partisans to destroy a train carrying troops and supplies to the Russian front. It was a troop train, which was both good and bad. On the plus side, they would have the opportunity to directly attack the Germans, but on the negative side, the partisans would be in much greater danger if something went wrong. Just thinking about it gave Jacob a knot in his stomach.

It was the first mission of this kind for about a third of the unit; they were excited and nervous but happy to be fighting the enemy. The newcomers were a motley group: a baker, an accountant, a carpenter, a lawyer, two merchants, two teachers, and a nurse, all now turned into budding partisans. They even had a rabbi with them. They were extremely conscientious and responsive to Jacob's commands, though he was much younger than most of them.

After traveling by foot much of the night and most of the next day, they arrived safely at the railway line in the middle of the afternoon. Twice they had detoured when scouts reported activity in front of them. The train was supposed to be along within the next two hours.

The railway tracks were about forty yards from the edge of the forest. Jacob sent out two reconnaissance teams—one up-track and one down-track. After half an hour, they reported back in: there was no sign of enemy patrols. Ideally, Jacob wanted a section of track that was going downhill with an outside curve. The down-track team reported that there was such a section a quarter-mile away. They hiked down to it.

Jacob wanted a downhill section of track because it would make it harder for the train to stop. He wanted an outside curve because it would be easier for a machine gun positioned up-track some distance to shoot in *enfilade*—down the length of the train instead of across from it. With the other machine gun positioned to fire across the tracks, the Germans would be caught in a cross-fire.

Jacob and his men needed to work quickly and avoid being out in the open as much as possible. He ordered most of the unit to take positions in the forest with weapons at the ready. He stationed several men as lookouts. He ordered Eliasz and Adam to cut the communication lines running alongside the tracks.

Sitting at the edge of the trees, Jacob asked Yitzhak to bring up the artillery shell and fuse they would use for the demolition. Yitzhak unloaded his knapsack, carefully placing the sixty-pound shell in front of them. Its tarnished brass jacket, pewter-colored charge, and sleek shape all gave it a lethal appearance. The fuse on the tip was not attached. Yitzhak placed it next to the shell.

"Is this a modified fuse?" Jacob asked.

Yitzhak was confused by the question. "This is the fuse I was given," he replied, hesitantly.

"This is a regular contact fuse, and it doesn't work for trains," Jacob explained. "It is a fuse that detonates when a shell at high speed strikes the ground or an object. You should have been given a modified fuse that detonates by pressure, such as what happens when a train rolls over the track with the shell buried beneath it."

"This is the only fuse I have," repeated Yitzhak.

"Are you sure?"

"Yes, this is the only one."

Jacob was dumbfounded. This *couldn't* be the only fuse they had. He called Samuel over. "Samuel, check with every person in the group and see if by chance we have another fuse."

Samuel nodded and left. He returned shortly and reported that there were no other fuses.

How could this have happened? Jacob had asked Yitzhak before they left if he had the fuse, and Yitzhak had said that he did. Now Jacob realized he hadn't been specific enough. Had they come all this way for nothing? How could he explain this to his commander? He could imagine himself saying, "Well, when we got there we discovered we didn't have the proper fuse, so we didn't accomplish the mission." He was reminded of an American movie he had once seen called *The Keystone Cops*. This felt like *The Partisan Keystone Cops*. Mentally he upbraided himself.

Jacob knew it would not help to get upset. As he sometimes did while digging the tunnel, he calmed down by quietly giving himself a pep talk. *You can do this. Get rid of the negative thoughts. Focus on a solution.*

Jacob decided he would call a "council of war." He called Samuel over as well as Aaron Bandt, men whose judgment he trusted, and explained the situation. "Somehow we did not bring a modified fuse with us. All we have is a regular contact fuse."

Aaron had a knack for boiling things down to their essentials. "We have to figure out a way to get the regular fuse to work, or derail the train some other way," he said.

Jacob could see the wisdom in starting on a backup plan for derailing the train while they debated if they could get the shell to explode. They probably didn't have enough time to do something else, but they had to try. They would work on the old-fashioned way of derailing a train: bending the rails out of position. He sent for Chiam, one of the experienced partisans, and told him, "Round up anyone with a crowbar. Then get them started pulling out spikes. Pull out as many as you can on both rails."

"Yes, sir," Chiam replied.

Meanwhile, Aaron and Samuel were discussing ways to get the detonator to work, trying to figure out how to hit it hard enough so it would explode. So far, they hadn't come up with an idea they were enthusiastic about. Overhearing the conversation, Moshe the baker made the most plausible suggestion. "Could we fire the shell by laying it on its side and shooting from the forest at its firing pin? If we could, the propellant in the shell would ignite, driving the charge and detonator forward. We could put something in front of it, like a big rock, that would actuate the detonator and set off the explosive."

The whole conversation was somewhat surreal to Jacob, but Moshe's suggestion was the best of the lot. Jacob quickly asked a crew of three men to excavate a trench between two railroad ties. They laid the shell on its side. The regular fuse was installed in the tip, which was pointed at a large rock they had buried about a foot away. The back end of the shell was exposed, poking out from underneath the rails.

"I've been thinking," Aaron said. "Rather than have several of us fire at the shell from the forest, let's place a rifle behind the shell with its muzzle right up against the firing pin. If we tie a cord to the trigger, we can trip it from the forest. Otherwise, we may miss or damage the firing pin; either one would be a problem. You can use my rifle if you want. I'll be manning one of the light machine guns."

"You realize you won't get it back if the shell explodes," Samuel said in jest.

"If it explodes, I don't think I'll care," Aaron responded with a grin.

Jacob was growing more incredulous by the minute, but he had to admit Aaron's suggestion had merit. "Let's do it," he said.

After securing the shell under the tracks, they positioned a rifle with its muzzle against the firing pin. They did their best to camouflage the rifle by covering it with gravel. Fortunately, it wouldn't matter too much if it were seen, since the train would be moving fast enough that it would be unable to stop in time.

Jacob called everyone together. "Remember the plan," he told them. "You will spread out in twos, everyone with your partner, for the next one hundred yards, staying behind cover. One machine gun should be in the middle and one at the far end. I don't know if the shell will go off, but if it does, make sure your ears are plugged, or you will wish they were. If it works, wait until you have a good target. The enemy troops will be confused and disoriented, and you will be tempted to start shooting immediately. I want each of you to carefully aim and fire your weapon. There is nothing like real fighting for experience, and one of the challenges is to make each shot count. If I sense the tide is about to turn, I'll give an order to withdraw. Samuel, Aaron, David, and Hertzel will cover for us. If anyone is hurt, pass the word for Masha. If the shell does not go off and the train does not derail, you will not fire. We will withdraw to fight another day. Any questions?"

"I would like to make a suggestion," said Zenek.

"Yes, go ahead."

"I suggest we have the rabbi say a prayer for us."

"An excellent suggestion. Rabbi Berkowicz, would you be willing?"

"Of course."

Everyone but Samuel gathered around. Samuel turned around and walked away.

Rabbi Berkowicz offered a prayer:

"Blessed are You, O Lord our God, King of the Universe,

We come before you as a small band of Your people
  who have suffered much.
Help us to remember Your mercy and lovingkindness,
Strengthen our arms and our hearts that we may stand
  against our enemy,
That we may destroy those who do evil in Your sight,
That we may uproot their wickedness and cast away
  their arrogance before You,
That we may yet see the redemption of Your people."

The group responded with a chorus of "Amen." As they dispersed to their positions, Jacob walked over to where Samuel was standing. "What's the matter?" he asked.

"What good has prayer ever done us? When has it ever saved us from the Germans? I've said a thousand prayers, and none were answered. I'd rather have a rifle than a rabbi. I'll put my faith in bullets, not in prayers."

Jacob didn't know how to respond. He had often leaned on Samuel for physical support. He wanted to offer Samuel spiritual support, but his own faith wavered sometimes. "I know many Jews who feel this way," he told Samuel. "I wish I could help. I am just glad to have you with me."

As Samuel turned and looked at Jacob, his anger softened. "We have been through a lot, my friend. Prayer or no prayer, I am also glad we can stand together and fight."

Now it was a waiting game. Everyone tried to relax until they could hear the train approaching. This was always the moment of highest tension for Jacob; his nerves were strung as taut as strings of a violin. Once the battle began, he was too busy fighting to be nervous. As the leader, he was responsible for the lives of these people, and the responsibility weighed heavily on him. He made himself not think about it. If he thought too much about it, he wouldn't be able to function.

It seemed to Jacob a lifetime since he had joined the partisans seven months ago. Nearly the only thing he knew then about guns was which end to point forward, and he barely knew that. But he was a dedicated student, and Bojarski was a patient teacher. Before long Jacob was given his own rifle, a badge of honor in the partisan world and an expression of trust by his leader. He looked down at the irregular line of his compatriots who were standing behind trees, kneeling behind boulders, or lying behind logs. Many had been just like him—they had never fired a gun before they joined the partisans. Now here they were, ready for battle. He had paired each new recruit with someone who was experienced. The older hands could steady the new ones.

The train was still a mile away when they first heard it. Everyone was on tenterhooks as they waited for it to appear. Finally, they saw it round a bend and approach their position.

Aaron had the assignment of pulling the cord when the engine was over the shell. Aaron timed things perfectly. To Jacob's astonishment and relief, the earth erupted with a tremendous explosion as soon as Aaron yanked the cord. The concussive force knocked anyone standing or kneeling flat to the ground. Clods of dirt and rock, shards of metal, and splinters of wood rained down on them. The engine was thrown up off the tracks; the boiler and firebox both ruptured, sending scalding steam and hot coals everywhere. The explosion left a crater thirty feet across. The troop cars right behind the engine careened through the crater, collapsed on their sides, and folded up against each other like a courtesan's fan. They were hit from behind as supply cars smashed into them. Fires broke out. It was an amazing spectacle.

Although stunned by the explosion, it took only a few moments for the partisans to recover. After a few seconds, the dust and debris began to clear a little, and the partisans could see German soldiers trying to free themselves through the doors and windows. Jacob wasn't sure who fired the first shot, but it was followed by an avalanche of bullets and several grenades. Bodies slumped over or fell back into the cars. The machine guns were raking the train from two different directions. The Germans were caught in a maelstrom of chaos and death.

Jacob began to pick off Germans with his rifle. Within seconds of pulling the trigger, he had cycled the bolt and was ready to fire again. His gun cracked five times, each time with effect, until the clip was empty. Then he loaded a new one and started again. At one point, Jacob aimed his rifle at a soldier who was slowly moving away from the wreckage, pulling something. He was about to fire when he realized the soldier was dragging an injured comrade. Jacob decided not to shoot someone trying to save a buddy. In an instant he moved his aim to a German unshouldering his rifle. He fired and saw the soldier drop. *For Samuel,* he thought, *this is a dream come true.*

With hundreds of Germans trying to escape the fires and fusillade, there were more targets than they could shoot at. Gradually the German soldiers established defensive positions and returned fire. It wouldn't be long before the partisans began suffering casualties.

"Pass the word to withdraw," Jacob told Chaim and Israel. People quickly formed into small, protective groups and began to move back. The Germans, picking up on a lull in the fighting, began to regroup. In a fury of anger, several German soldiers burst from the cover of the train and charged towards the forest. They were joined by several dozen others.

Jacob, seeing what was happening, understood he and the other partisans were in a precarious position. Once the Germans reached the woods, it would be one-on-one combat. The partisans would no longer have any advantage. They had to stop the Germans now.

No command was needed. Everyone turned and rejoined the battle. Not one person broke and ran. Here was a chance to live or die with their heads held high. They stood against the onslaught like a sea wall standing fast against the waves of a storm. Samuel, who was racing up from his position on their left flank, dropped to the ground to put his machine gun in action again. He looked down the entire length of the German attack, parallel to the edge of the forest, and raked their entire front with fire.

The Germans were met by a withering hail of bullets and grenades that seemed to stand them up and push them backwards. All along the line soldiers crumpled and fell. The charge was blunted and then broken. Only a few were able to crawl back to the safety of the train. There would not be another attack, at least not on this day. On this day the partisans owned the forest.

While the four covering their retreat made sure they were not followed, Jacob's small force reformed. Moshe had been hit in the shoulder; the bullet had gone clean through. Masha was plugging the wound to staunch the bleeding. Then, to his great sadness, Jacob saw two men run up carrying Anshel. He had been seriously wounded in the chest and was bleeding badly. Masha yanked a man over to finish the work on Moshe while she tended to Anshel. "We need to get out of here," Jacob said. "You'll have to tend to him on the move." Masha nodded. They rigged up a stretcher, and while four men carried Anshel, Masha walked or ran alongside, compressing his wounds with bandages even though she knew it was hopeless. They hiked back quickly towards their base. After an hour, Jacob called a halt.

As the adrenalin rush began to subside, they stood in awe at what they had done. They had dealt a blow to and pushed back their hated enemy. Gerszon, the lawyer, summed up many of their feelings when he said, "I will never forget this day as long as I live." It was, however, a subdued celebration—it had been a close-run thing, and they had lost Anshel. Even so, they clasped hands and passed around bottles of vodka. They were passive victims no longer.

It was Jacob who had the last word. "Not bad," he said half seriously, "for a bunch of amateurs."

Chapter 62: The First Battle in the Ghetto
Rachel, Western Poland, April 1943

Rachel realized how naïve she had been. Her escape route on the western side of the ghetto was closed. She had expected to get in and out of Warsaw before anything like this happened. Although she had missed being able to do that by only a few hours, she should have been a little less confident she could predict events. Now she did not know what the future held for her or Rebeka.

Have I been not only naïve, but foolish? Rachel did not know how to answer this question. *Still,* she thought, *if I can save Rebeka's life...* She settled down to wait, practicing using her pistol and getting to know Rebeka and the other fighters.

Rachel noticed rows of bottles standing on the floor around the windows. All the bottles had corks in the top, some with wicks of cloth and some with steel wires sticking out from the corks. When she asked Julian about them, he said, "These are our homemade firebombs. They are filled with gasoline. We soak the wick in kerosene or alcohol, light it, and throw the bottle. When the bottle hits the target it shatters, covering everything around it in flames."

"What about the ones with wires?" she asked.

"The wired ones don't need to be lit. Pulling the wire mixes two chemicals in the bottle that start to burn. It's helpful to have some chemists in our midst."

Rachel realized the possibility of her successful escape with Rebeka was becoming less certain by the hour. The fighters had learned that security had now increased around the entire ghetto, including around Muranowska Street, with police stationed every twenty feet. Sensing her concern, Halinka said, "Don't give up hope. The Muranowska tunnel is well camouflaged. I think we'll still be able to get you and Rebeka out." Rachel settled down to spend the night, curling up with a blanket on the floor next to Rebeka, who was on the couch.

At five a.m. Monday morning they were awakened by the muffled sounds of diesel engines and shouts some distance away. They could hear soldiers' boots stamping on cobblestones as they entered the ghetto at the gate on Gęsia Street. The soldiers were headed in their direction.

The ominous stamp of boots got louder until several hundred German soldiers, marching in formation and stretching the length of the entire block, came into view. Seeing them took Rachel's breath away. They were like a dark swarm of insects crawling toward them. Their marching in the open expressed their disdain for the Jews. There was no need to take cover. What could the Jews do?

The soldiers halted at the intersection of Zamenhofa and Miła streets, exactly where the Jews expected them to come. There were teams of fighters at every attic window ringing the intersection. Each team was ready with firebombs, grenades, and pistols. Only two of the fighters had rifles.

"Light the wicks," Halinka ordered, "but wait until the signal is given from across the street." The German soldiers below them were now at ease, unsuspecting, waiting for further orders.

Rachel had Rebeka crawl underneath one of the sofas and then packed cushions around the little girl. "It's going to get loud," Rachel told her, "so cover your ears. But don't worry; I'll be checking on you. Do you think you can be brave?" Rebeka nodded. Before this trip, never would Rachel have imagined being in a battle with her fellow Jews *and* having a child with her. The only thing that eased her worry a little was knowing that if not here, Rebeka would be hiding in a dark bunker.

The fighters saw a bottle sail out of an attic window across the street and spiral down to the pavement before exploding among the soldiers. A sea of flame spread where it hit, and men began scattering. One man was screaming, covered in flames. A dozen more bottles and grenades followed, filling the street with explosions and fire. Pistols fired all around. The Germans, stunned and unbelieving, looked up. They were being attacked by Jews!

It was pandemonium in the street. The Germans ran for cover, leaving their wounded lying where they fell. The soldiers fired back, but it was not an even playing field, for the Jews were well protected by their window parapets while the Germans were exposed.

"Come here," Julian yelled at Rachel. "See the knot of men taking cover behind the wagon? Fire your pistol at them—just one or two shots." Rachel took off the safety and then, as she had practiced, lowered the gun until the sight lined up with the back side of the wagon. She pulled the trigger. She expected the loud bang, for pistols were firing all around her, but the kick of the pistol surprised her. She had no idea whether she had hit anything. In the excitement of the battle, she found shooting the pistol wonderfully thrilling. She not only felt as if she were truly one of the fighters, but she reveled in striking back. In fact, she couldn't help but aim and fire again.

"Okay, that's good," Julian told her. "Keep lighting those bottles." Rachel had assigned herself the task of lighting the wicks so the others could throw the bottles faster. First, she ran over to Rebeka and removed a few of the cushions. Rebeka had her eyes closed tightly and her hands over her ears.

"Are you all right?" Rachel asked. She had to yell to make herself heard. Rebeka didn't answer but just nodded slightly. "You are doing great. Keep it up! I'll be back soon," and she pressed Rebeka's arm and re-bundled the cushions around her.

Suddenly they heard a clanking noise coming up the street as a tank crawled into the intersection. Within the narrow confines of the street, it could not elevate its gun enough to fire on the upper stories of the buildings around it. Instead, it fired a shell into the ground floor of one of the corner buildings, blowing out walls and leaving a gaping hole in the façade. Rachel realized that a few more hits like that and the building would collapse, taking the upper floors with it.

But no sooner had the tank fired than it was engulfed in firebombs from all sides. A few of them shattered on the rear deck where the flaming gasoline seeped into vents of the engine compartment. Within minutes the tank was on fire, sending a plume of smoke billowing into the sky. Rachel saw hatches open and the crew trying to escape. Shots rang out all around her; she heard the pinging of bullets ricocheting off the tank turret, yet the crew managed somehow to stumble to safety. If only the fighters had more rifles or a machine gun, the crew would not have gotten away!

The battle raged for some thirty minutes before the Germans withdrew, dragging their wounded with them. For the first time, Jews in the ghetto had fought and beat back a German assault. Their victory, and victory in two other battles fought about the same time at other intersections, was heralded by the raising of two flags high above Muranowski Square—one the Polish flag, the other a flag of blue and white.

The Jewish fighters had, for the moment, triumphed. They allowed themselves a few minutes to celebrate with hugs and backslapping and excited recounting of events. Rachel had rarely felt such exhilaration, and the fighters seemed to enjoy having a pretty girl they could hug and kiss! It was a grand moment.

Halinka eventually brought them back to earth. "We need to leave this spot. The Germans will surely target it when they return. We'll go to the strongpoint at Kupiecka 18. Let's get moving. We'll need to pack all the bottles carefully." Not even ten minutes later mortar shells began dropping on the intersection, smashing rooftops and blowing craters in the street.

Because many of the buildings in the ghetto were roughly the same height, paths had been created through attics of adjacent buildings. Often the buildings sat right up against each other, so it was easy to move from one building to another. But sometimes they had to rely on ladders or planks thrown down between the buildings to cross a gap of several feet or more; those few steps high above the ground could be terrifying for anyone who didn't like heights, including Rachel. She quickly learned not to stop or look at the ground, but to look only straight ahead. Fortunately, Rebeka had her sure-footed brother to carry her.

The fighters moved through the attics of several buildings before dropping down to street level, then down into a cellar and through a tunnel that took them across the street to Kupiecka, a side street off Zamenhofa. "The whole ghetto is now a catacomb of tunnels and passages," Dolek told Rachel. "That's how we'll get you to the tunnel at Muranowska."

That afternoon the Germans returned, but they had learned from the morning's debacle. They operated in small groups and spread themselves out, running from doorway to doorway. An armored car in the lead rolled into the intersection, and while the fighters watched from half a block away, a torrent of flame gushed from the side of the armored car into one of the corner buildings, setting the interior ablaze. The fighters realized the entire building would soon be enveloped in flames. They knew that any remaining fighters could move through the attics to safety, but those in the bunkers would be trapped. If they didn't have an alternative source of air, they would be asphyxiated; if they didn't have another escape route, they would be burned to death. The Germans set every corner building on fire and then began to move slowly down the street, searching for bunkers, yelling for the Jews to come out, and burning the buildings on both sides.

"Runner," cried Halinka. His face alight with eagerness, Jakub, the boy Rachel had seen earlier, came to Halinka's side for instructions. "Get to Miła 18. Tell Mordechai where we are and ask him what he wants us to do. Tell him the Germans are burning down the central ghetto with a flamethrower. Ask if the tunnel out of the ghetto at Muranowska is still open. Now repeat the message back to me." Jakub did so. As he finished, Halinka said, "On your way. I hope to see you back here this evening. If we have to leave here, we'll go to Kupiecka 4, so if we're not here when you return, meet us there."

Jakub was back within two hours. Digging something out of his pocket, he told Halinka, "Mordechai gave me this note for you." Halinka opened it and read, *We expect an attack at the brushmakers' ghetto tomorrow morning. Position yourself across from the main entrance on Wołowa Street. Wait to fire until those inside start shooting.*

Halinka looked up at Jakub and said, "Good job. Anything else?"

"I asked about the tunnel. Mordechai said the only way out of the ghetto now is through the sewers."

The web drew tighter.

Chapter 63: Passover

Rachel, Western Poland, April 1943

That night—Passover evening—the ghetto was quiet, giving the Jews an opportunity to gather for their Passover Seder. It was perhaps the most unique Passover in Jewish history. They had only water for wine and potato peels for matzos, but they were determined and willing to improvise, and among them the fighters were able to piece together the Haggadah.[*]

It was a joy to have Rebeka there. By tradition, the youngest person present asks four questions. As she sat on her brother's lap, her sweet voice called out: "Why is it that on all other nights we eat leavened or unleavened bread, but on this night we eat only unleavened bread?"

A voice from the group responded, "The unleavened bread reminds us of when we were slaves. It also reminds us that we had to take flight so quickly bread did not have time to rise."

"Why is it that on all other nights we eat all kinds of vegetables, but on this night we eat only bitter herbs?"

Another person replied, "The bitter herbs remind us of the bitterness of slavery."

"Why is it that on all other nights we do not dip our food once, but on this night we dip it twice?"

"The salt water into which we dip the vegetables represents the tears we cried while in Egypt. The fruit-nut paste reminds us of the clay we used to create bricks in Egypt."

"Why is it that on all other nights we eat either sitting up or reclining, but on this night we only eat reclining?"

"On this night we remember our freedom by reclining like royalty."

The Seder was deeply moving to Rachel, as she guessed it was to all who were present. As they celebrated the redemption of the Jews from Pharaoh, ruler of Egypt, she thought about how she was now witnessing—in fact, how she was now *living through*—the redemption of the Jews from the Nazis, rulers of Europe. What a different redemption it was!

---

[*] The *Haggadah* gives the steps and words recited at the Passover meal.

The fighters hoped they could hold out for at least a week. They expected to die fighting; they expected that everyone in the ghetto would be killed. There would be no parting of the Red Sea during this redemption. If a score was kept of Jewish and German casualties starting that day, and if each side was given a point for each casualty it inflicted, they knew the final score would be something like Germans: 50,000; Jews: 200. Despite these numbers, Rachel knew it was nevertheless a redemption—a liberation from slavery, a victory for the Jews.

As the Seder drew to a close, Halinka announced, "We are going over to Wołowa Street to help with an expected attack tomorrow on the brushmakers' ghetto. It won't take long to get there, because we can move through the streets—the Germans seem to have abandoned the ghetto for tonight." As they moved to their new location, their way was partially lit by the reflection of flickering flames off the low clouds in the sky. The air was tinged with smoke and ash.

After reaching their new base, Halinka said, "Teresa, I need to speak with you." Halinka drew her aside and lowered her voice to afford Rachel some privacy. "The tunnel at Muranowska won't work. Mordechai says the only way out is the sewers. For that we will need a guide—it is a maze of passages down there, and some are flooded. There is still some hope, but right now I don't know how much."

"It is all right," Rachel quietly replied. "It is my fault. I will take what comes. I only regret . . ." she said, her voice trailing off.

"Esther?" Halinka asked.

"Yes, Esther, and now maybe Rebeka."

"If it's any consolation, Rebeka would be no safer with her family. In fact, she would have no chance at all. There will be nothing left when the Germans are done."

"I will pray she might still get out, regardless of what happens to me."

The fighters explored their new location across from the gate to the brushmakers' ghetto. They looked out on a plaza about fifty yards wide. They needed at least one escape route through buildings, either through the cellar or the attic. Halinka detailed two fighters to scout out these routes and stationed sentries all around.

The ghetto was now like a ghost town. The fighters could enter virtually any door and find an empty, furnished apartment behind it.

All the occupants had either been deported in the *Grossaktion* or were hiding in bunkers. They took up positions on the upper floors, as they had the day before.

Rachel was surprised at the mundane things needed for war, such as brushes. Paintbrushes, brooms, brushes for applying grease, brushes for cleaning weapons—these were the products the Jews made in the aptly named brushmakers' ghetto. Most of the workers lived in barracks next to the factory; it did not occur to the Germans that the workers would now be in bunkers and that the people in the factory would be squads of fighters.

As they relaxed and waited, Halinka and Rachel had a chance to talk. "How did you feel about today?" Rachel asked.

"Today was very satisfying," Halinka replied. "I wasn't sure we'd even be able to bloody the nose of the Germans. I think we did that and more, but I don't know how many days like this we'll have left."

"What do you think will happen tomorrow?" Rachel asked.

"The battle tomorrow should be especially interesting. You see the plaza in front of the brushmaking factory? We've planted a bomb under it."

"A bomb?" Rachel repeated in surprise. "How did you get hold of a bomb?"

"We made it," Halinka explained. "Antek was able to smuggle in a 'cake' of TNT. We packed it into a four-inch-diameter pipe and put the pipe in a box of nuts, bolts, and scrap iron, just to make it more exciting. It will be detonated from inside the factory if and when the Germans show up. Let's just hope the Germans decide to enter in a good-sized group. It would be a shame to waste it on two or three."

"That explains why earlier I heard some fighters betting on how many Germans would enter the plaza," Rachel said.

"Whatever happens," Halinka added, "we'll have a ringside seat from where we are."

***

The next day the fighters were ready by five a.m., but all they could do was wait. It was past ten before they heard anything coming their way. A scout reported that a group of fifty Germans, marching in formation, was approaching the entrance to the brushmakers' ghetto. In front of them were some members of the Jewish police force, being prodded by bayonets. The Jewish police had always assumed they had protected status. As fellow Jews, they were hated because of the active part they played in rounding up families for deportation during the *Grossaktion*. Having betrayed their countrymen, they were now being betrayed by the Germans. It was, Rachel thought, poetic justice.

Halinka warned everyone to stay back from the windows. Rachel took Rebeka and sat on the floor at the back of the room, hugging the little girl tightly and covering her ears and eyes with her hands and arms.

As the mixed Jewish/German contingent approached the entrance to the factory, the Jews were halted outside the gate. A group of thirty to forty Germans stepped into the plaza and approached the factory doors yelling, "*Juden, raus! Juden schwein raus!**"

The air inside the building was electric with tension. Rachel could hear many of the fighters saying under their breath, "Now! Now!"

The building in which the fighters were hidden was rocked by an explosion. All the windows shattered, and glass flew everywhere. Rebeka screamed, and Rachel toppled over with her from the force of the blast. They were pelted with debris—pebbles and dirt, fragments of metal, bits of red slime. It took a moment for Rachel to realize that the slime was what was left of bodies.

As the dust settled, the fighters crawled to the windows. They could see a large crater where the soldiers had been, with bodies of German soldiers scattered around the perimeter. Some of the Jewish policemen were also on the ground. There were still a few soldiers staggering about. Without hesitating, Halinka ordered, "Open fire!" As if they heard her, the fighters inside the factory began firing as well, catching the Germans in a deadly crossfire. They had no choice but to withdraw.

---

* Jews come out! Jewish swine come out!

Chapter 64: The Train, Part Two
Helmuth, Eastern Poland, April-July 1943

Shortly after Helmuth's experience with Rachel, Halinka, and the children, Helmuth approached Paul.

"I don't want to be here anymore. I'm putting in for a transfer to the eastern front, back to the *Waffen SS*. I'm not sure they'll take me with my injury, but with the defeat at Stalingrad, I'm guessing the generals are hungry for men. If I can't get into the *Waffen SS*, I'll go as a regular soldier."

Paul considered this. "Does this have something to do with the killing of children?" he asked.

"It has everything to do with the killing of children. What is being done here makes me sick. How have we as a people come to this—killing old men and women and *children*?"

"If they'll let me, I'll come with you," Paul replied.

Several weeks later, they were in the middle of a long, slow train journey of more than seven hundred miles to the front in Russia. The train car rocked with a gentle rhythm, accompanied by the clacking of the wheels on the track. They were passing through a forest, and though patches of snow still covered the ground, there was a warmth in the air that presaged spring. Helmuth looked around. Men were chatting and playing cards; a group of men was singing to tunes played on an accordion.

Suddenly a huge explosion came from the front of the train. Before Helmuth could register what was happening, the car flipped over and began skidding down the track, ramming violently into other cars. Seats came loose, luggage and gear were thrown all over, and windows were smashed. The car came to a stop on its side with another car partially on top of it. The car filled with smoke, and Helmuth could hear steam hissing.

Shouting and yelling for help, men began to crawl out windows and through a jagged hole in the ceiling (now one of the sides) of the car. Several soldiers managed to kick one of the doors open enough to squeeze through.

For few moments there was silence. Then a wave of noise rolled over them as they were hit with an onslaught of bullets and grenades. Men fell from the windows, wounded or dead. Bullets penetrated inside the car, causing everyone to seek cover behind broken benches or to lay on the floor.

Helmuth was battered but able to move. He looked over at Paul and saw he was pinned on the floor under some wreckage. Seeing that Paul needed help, several men crawled over and lifted the wreckage enough that Helmuth could pull him free. "Are you badly hurt?" he shouted.

"I think my leg is broken," Paul yelled back. The smoke was getting worse, and bullets were pinging around them.

Helmuth knew they had to get out before everything caught on fire or they were hit. They would have to get out through the jagged hole in the side. Unfortunately, that would bring them into the open, exposing them even more to the partisans' fire, but he had no choice.

"I'm going to get us out of here," Helmuth yelled. Paul nodded. Helmuth wrapped the arm of his good shoulder around Paul's chest. He began to drag him out of the car and up the embankment. He didn't stop until he reached the other side and they were safe.

Somehow, they escaped being hit, even though they felt bullets zing past them. A man next to them who was unshouldering his rifle was killed.

The wounded, including Paul, were taken back to hospitals, while the rest of the division regrouped and secured new transport. This time they were able to finish their journey, disembarking several hundred miles southwest of Moscow. They were getting ready for Operation Citadel, planned to begin in the summer.

Chapter 65: Again In Russia
Helmuth, Russia, July 1943

Helmuth was back in the *Waffen SS*, but just as a regular infantryman. Things were very different now than they were before Helmuth's injury. Then the soldiers had been brimming with confidence. They were the vaunted German army—they were invincible. Now things had changed. Now they were backing up across ground they once had conquered, retracing their steps. The destruction wrought by the Germans and the Russians' scorched earth policy meant nothing was left. There were no villages, no crops, no people. All was barren.

Helmuth could not help but think that what had happened in Russia was a type of what had happened in his life. Initially he had been so confident Germany was right. The Germans were morally superior; they deserved this land as *lebensraum**, and they were justified in destroying supposedly inferior peoples. But now he was backing up; now he doubted everything—now all was barren. He felt only emptiness.

As he considered what he had done in Warsaw, he no longer cared whether he lived or died. How could he have become so lost? Perhaps if he died, he could atone for the sins he had committed.

On July 16, during the battle of Citadel, his wish was granted.

---
* living space

Chapter 66: The Ghetto in Flames
Rachel, Warsaw, April 1943

The battle at the brushmakers' ghetto was the high-water mark for the ghetto fighters. They subsequently fought a long, losing battle against superior forces with superior weapons. It was impossible for their pistols and firebombs to compete with machine guns and howitzers, tanks and flamethrowers.

On the third day of the uprising, the Germans settled on their strategy to subdue the ghetto. They brought in dogs to sniff out the Jews, and they bribed or tortured captives into revealing where the bunkers were. Jews flushed out of bunkers were forced at gunpoint to the *Umschlagplatz*, from which they were taken to labor or extermination camps. The Germans then burned the ghetto down, street by street and house by house. People caught in burning buildings leapt from balconies to their deaths, sometimes holding children in their arms. People caught in the ever-increasing heat of the bunkers, buried underground in the dark, sometimes went mad before they died.

***

On the third night, Halinka gathered her group in the interior courtyard of an apartment complex. They needed to move again. The buildings all around them were on fire, making it light as day. They were going to try to make it to their headquarters at Miła 18. There they would try to find a guide to take Rachel and Rebeka out through the sewers. Rachel knew that one way or another, her time here would soon be over.

They ran through the cellars of burning buildings. The walls radiated such heat that they felt they would burn up. The floor was covered in a soft, spongy ash. Looking down at her feet, Rachel could see the ash contained charred bodies.

They managed to make it to some buildings that were not on fire, where they decided to rest for a few minutes. They gathered in a sub-basement that had some small windows about six feet from the floor. The fires outside cast flickering shadows through the windows onto the walls. As Rachel looked at the windows, something caught her eye. She noticed a shadow come over part of one window and then stop.

Suddenly the window was smashed by the muzzle of a rifle. The protruding barrel was pointed directly at Halinka. There was no time—no time to think, no time to aim a pistol. Rachel acted instinctively; she couldn't help herself. What she did was because of who she was. "No!" she screamed, and she threw herself in front of Halinka.

There was a sharp crack as the German rifle fired. The bullet hit Rachel in her right side, and she collapsed to the floor. Several pistols around her fired back, silencing the intruder.

Fighters ripped off shirts to use as bandages. Halinka cradled Rachel's head in her lap and tried to comfort her while others tried to stop the bleeding. There was very little they could do. As Rachel struggled to breathe, Halinka was beside herself. "Teresa," she said in a whisper, "How can I lose you in this way? Oh, Teresa, Teresa. . . ."

As Halinka held her through the night, Rachel slipped in and out of consciousness. At one point, she asked for some water. Another time she gasped out Esther's name. "Shhh . . . don't worry," Halinka said, with tears streaming down her face, "I will take care of Esther."

Around four a.m., Rachel's breathing became shallower. Knowing what this portended, Halinka comforted her friend. "It is all right. You can go now. You will be remembered in the halls of the righteous. I will take care of Esther and Rebeka." With a gurgle and one last breath, Rachel was gone.

It was almost dawn.

Chapter 67: Rachel's Letter
Father Sobieski, Western Poland, May 1943

Several weeks after Rachel failed to return from Warsaw, *Frau* Kohler visited Father Sobieski in his office. "We were so very sorry to lose Julia," she told him. "The children miss her very much. You say she was killed in an accident? Did the accident have anything to do with the Germans?"

"You are perceptive. Yes," he said, nodding, "I'm afraid it *did* have something to do with the Germans. She was a very brave woman. A true patriot." The Father's voice broke and he paused to compose himself. "I will also miss her very much. I thought of her as I would a daughter."

"She didn't have a lot, but I have brought her things with me. I thought perhaps you would know someone who could use them—the clothes, I mean."

"Yes, I'm sure we can put them to good use."

Reaching into her purse and retrieving an envelope, *Frau* Kohler said, "She also left a letter addressed to you."

As Father Sobieski took the envelope, he was struck by seeing his name on the outside. It was written by Rachel—he realized it was the only personal thing he had from her. What he would have lightly thrown away before he would now keep and cherish.

"Let us know if you find another governess, especially if she is like Julia."

"*Frau* Kohler," the Father said, acting on impulse. "I hesitate to ask this, but Julia was supporting an orphan. Someone who lost both parents in the war. If you had any inclination to help—"

"Yes, of course, Father. It would give me great pleasure to help a child, especially on behalf of Julia. Please send me a note about this, giving details and an amount."

"Thank you," he responded.

Then *Frau* Kohler said something that gave even the unflappable Father a start. "I will be going now. I don't suppose, Father, there will be any more suitcases. I am sorry for that."

After taking a few seconds to recover, he bid her goodbye, adding, "God bless you."

***

With trembling hands and an aching heart, Father Sobieski opened the letter. In Rachel's handwriting, he read:

>Dear Father,
>
>If you are reading this, it means I did not return from Warsaw. I am very sorry for that, for I love you and Maria, the Kohler children, and Esther. Know that I didn't give you up willingly. I will miss you very much.
>
>I'm sure I don't need to ask, but please take care of Esther. I know she is very special to you as well as to me. Tell her how sorry I am. I had hoped I would have a chance to be with her for many years, acting in place of her mother. It grieves me to think of the loss she will again feel.
>
>Father, there is a young man who I deeply care about. If he survives, I believe he will come looking for me. His name is Jacob Liebman. The only address he has for me is the address of my home before we were taken to the ghetto, and which I enclose. Please see if you can arrange for some means of letting him know what has happened to me.
>
>You have been like a father to me, and for that I am truly grateful.
>
>With love, your adopted daughter,
>Rachel

Chapter 68: A Meeting at the Synagogue
Father Sobieski, Western Poland, May 1945

The war was over. Although Europe was free from Nazi tyranny, the continent was in ruins. Millions of lives were broken and shattered, none more so than those of the Jews who survived. Father Sobieski's mission in the resistance had ended, but new service in rebuilding lives would more than take its place.

When it came to sheltering Jews, he had not hesitated. With his long life of service and dedication, he had fitted himself to be an instrument that resonated with God's Spirit. From his life of saving souls, it was no big leap to saving bodies. He had taken on that mission without looking back, despite the risks and consequences. If a child was in trouble, he helped.

There were five hundred people in the synagogue that day. Few had been untouched by Father Sobieski. All knew who he was. These were people whose souls had been scarred by the deepest suffering. For years they had lived lives of fear and brutal hardship. Treated like animals. Betrayed by fellow countrymen. Humiliated, beaten, starved. Friends, neighbors, and family gone forever. Somehow, they had survived, but they were the very few. It was easier for them to assume their children were gone.

But those children were not gone—through the goodness of a man most had not met, and many others, their children lived. Now parents and children were together, worshipping as Jews. These miracles were enough to fill one's soul. It was a transcendent moment.

Suddenly the Rabbi paused and announced that Father Sobieski had just entered at the back to say goodbye to "his children." There was a noticeable hush. All faces turned to see him. There he was—a slight figure, looking a little embarrassed for having disrupted the service. He nodded his head as an acknowledgment to the congregation.

What do you do when you meet the person who saved your child and a hundred others? A silence of reverence and gratitude permeated the room. Then from the pews a young girl, perhaps five years old, ran to Father Sobieski and hugged him around his legs. He called her by name and lifted her up. With that simple act of compassion and familiarity, the floodgates opened. Children began to fill the aisles and run to him. Everyone rose to their feet in a sudden, spontaneous acclamation. They clapped and cheered, but more than anything, they unashamedly wept. Amidst all the evil, here was a pillar of goodness triumphant. Father Sobieski came forward to meet his children, and the congregation surged toward him. Many reached out to touch him, to say they had once been in his presence.

  The room felt as if the walls would cry out, as if the roof would be blown off.

Chapter 69: Jacob Returns
Jacob, Western Poland, June 1945

Jacob finished the war fighting in the Russian army. It had been a long, hard slog. He was present when Warsaw was liberated, but it was not a joyous occasion, for the city had been devastated and the former ghetto was a moonscape. Now that the war was over, he could try to find Rachel.

With fear in his heart, he knocked at the door of her home, the home he had known before his family left for eastern Poland. He doubted she would be there—all Jews had been forced into ghettos just like his family had, and their homes had been left empty for others to take. But coming here was a starting point in his search.

A young girl with blond hair and blue eyes answered the door.

"Hello," Jacob said. "Is your mother at home?"

"I will get her."

A petite, smiling woman came to the door, drying a plate with a dishtowel. "May I help you?" she asked.

"I am looking for a woman named Rachel Auerbach. Her family lived here before the war. Would you know anything about where I could find her?"

She stopped drying the plate. She looked up at him and studied his face for what seemed like minutes. Her eyes shimmered as she asked, "Are you Jacob?"

Jacob was visibly taken aback. "My name is Jacob, yes; Jacob Liebman. But how do you know me? Have we met before?"

"No, but I knew your Rachel. In fact, your Rachel saved my life."

Jacob was momentarily speechless. "You knew my Rachel? How . . . how is that possible?"

"Please come in. I have both prayed for and dreaded the coming of this day. We have much to talk about. I was a friend of Rachel's, and I also need to tell you about two little girls named Esther and Rebeka."

The day Jacob learned of Rachel's death from Halinka was the hardest of his life, for it took away his hope. His hope for Rachel, although he knew it was against long odds, had carried him through dark nights and bleak days. Sometimes thinking of their future together had been all that had kept him going. Now that hope was gone.

He had loved her so! He had held her hand only once, and he had kissed her only once. Many nights he had dreamed of taking her in his arms. Now, he realized, dreams were all he would ever have.

Jacob's heart overflowed with pain. He had felt this kind of debilitating, overwhelming pain when he had learned his family was gone, but that wound had mostly healed over. Now a new wound was opened, and the pain came back, drowning him, crushing him.

Halinka suggested he stay with them for a while. The small farm attached to the house had been neglected. The garden was full of weeds; the fence was broken down; the machinery needed repair. There was a lot for him to do. He didn't realize it then, but working with his hands in the warm summer sun would be therapeutic for him.

But it was Esther and Rebeka and Halinka that helped him most to heal. After dinner, the girls each took one of his hands, and they walked to a nearby pond to feed the ducks. Some evenings he held them both on his lap while they read stories. They had also known Rachel—indeed, they were here because of her, and he saw in them part of her. And Halinka, with her bright, cheery, no-nonsense attitude, struck a good balance between empathy and toughness. They often sat up at night and talked around the fireside. He came to realize she had also suffered deep wounds. They all had initially been bound together by ties to Rachel, but gradually they were knitted together by bonds of love for each other.

Esther sometimes suffered from nightmares. One night, when she woke up crying, Jacob offered to sit with her. "Were you having a bad dream?" he asked. She nodded. "Would you like me to stay here with you?" She nodded again. Sitting in a chair by her bedside, he held her hand while she fell back asleep.

Some hours later, Esther again cried out. "I don't like the dark. When will it be morning?"

Jacob felt a presence enter the room. He felt a voice whisper inside him, "It won't be morning for a while, but I am here, and I love you." Esther seemed to have felt it as well, for she snuggled into her covers and rolled over, content and secure. Unexpectedly, Jacob's heart was filled with gratitude—gratitude that he had loved, and had been loved by, such a person as Rachel.

A few hours before dawn, Jacob felt a heaviness steal over him, and he slumped down in his chair. When he awoke, rays of sunshine were just touching the panes of the window and peeking into the room.

It was morning.

Notes

Chapter 1: The Loading. A description of what it was like inside the cattle car can be found in numerous sources. Some are Gilbert (1986, pp. 294-328), Yad Vashem ("Deportation to the Death Camps") and United States Holocaust Memorial Museum ("Deportation to Killing Centers"). The striking image of the diapers hung out to dry on barbed wire is taken from Levi (2008).

Chapter 3: The Jump. The account of Rachel jumping from the train is inspired by the autobiographical account of Ruth Cyprys (Cyprys, 1997). In her extraordinary story, Ruth did hide a hacksaw blade in her boot and did cut through the bars of the windows in the cattle car. She jumped out as Rachel did. However, it was a not a six-year-old girl who followed her, but her own two-year-old daughter, in the middle of winter.

It may seem unrealistic for a mother to give up her daughter to the care of another and have her thrown from a moving train. However, there are numerous accounts where something similar happened. Alicia Appleman-Jurman recounts how, as an eleven-year old child, she was pushed out of a train, without her parents, when the occupants were able to hammer loose two bars that were fastened over the window. Before she jumped several parents pushed their children out the window, alone, including an eight-year old boy. The opening was not big enough for adults. (Appleman-Jurman, pp. 31-33).

Chapter 6: Morning. "When Will it be Morning?" is an adaptation of an experience that happened in my own family.

Chapter 7: Leaving. The account of the neighbor showing up to ask for the sofa is taken from Kramer (2009, pp. 64-65)

Chapter 8: The Ghetto. The description of the ghetto, where they took the bathtubs and stoves, etc. outside, is similar to the ghetto described in Bitton-Jackson (1997).

Chapter 9: Pails of Water. The selection of the Judenrat using the pails of water is briefly described in Kagan and Cohen (2000, p. 40)

Chapter 10: Books and Scrolls. The burning of all the books and documents in the ghetto is taken from Livia Bitton-Jackson (1997, pp. 57-60) Livia also wrote poetry, and in an attempt to save her poems, she hid them and gave them to a Hungarian soldier, who was escorting them to be deported. She never saw them again.

Spitting into the mouth of the Rabbi is described in Gilbert (1986, pp. 105-106).

Chapter 11: Samuel. Removing the fence sections and transporting them to wall in the "shops" ghetto is taken from Kagan and Cohen (2000, p. 46)

Chapter 12: The *Aktions*. The tactic of giving out loaves of bread and a jar of marmalade was used in the Warsaw Ghetto to persuade people to come for deportation (Engelking and Leociak, 2009, p. 711).

Chapter 13: Outcast. The description of Rachel working and living in the fields is adapted from the experiences of Alicia Appleman-Jurman (Appleman-Jurman, 1988).

Chapter 15: Father Sobieski. The prayer of Father Sobieski is based on an account of David Prital with a Ukrainian peasant as told in Gilbert (2003, p. 13).

Chapter 22: The New Ghetto. The segment of the poem quoted in the story after Jacob learns his family is gone is named, "The Day of My Great Disaster," and is by Yitzkhok Katzenelson. He wrote the poem after he came home and discovered his sons and wife had been taken for deportation. See the Bibliography for the full reference.

The story of mass executions, the destruction of the ghetto, the formation of the small ghetto comprised of artisans and shops, and the building and escape through a tunnel is based on the accounts of Jews at Novogrodek, in what was eastern Poland. These events are recounted in Kagan and Cohen (2000) and Duffy (2003).

Chapter 23: The Tunnel. Virtually everything about the tunnel is based on real events, including how it was built, the lights, the cart to haul dirt, the disposal of the dirt, the wheat field, the rain, and the guards opening fire during the escape (Kagan and Cohen, 2000, pp. 77-83, 172-180), (Duffy, 2003, pp. 198-203) and Gilbert (1986, pp. 608-609). One of the above authors, Jack Kagan, is the boy whose toes were amputated. Unfortunately, unlike the story, he had to walk the whole way to the partisans on his sore and bleeding feet. For the sake of the story, I have moved the events forward a year to 1942; although they actually occurred in 1943, the events could have happened in 1942 as other nearby ghettos were liquidated then. The war-time tunneling escapes mentioned by Brickhill (1950), and Williams (2005) were also used for reference. The tunnel is also mentioned by escapees

Rae Kushner and Sonya Oshman in oral interviews. Documentaries discussing the tunnel include "Tunnel of Hope," released in 2014 by Michael Kagan, son of Jack, and "A Partisan Returns: The Legacy of Two Sisters," about Rae Kushner and Lisa Reibel, who both escaped through the tunnel. See the Bibliography for these references.

Chapter 28: A Step Into the Unknown. Rachel's role as a courier was inspired in part by Sonia Games (Games, 2002). Speaking of couriers, Emanuel Ringelblum, the Jewish archivist of the Warsaw Ghetto, wrote:

> The heroic girls, Chajka [Grosman], Frumke [Plotnicka] and others, theirs is a story that calls for the pen of a great writer. They are venturesome, courageous girls who travel . . . across Poland to cities and towns, carrying Aryan papers, which describe them as Polish or Ukrainian. One of them even wears a cross, which she never leaves off and misses when she is in the ghetto. Day by day they face the greatest dangers. . .
>
> They accept the most dangerous missions and carry them out without a murmur, without a moment's hesitation. If there is need for someone to travel to Vilna, Bialystock, Lvov, Kowel, Lublin, Czestochowa, or Radom to smuggle in such forbidden things as illegal publications, goods, money, they do it all as though it were the most natural thing. If there are comrades to be rescued from Vilna, Lublin, or other cities, they take the job on themselves. . . . (Arad et al., 1981, p. 239)

Chapter 29: The Train to Warsaw. The incident with the SS officer on the train is adapted from Sonia Games (2002, pp 212-217). Sonia was trapped on a train, like Rachel, with an SS officer next to her, police opening luggage in front of her and *Wehrmacht* soldiers behind her. The SS officer did take her to an outside platform at the back of the car where Sonia pushed him off the train.

Chapter 33: Helmuth. The events leading up to Hitler's rise to power in Germany, and his consolidation of power after becoming chancellor, can be found in Evans (2003) and Evans (2005). The experience of Helmuth in a *Waffen SS* unit under attack is inspired by Hartinger (2019).

Chapter 34: Joining the SS. The ideology of the SS explained here closely follows that given in Stein (1966). The statement by Himmler—"Germans had the moral right, *they had the duty* to destroy this people which wanted to destroy them"—is quoted in Sidman (1977, p. 342) and Arad et al. (1981, p. 345). Italics added.

"The Jews' blood spurting from the knife makes us feel especially good," can be found in several sources, including Johnson and Reuband (2005, p. 26)

The description of the Jew ("the Jew is filthy…") is paraphrased from that given by a Jew, Chiam Kaplan, explaining how they were looked on by the Germans. This is taken from Arad et al., (1981, p. 201) and Stanislaw Adler, (1982, p. 7)

Personal accounts of the training of SS soldiers, including the incident of marching into the lake, can be found in Williamson (1999, p. 34).

Chapter 36: The Aryan Side of Warsaw. Counting of the windows by the SS captain is mentioned by Ringelblum (1974, p. 342).

Chapter 37: The Warsaw Ghetto. The policeman beating a child smuggler to death is based on a first-hand account given in Szpilman (1999, pp. 12-13).

Details of the Warsaw ghetto can be found in many sources. Two used here are Engelking and Leociak (2009) and Schwarberg (2001). The Schwarberg reference is a book of extraordinary photographs of the ghetto taken by a German soldier.

Chapter 38: The Orphanage. Although the interaction with Helmuth is fictional, virtually everything about Janusz Korczak and Stefania Wilczuńska is based on fact. See for example, (Lifton, 1988), (Farrar et al., 1988), (Marrin, 2019), and (Jaworski, 1978). A description of the march and *Umschlagplatz* is also given by Szpilman (1999).

"Am I standing up straight enough, Uncle?" comes from an account of a Latvian SS officer as given by Bielenberg (2011, pp. 258-259).

Chapter 41: A Courier and an Escort. One of the great stories of the Holocaust and the Warsaw Ghetto is that of Irena Sendler, a non-Jew who saved an estimated 2,500 Jewish children by smuggling them out of the ghetto and placing them with non-Jewish families or at convents (Mazzeo, 2016), (Mieszkowska, 2011).

It may be surprising that Rachel escorts children to a convent quite a distance from Warsaw. However, this did happen. Children from Warsaw were placed in convents all across Poland (Mazzeo, 2016, p. 165). For example, the convent at Turkowice, where a number of children were placed, was approximately 185 miles from Warsaw.

The placing of Jewish children in Catholic convents was complicated. As mentioned by Bogner (1999), summarizing Ringelblum, there were at least three objections by Jews to placing children in convents: 1) some suspected the Catholic clergy of taking advantage of the Jews' plight to proselytize and convert their children, 2) some felt the convents, by requiring payment in advance, were seeking to make money, and 3) some accused the Catholics, who had done little to help Jews to this point, of wanting to obtain a "seal of approval" by saving some hundreds of their children.

Chapter 42: The Streetcar. The incident on the streetcar is adapted from Mazzeo (2016, p. 150) and Mieszkowska (2011, p. 82).

The method of taking children out of the ghetto through tunnels was one of the four main ways that were used, according to Irena Sendler. (Mieszkowska 2011, pp. 7, 8). Not all of these methods were feasible after the January 18 *Aktion*.

Chapter 44: On Their Way. The Kozlovsky farm the partisans went to was real. I have moved it somewhat east for the sake of the story. Konstantin Kozlovsky and his sons were recognized as "Righteous Among the Nations" by Yad Vashem. See (Kagan and Cohen, 1998, pp. 58-59) and the Bibliography for more information.

Chapter 45: The Camp. The description of the Bielski Brothers and their encampment in the forest is taken from Duffy (2003, pp. 212-228), Kagan and Cohen (2000, pp. 191-195) and Levine (2009, pp. 259-291).

Yakov Fyodorovich was a real person. A Jew from Gomel in Belarus, he led the first all-Jewish 51st brigade. He did receive the Order of Lenin in the war between Russia and Finland.

Chapter 46: Training. The formation and training of the 51st Brigade is taken from Shner-Nishmit (2015), Ainstein (1974), Alpert (1989), Nachum (1989), and Grau and Gress (2011).

Chapter 47: First Mission. The raid on the peasant's farm is adapted from Duffy (2003, pp. 123-124)

Chapter 51: The SS Officer. The interaction between Helmuth, Rachel, Halinka and some children is fictional. That a SS officer might feel this way and let children go free is based on an account, mentioned in a previous note, of a Latvian SS officer (Bielenberg, 2011, pp. 258-259). When a child asked him, right before the child was shot, "Am I standing up straight enough, Uncle?" he felt convicted by his conscience. Eventually he volunteered for the eastern front, in the hopes he might be killed there to atone for his crimes.

Chapter 54: Clarity. A suggested price for a convent to take a Jewish child was 600 złoty per month, payable in advance (Ringelblum, 1974, p. 336).

Chapter 55: The Bridge. The battle to take the bridge and free the ghetto is actually a combination of two different battles fought by the 51st brigade as described in Shner-Nismit (2015) and Ainsztein (1974, p. 332). Their leader Yakov Fyodorovich was wounded in the battle for the bridge and did ask to be killed. His final words are closely paraphrased from Shner-Nismit (2015, pg. 179).

The woman leading the charge on the bridge is inspired by the life of Żenia Eichenbaum, a woman partisan who fought in the battle for the Kosovo ghetto and the bridge and who later led her fellow soldiers in repulsing an attack when they were ambushed (Ainsztein, 1974, pg. 337), (Shner-Nismit, 2015, pg. 331). She was killed in battle. She was posthumously recommended for the Soviet Union's highest military honor, "Hero of the Soviet Union."

Chapter 61: The Train. The incident of exploding the shell with a rifle aimed at the firing pin is taken from Levine (2009, pg. 194) and Kahn (2004, pg. 84-85). Ainsztein (1974, pg. 323) also mentions converting artillery shells into mines to blow up trains.

Chapter 62: The First Battle in the Ghetto. The description of the Warsaw ghetto uprising is based on numerous sources. Chief among them are Engelking and Leociak (2009), Ber (1975), Ringelblum (1974), Ainsztein (1979), Rotem (1994), Zuckerman (1993), and Gutman (1994). The last four sources are memoirs by those who actually participated in the uprising. The battles described here are representative of actual battles, including the explosion of the bomb at the entrance of the brushmakers' ghetto. The German *Aktion* did begin on the first day of Passover, April 19, 1943.

Chapter 67: The Ghetto in Flames. The incident where Rachel looks down into the ash and sees that it contains charred bodies is taken from Rotem, (1994, pp. 39–40).

Rachel's sacrifice to save Halinka is based on a real event described in Ber (1975, p. 56), whereby a fighter named Halinka Rochman gave her life to save the life of her commander, Ruzha Rosenfeld. Before she died, Halinka is quoted as saying, "My life is less important than Ruzha's; she's the commander; we need her more." Brief reference is also made in the database maintained by the Polish Center for Holocaust Research. See the Bibliography.

The name *Antek* was the code name for Yitzhak Zuckerman, one of the leaders of the Jewish fighters (Zuckerman, 1993) who survived the uprising. The name *Mordechai* is in honor of Mordechai Anielewicz, the twenty-four-year-old leader of all the Jewish fighters. Morcechai took his life on May 8, 1943, after German troops closed in on their command post at Miła 18.

Chapter 68: A Meeting at the Synagogue. The description of Father Sobieski in the synagogue is inspired by a Belgium priest named Father Bruno (the Reverend Henri Reynders). Father Bruno helped save 320 children. When he entered the synagogue to say goodbye, children "were clinging to his arms and tearful parents were showering him with thanks and blessings." (Gilbert, 2003, pp. 309-315)

Chapter 69: Jacob Returns. The reader may wonder how Halinka and Rebeka escaped from the ghetto. A few of the fighters were able, eventually, to escape through the Muranowski tunnel and through the sewers. (Engelking and Leociak, 787)

Bibliography

Adler, Stanislaw, *In the Warsaw Ghetto, 1940-1943, An Account of a Witness*, Yad Vashem, 1982

Ainsztein, Reuben, *Jewish Resistance in Nazi Occupied Europe*, Paul Elek, 1974

Ainsztein, Reuben, *The Warsaw Ghetto Revolt*, Holocaust Library, New York, 1979

Alpert, Nachum, *The Destruction of the Slonin Jewry, The Story of the Jews of Slonim During the Holocaust*, Translated from the Yiddish by Max Rosenfeld, Holocaust Library, New York, 1989

Amarant, Shmuel, "And the Bravery, The Partisans of Tuvia Bielski," https://www.jewishgen.org/yizkor/Novogrudok/nov333.html

Appleman-Jurman, Alicia, *Alicia, My Story*, New York: Bantam Books, 1988

Arad Yitzhak, Yisrael Gutman, and Abraham Margaliot, *Documents on the Holocaust,* Yad Vashem, 1981

Bartoszewski. Władzsław and Antony Polonsky, *The Jews in Warsaw, A History*, Basil Blackwell in association with the Institute for Polish-Jewish studies, Oxford, 1991

Bielenberg, Christabel, *The Past is Myself, and The Road Ahead*, Omnibus Edition, Corgi Books, 2011. *The Past is Myself* was originally published in Great Britain in 1968 by Chatto and Windus Ltd.

Bitton-Jackson, Livia, *I Have Lived a Thousand Years, Growing Up in the Holocaust*, Simon Pulse, 1997

Bogner, Nahum, "The Convent Children: The Rescue of Jewish Children in Polish Convents during the Holocaust," *Yad Vashem Studies* Vol. XXVII, Jerusalem, 1999, pp. 235-285. Available on-line at, https://www.yadvashem.org/righteous/resources/rescue-of-jewish-children-in-polish-convents.html

Brickhill, Paul, *The Great Escape*, Norton Paperbacks, 1950

Cyprys, Altbeker Ruth, *A Jump for Life*, originally published in Great Britain by Constable and Company. Continuum Publishing Company, 1997

Duffy, Peter, *The Bielski Brothers*, Harper Perennial, 2003

Engelking, Barbara and Jacek Leociak, *The Warsaw Ghetto, A Guide to the Perished City*, translated by Emma Harris, Yale University Press, 2009

Evans, Richard J., *The Third Reich in Power*, Penguin, 2005

Evans, Richard J., *The Coming of the Third Reich,* Penguin, 2003

Evans, Richard J., *The Third Reich at War*, Penguin, 2008

Games, Sonia, *Escape Into Darkness*, Xlibris, 2002

Gilbert, Martin, *The Righteous*, Owl Books, Henry Holt and Company, 2003

Gilbert, Martin, *The Holocaust*, Owl Books, Henry Holt and Company, 1986

Grau, Lester (editor), Michael Gress (editor), *The Red Army's Do-It-Yourself, Nazi-Bashing Guerrilla Warfare Manual: The Partizan's Companion*, 2011, originally written in 1943.

Gutman, Israel, *Resistance, The Warsaw Ghetto Uprising*, Houghton Mifflin, 1994

Haffner, Sebastian, *Defying Hitler*, Picador, 2000

Hartinger, Andreas, *Until the Eyes Shut, Memories of a Machine Gunner on the Eastern Front*, 1943-1945, 2019.

Heck, Alfons, *A Child of Hitler, Germany in the Days When God Wore a Swastika*, Renaissance House, 1985

Hersey, John, *The Wall*, First Copyright 1950, Vintage Books copyright, 1988.

Jaworski, Marek, *Janusz Korczak*, Interpress, 1978

Johnson Eric, and Karl Heinz Reuband, *What We Knew*, John Murray, 2005

Katzenelson, Yitzkhok, "The Day of My Great Disaster" The version quoted is taken from: https://poetryinhell.org/ghetto-hunger-struggle-2/yitzkhok-katzenelson-the-great-day-of-my-disaster/ Another partial version can be found in Engelking and Leociak (2009, p. 545). They cite *The Ringelblum Archive: The Warsaw Ghetto*, July 1942-January 1943, R. Sakowska, Editor, Warsaw, 1980, pg. 207-212)

Kagan, Jack and Dov Cohen, *Surviving the Holocaust with the Russian Jewish Partisans*, Vallentine Mitchell, Second Edition, 2000

Kagan, Michael, "Tunnel of Hope," a filmed documentary. For this documentary survivors and their families returned to the site of

the tunnel (now in Belarus) to try to find it again.
See https://www.youtube.com/watch?v=4rwLN5ZGbQw

Korczak, Janusz, *Ghetto Diary*, Yale University Press, 2003

Kozlovsky, Konstantin, recognized as "Righteous Among the Nations" by Yad Vashem. See https://righteous.yadvashem.org/?search=Kozlovskiy%20Konstantin%20&searchType=righteous_only&language=en&itemId=4042667&ind=0

Kramer, Clara, *Clara's War, One Girl's Story of Survival*, HarperCollins, 2009

Kurzman, Dan, *The Bravest Battle*, De Capo Press, 1993

Kushner, Rae, oral interview, United States Holocaust Memorial Museum Archives, Accession Number: 1993.A.0088.15 (RG-50.002.0015)

Kushner, Murray, executive producer, "A Partisan Returns: The Legacy of Two Sisters," documentary can be accessed from https://www.jewishpartisans.org//films

Levi, Primo, *Survival in Auschwitz*, Classic House Books, 2008.

Levine, Alan, *Fugitives of the Forest*, Lyons Press, 2009

Lifton, Betty Jean, *The King of Children*, Farrar Strauss and Giroux, 1988

Malinas, "The Jews of Vilna in Hiding," https://www.yadvashem.org/education/educational-materials/lesson-plans/malinas.html Yad Vashem, 2020

Mark, Ber, *Uprising in the Warsaw Ghetto*, translated from the Yiddish by Gershon Freidlin, Schocken Books, 1975

Marrin, Albert, *A Light in the Darkness*, Knopf, 2019

Mazzeo, Tilar J., *Irena's Children*, Gallery Books, 2016

Mackinnon, Marianne, *The Naked Years, Growing Up in Nazi Germany*, Chatto and Windus, 1987

Mieszkowska, Anna, *Irena Sendler, Mother of the Children of the Holocaust*, Praeger, 2011

Oshman, Sonya, oral interview, United States Holocaust Memorial Museum Archives Accession Number: 1993.A.0088.21 (RG-50.002.0021)

Rochman, Halinka, Polish Center for Holocaust Research, 2011
https://new.getto.pl/en/People/R/Rochman-Halinka-Nieznane

Ringelblum, Emmanuel, *Notes from the Warsaw Ghetto, The Journal of Emmanuel Ringelblum*, Translated by Jacob Sloan, Schocken Books, New York, 1974

Rotem, Simha ("Kazik"), *Memoirs of a Warsaw Ghetto Fighter,* The Past Within Me, Yale University Press, 1994

Shner-Nishmit, Sara, *The 51st Brigade, The History of the Jewish Partisan Group from the Slonim Ghetto*, JewishGen, Inc., translated from Hebrew by Judith Levi, 2015

Shumann, Willy, Being Present, Growing Up in Hitler's Germany, Kent State University Press, 1991

Schnibbe, Karl-Heinz, *The Price*, Bookcraft, 1984

Schwarberg, Günther, *In the Ghetto of Warsaw*, Heinrich Jöst's Photographs, Steidl, 2001.

Szpilman, Wladyslaw, *The Pianist*, Picador, 1999

Stein, George H., *The Waffen SS, Hitler's Elite Guard at War*, 1939-1945, Cornell University Press, 1966

Stroop, Jürgen, *The Warsaw Ghetto: The Stroop Report* - "The Warsaw Ghetto Is No More" https://www.jewishvirtuallibrary.org/the-stroop-report-may-1943 , 1943

Tubach, F. C., *German Voices, Memories of Life During Hitler's Third Reich*, Univ. Calif. Press, 2011

United States Holocaust Memorial Museum, "Deportation to Killing Centers," https://encyclopedia.ushmm.org/content/en/article/deportations-to-killing-centers

Williamson, Gordon, *Loyalty is My Honor, Personal Accounts from the Waffen-SS*, Bramley Books, 1999

Wiesel, Elie, *Night*, Bantam Books, 1960.

Yad Veshem, "Deportation to the Death Camps," https://www.yadvashem.org/holocaust/about/final-solution/deportation.html#narrative_info

Zimmerman, Joshua D., *The Polish Underground and the Jews, 1939-1945*, Cambridge University Press, 2015

Zuckerman, Yitzhak ("Antek"), *A Surplus of Memory, Chronicle of the Warsaw Ghetto Uprising*, Translated and edited by Barbara Hershav, University of California Press, 1993

Made in United States
Orlando, FL
15 November 2023